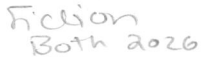

CW01509919

JUDITH TRUSTMAN

How Like A Winter

First published by Shaking Grass Press 2025

A CIP catalogue record is available for this book on request from The British Library.

First edition

ISBN (print): 978-1-9192604-0-2
ISBN (digital): 978-1-9192604-3-3

Illustration by Eva Polakovicova

This book was professionally typeset on Reedsy.
Find out more at reedsy.com

For Sarah and Rose

How like a winter hath my absence
been from thee..
~ Sonnet 97, William Shakespeare

The good-enough mother… starts off
with an almost complete adaptation
to her infant's needs, and as time
proceeds she adapts less and less completely, gradually, according to the
infant's growing ability to deal with
her failure.
~ D. W. Winnicott

I

Part One

Two Mothers

1

The Social Worker

Tara woke and felt the sun across her leg, an uncommon feeling, warm as touch only safer. Dylan, lying like a small hillock beside her, didn't stir. Drowsy with sleep she pulled the cover in closer, relishing the heat, not ready for the day or the hunger. Everything could wait. It would come around right with a little more sleep for them both.

But Dylan was not beside her. His baby feet had carried him away, into the prairie of the room where he would often shamble, familiar with the shapes, the low light through the half-dressed window. Cloth mountains rose from the ground in an ever-changing landscape, where the smell of his mother's milk fed him rags to pull on and suck. But they were not his mother. His mother was big and warm. He knew her voice. Smell took him to the darkness beyond the door, where shapes and shinies lay. Shinies slick with smell.

No light gave onto the hallways of the houses in Denley

Avenue, an economy forced upon the builder by a cash strapped council and a cheat's architect. Residents, who came and went with regularity, complained about the darkness, the damp in the walls, black mould blooming behind furniture, beneath sills. The estate itself resembled a mottling upon a sparse upland which gave out to the north of the city, set above the older Victorian streets like a cluster of sheep. The area had been staked out by discard and poverty. Here was where the shopping trolley gardeners lived.

Tara's feet were cold, her fogged head made them worse. Two months with only pity money had reduced her to sleep whenever the chance was available. Cocooning herself tighter within the fold of blankets, the thought occurred to her that a visit from the social might actually help. The name of the current social worker lay somewhere beneath the jungle. Her day-to-day thoughts, fears for Dylan, the cold, the milk disappearing down into his beautiful body that seemed never to be enough, a mesh of worry in her head; she had named it all The Jungle. Carol. That was it, the woman with the lopsided hair who said she was here to support.

Perhaps, said her jungle, it was time to get up and find the food vouchers. They shouldn't have been lost like they were, stupid little chits. A good sleeping boy was Dylan. Her hand reached for his sleeping form, but stopped short for fear of waking him. Another hour and she'd have it figured out for today. Another hour.

Dylan's eyes fixed upon the shinies, a waterfall of gooey shapes climbing out of the black hulk down towards the floor. He took a step towards the smell of it, the salt sweet wetness.

At half past eleven on Tuesday morning, Carol was making her way to Denley Avenue to make an unannounced visit. This was the second weekend in February and it was cold and overcast. Monday had been disastrous, and today was looking like *another day, another messed up kid*. The house was at the end of a street where every property looked in need of some tlc. No one here tended the gardens.

She put her face to the narrow oblong letterbox of number 58 and peered inside. The hallway was dark, Dylan standing there swaying a little, wearing only a vest and a sodden nappy. Hello Dylan, is your mummy there? He was unsteady on his feet but took a step towards the direction of her voice until his legs gave way all at once and he was down on the bare floorboards, the space littered with black bin bags and assorted debris.

Hello, is anyone in? Tara? Carol fumbled in her bag searching for her phone whilst she propped the flap of the letterbox open with her other hand. Dylan go get mummy for me. Get mummy there's a good boy. He said nothing and chewed on his hand which was shiny with dribble. It had slathered down his arm towards his vest where a bloom of damp was growing across his chest. He leaned forwards, arms waving, scissoring unevenly at a black bin bag which had spewed its contents onto the hall floor. His hand came away with a crumpled takeaway dish which went straight to his mouth.

Carol was on the phone, Bob, I can't raise anyone here at all and the baby's in the hallway chewing on the rubbish. It's the third time I've tried to gain access, but the last two visits mum's been out or made an excuse. I think we're going to have to get the police and take the boy out.

Have you rung the bell?

I've been trying Bob, but there's no answer. The baby's in the hallway with a mouth full of crap and I've been here shouting through the letter box for twenty minutes and can't raise anyone. It looks pretty filthy in there.

When did you last manage to see her, Carol, get a proper look at what state the place is in? I mean, we're in the second period of registration here and this baby's not yet two.

I've tried, Bob, but she always has a headache or something, I've been trying to work with her to build some kind of trust, but I don't think she's being open with me.

Bob was going through the motions with her. He'd agree in the end because this was the first time she'd managed to get hold of him, despite trying before on other nightmare cases. He'd have to carry the can anyway if it all went tits up.

It's such a shame. I liked Tara you know, Bob. I've tried hard to work with her you know.

I know, I know, you always believe in them Carol, but it sounds to me like you're working with too much risk here.

Yeah, it's going to have to be police protection, because the baby's on his second piece of rubbish now. Thanks Bob.

I'll wait by the doorway until the police get here, because the best I can do is try and stop him eating all the crap off the floor. Even if mum wakes up or whatever, I think we've got to take Dylan out anyway. She's not minding him.

Green light from me, Carol.

Okay, bye. She tugged on her hair, pulling it down on one side. It boosted her image, the haircut. Asymmetrical, quite funky. She wished she'd worn trousers now the cold was biting round her legs.

She looked in, lifting the flap of the letterbox, pressing on the doorbell with her other hand. Dylan, put the box down darling. Go and get mummy for me. He said nothing but he did look up. His nose was visibly snotty even from a distance. He was a mess, making no noises which was plain not right. That baby's too quiet. Where's the babble? She kept her hand on the doorbell, listening to it buzzing inside then letting it go suddenly in case it frightened him. More worryingly, he didn't seem to react.

The police car drew up outside the house. Two uniformed officers, man and woman, get out of the car. Heading back down the steps towards them she missed the door opening behind her. It was the first police officer, the man, who signalled with a nod to look behind her.

Tara was framed in the open doorway wearing only a long grey tee shirt; her hair was twisted untidily behind her head and strands of it hung down either side of her face, still crumpled with sleep. Hullo? What's going on? she said, her voice thick. What are you bringing police round my house for, Carol? She was angry. Dylan, get back inside, she shouted at the toddler who was grasping at her legs and shuffling along on his bottom.

I've been here twenty minutes or more Tara, trying to get you to answer the door. What's been the problem? Dylan was in the hallway on his own you know.

I was asleep that's all, Carol. You didn't need to bring the fucking police round here just cos I was asleep you know. What the hell. You people are all the same. She turned and picked up the baby, her hip taking his weight. What do you want? she shouted at the police over her shoulder.

The police officers were standing behind Carol, all three of them on the doorstep by now. Can we come in and have a look round then, love? Only Carol here's been worried you weren't hearing the doorbell and the little lad was not being minded, said the policeman. He looked at Carol and said PC Routledge, miss. Shall I take it from here?

Well, let's all go in, if that's alright with you Tara? I'm afraid we've got to have a look round now that we're here. We were worried about you and Dylan.

How can I say no? Eh? Carol, you've done it to me now. Well, what the fuck, I don't have a say do I? I don't have no privacy any more. Yeah, help yourselves, come in, look round. Whatever you want. She headed back down the hallway and disappeared through an open doorway.

We might still be looking at the taking the baby out, miss, if it's not right in there. PC Routledge knew the form, he'd been there before. The police woman looked young, but she'd taken in the state of the front garden already. There was a sofa jammed underneath the hedge that bordered next door, its guts ripped out, a big chunk of foam hanging forwards. It didn't look good, Carol could see that, but then last time she'd been in the house it had been better.

Something was not right about the house. As soon as she set foot inside the door, she could sense it. The cold hit her first, followed by the smell of nappies, until the smell of something worse hit her nostrils.

The living room was bad as hell, two full bin bags lurked inside the door, dirty nappies everywhere, some folded up, one unfolding on the arm of the sofa with a hard dry poo hanging inches away from a cushion. A bottle lay derelict on the other cushion, the contents crusty with age. Tara was sitting down in the chair rocking Dylan who looked sad and tired. Piles of clothes littered the back of the chair with more

8

strewn on the floor behind it. The remains of what looked like a Chinese takeaway was spread out on the coffee table beside an ashtray overflowing with butts. Was there a drug problem developing here?

Tara, has he had his breakfast? she asked as she peeled back one of the curtains looking for the source of the smell. Only he looked hungry to me when I was trying to get you to answer the door. The police officers were banging about in the kitchen opening cupboards.

I don't get my benefits till tomorrow. I've run out of money if you must know, she said rocking. But he's alright, he's had milk. That's what he likes for his breakfast anyway, isn't it Dylan? She spoke as if to the floor, not Dylan. You're not taking him, Carol, you know I've been engaging with you lot. You know you can't take him if I'm engaging. Her voice had become raised, edgy with anxiety.

I know you have Tara, but what happened this morning.... Gingerly, she lowered herself onto the sofa, moving the bottle to the table. It's not looking right in here is it, love? You know that it's not right for Dylan. Tell me what's been happening. Something sticky on the edge of the sofa was under her leg, so she shifted to one side and swung her knees the opposite way. Should've worn something else. She began tucking the edges of her skirt around her legs.

Nothing's happened Carol. I was asleep that's all. Dylan knows not to touch stuff when he wakes up first. She stopped rocking and shifted his weight up her body. Her tee shirt had a wet patch on it where his face had been pressed up against her.

Is he making sounds yet, Tara? You remember we spoke about it? Watching as she spoke, he returned her gaze unfocused and dreamy. Hello Dylan. How are you today? Her voice didn't seem to register on his face at all. He just carried on sucking his hands.

You're alright aren't you, Dylan? Tara moved him to the front of his knees and bounced him vigorously up and down, up and down, until he began to whimper, his cry shaking as she jogged him.

Can you come through please miss? PC Routledge called her from somewhere in the flat. Carol got up. I'm going to have to have a look round Tara. Do I have your permission?

A nod was all she got, enough, given that it had to be done anyway now that the police were here, but anyone could see where this was heading. Out in the kitchen the two police officers were watching something outside the backdoor. It was a stocky brown dog, tethered in the back garden on a long rope, lunging repeatedly at the back door and barking. The rope was too short. Every time he lunged he crashed in a stranglehold, inches out of reach. He was repeating it over and over, as if it had been going on a while. He's sore on his neck look, I don't know how long that's been going on for, the woman police officer said. What do you think, Brian, get the RSPCA in?

There'll be a prosecution in it if we go down that route, he replied. I dunno, maybe we can improve things for the dog at least while we're here. Is it hers miss?

I don't know, I'm pretty sure it wasn't here last month when I came round, otherwise I'd have said something.

The kitchen was a bigger disaster. Dishes encrusted with food were stacked high on every surface. Plastic cartons littered the kitchen sink and Carol spotted the chicken carcass before anyone else said anything. How long's that been there

10

I wonder, she said grimly.

Don't know but I'd say it's not recent, the woman police officer said. Nothing in the cupboards either.

I'd better check out the bathroom and bedroom, hadn't I, but I don't suppose it gets any better.

There was only one bedroom and Carol knew there was only one mattress for them both. Dylan was not long out of a cot. They'd spoken about getting help from one of the charities towards his first bed. The smell of urine was overpowering in the bedroom and it was obvious the bed had not been slept in for some time. The smell in the room was foul. There was a large stain in the middle of the mattress and sheets were nowhere to be seen. Newspapers covered the floor and dirty clothes were scattered in every corner of the room. Something brown had been deposited on the newspaper: the source of the smell, dog faeces. The bathroom was worse, but one look was enough. The smell made her want to retch.

It's going to have to be police protection isn't it? she said to the two officers back in the kitchen who had found the key to the backdoor and were outside fussing over the dog. It was jumping up all over them, yelping. I think so, miss. We can't let the young lad stay here in this state, said PC Routledge, I'll make a phone call and my colleague will explain to mum.

She hated this bit, this taking children away from mums. No matter how many times she'd done it and there had been plenty, it didn't get any better. Sometimes there was no alternative, and whatever they said on the spot, there was too much wrong here to risk leaving him. Tara had not moved, but Carol could see that she was crying, attempting to force a bottle into Dylan's mouth.

He probably doesn't feel like it now, Tara, she said as gently as she could. She was upset for Tara already, even though no one had told her what was going to happen yet.

I'm sorry miss, but I'm afraid your place is not safe for your son, PC Routledge said. We are exercising our powers of police protection and we have to take him to a safe place. Tara looked at him dumbstruck and stopped rocking, then her head shot round to Carol. What's he saying, Carol? You told me we were working cooperatively. Tell me what I need to do and I'll do it.

I'm sorry Tara, but they've made their decision. Tara wasn't listening. By now there was a wild look on her face.

Tell me what to do! You're not taking him. You're fucking not taking him, Carol, you can't, I know my rights.

Carol knew the drill: don't get upset, tell them what the decision is and stay professional. Dylan's got to go and stay elsewhere, Tara, and it's not my decision, it's the police making this call. We're going to have to find an emergency placement for him. As soon as the words were out, she waited for Tara's reaction. For a few seconds there was silence and no one in the room moved, expecting Tara to erupt; she focused her mind on her manager's last words: do what you have to do, he'd said, which had made her feel like it was a team effort. She didn't always feel that though, if they were shouting or crying or when they stood up and said right in your face *you're a liar Carol Leadbeater that's what you are, a liar.* And when they told her to go to fucking hell as she was taking their child into her own arms, gently and softly so that there was no wrestling them away, she did feel like someone who might be a liar. If they said to her *Carol you know you said you'd work with me, you promised, promised me you would* and they cried and wailed like an animal who'd lost its young, then she began to think maybe she *had* lied to them and it was all too terrible. Terrible and ferocious, but someone somewhere who made the rules believed it had to be done and so she got paid to take children away because of that.

But Tara didn't erupt. She was down on the floor sobbing. The woman police officer said to Carol, here, let me take the lad out to the car, you try and help mum. She reached down to where Tara was crouched on the carpet and put an arm through hers, helping her to her feet. It was this, this broken-hearted job that got to her every time. You have to help when someone has shattered into pieces before your very eyes, but there is nothing you can say that will make a difference.

Don't worry, she said, hearing how hollow her own words sounded, because Tara had crumpled in on herself. We'll sort out some contact for you as soon as we can and he'll be well looked after tonight. Tara was still staring at the floor so that Carol only half caught her words, barely a whisper. Please, please let me go with him.

I'm sorry Tara, you know I can't do that. But he'll be somewhere safe, with foster carers tonight…. She trailed off looking at Tara's face which was shuttered with pain. I've got to get out of here. The other police officer who was worried about the dog came inside, needing Tara's permission to take it away. He liked dogs, did PC Routledge. She'd met him before.

By the time she was outside twenty minutes later, she'd managed to scrape together the bare essentials for Dylan's first night away – some pyjamas, a pair of shoes, a ragbag of toys, scooped into the arms of the policewoman who headed out towards the car where Dylan was being entertained by the other police officer. The weather had turned to a bitter squall, the sky was grey and the wind whipped scraps of leaves high up above the gutter along the street. Out on the road, the policewoman was placing Dylan into the back seat, wrapped in a blanket. He was not crying, but it would break any second. She turned away. Best avoided. They would take him to the station, but it was her job to find him an emergency foster placement, the next job on the list. With a bit of luck, Bob might have flagged this to the placements team already.

The policewoman was putting the ragbag of toys dangling from her arms into the back with Dylan. There had been no goodbyes. Carol's phone pinged with a message. A placement had been found.

Once it was all over and the police car had left, she went back in. She had to. It took ages to find a cup that was not filthy, and a teabag, but she made a drink for Tara. The sobbing from the other room was so bad her own hand was shaking as she poured the boiling water from the kettle. She was sick as a dog. When she placed the mug down beside Tara she didn't look up. Carol told her she would ring later, that they could speak about it all then, but for now she needed a bit of space. Before she could say more, Tara told her to get out. I'm never fucking speaking to you, she screamed as Carol retreated down the path.

Afterwards, it was if the life had been sucked out of her, which wasn't new. It was something in the pit of her stomach that had to do with her past. She couldn't face the office and the comments. Always the comments. It was a way some of them tried to make sense of it: they had to *believe* they'd done the right thing when they were sick in the gut. It made them feel better about it.

14

She sat in the car a long while with the engine still, staring out at the dirty sky through her windscreen. She'd see if Hen was in before going back to the office. She wasn't supposed to skive off in the middle of the day, but today maybe Hen would appreciate a quick hello. When she dropped in last week Hen was still in bed, so it had been pointless, maybe not today.

Hen was in the kitchen making tea and fussing about the sink. What are you doing here? she said, which wasn't what Carol hoped for as a welcome. She reached up for a kiss anyway, expectant. Hen was taller, of bigger build and inflexible by nature so it was generally Carol who made the running, at least when it came to physical affection. Hen smiled a little and the tension eased off. The air had been stiff between them for days. She wondered if Hen might be on the verge of a great writing breakthrough, but in the end decided that she was more likely to be depressed instead. It was the way she wouldn't talk for days on end that made her so confused. Carol made herself a cup of tea and sat down at the kitchen table.

Had a pretty grim morning Hen, if I'm honest. I thought I could check in at home for a couple of hours and see a friendly face. No answer came from Hen's back as she stood by the sink. Hen was broad shouldered, strapping even, so moved around the kitchen slowly.

You're not still brooding are you? She wanted Hen to shrug in that great bear way she had of lumbering around, then come over and give her a hug. You know I didn't mean it, I'm happy with the financials, give me time to get used to it a little, that's all I need.

Well, you know, I'm not happy with it. Hen remained still, her back to Carol, hands unoccupied resting on the side of the sink. The thing is Carol, now that you're here... I've decided to move back in with my parents for a while.

Carol looked at Hen's back and wondered if she should go and hug her. Was that it? Was this a ruse? She couldn't believe what she had heard, but when Hen didn't turn, didn't in her broad backed way show a flicker across her steady self of any movement, Carol's heart tightened in her chest. What do you mean move out? she said and stood up, cup in hand. Are you saying you're moving out from here, from us? Her voice sounded off register.

Was this that trouble with the neighbours? Hen said she'd been upset by it, that it stopped her being able to hear herself think. Hen was a bit snobbish about living in an ex council house. The neighbours were a nasty bunch and there had been run-ins with them before, but she had protected Hen from it, from the worst of it anyhow.

Yes, I'm sorry, it's not, well you know... this arrangement it's been great but it isn't working for me with the writing.

It was becoming hard for Carol to breathe. It was like watching a plane crash in slow motion, ripping through branches, tearing up the ground, the undercarriage shattering as it screamed across the rocks.

While Carol struggled to hold onto herself, Hen's back was a statue at the sink. Carol would remember this forever, hold a screen shot of this moment, Hen's back still as marble. She didn't want to realise how bad it was, yet it was there in front of her. Last week had been dreadful enough, a heated row that left them both in tears. Of course it had been fragile from the start, but she'd always believed it would never come to this. They were too sussed, insightful. Was it her, something she'd done? She was hard-wired to self-blame. Stop doing that, Hen had always said, stop being self-pitying. So no, maybe it was Hen and she'd made the wrong choice. And the tears began to roll, big generous useless tears while Hen left the room.

2

The Therapist

The fields at the back of Jo Juniper's house were undulating shoulders of the ridgeway. At this time of year, the mud upon every path became puddled with footprints, but after three weeks of uncommonly dry weather the cracked soil had hardened into ridges. Jo could cut straight across it without wellies and today, standing high on the breast of the hill, the earth was breathing with early signs of spring. The ground fell away in a steep dip towards the woods and, if you were lucky, small deer would sometimes venture out into the open. They were fleeting and swift, but the sight of them made her feel as if she too belonged to nature. So all the while, she scanned the treeline expectantly.

Cold air swept around her head. Though she regretted not wearing a hat, she didn't like the way it flattened her hair. So pale and fine like a child's it gave her an air of fragility. When she was small her parents thought she was delicate. In protest she became sporty, hardened to being outdoors.

Red kites were circling high above in a large group, possibly three or more, and she wondered about prey and praying. They were looking for something, but their cry sounded like keening as it carried on the warm air currents.

All week she had been uneasy. It was something that came from before she trained as a psychotherapist. It didn't disturb her, but it was enough to make her constantly struggle to find some equilibrium.

It seemed as if one of her clients had got hold of her in a way she least expected. A younger woman called Tara who had turned herself inside out in their sessions over the past few weeks. Plucky perhaps, but her life was a mess. It was about the baby, maybe that's why it had got to her. And it was always uncertain whether any of them would ever make it. The third client this week with relationship difficulties had tipped Jo over, as if she was trying to sidestep a shadow from her own past. The walk might help.

Despite a bright blowing wind chafing at Jo, Tara and her problems wouldn't let up. From her first appointment, it was pretty obvious she was scraping along below the breadline. She made no secret of her fruitless attempts to get help from social services to pay for the sessions. Now there was a chance she might not come at all today, despite being in trouble up to her neck. Poor Tara, it was social services telling her to get the therapeutic help in the first place.

Jo worried that the five weeks so far had only been enough time to get going, nothing more. The stakes were too high: her child taken into care by social services and the long-term plan was uncertain. She might keep him or lose him. It was that stark. If she did come today, the funding problem, likely unsolvable, was the last thing Tara needed. Not knowing from week to week whether she could continue was like cutting the lifeline at the end of every session. Tara's previous sessions always seemed to coincide with a court hearing, and she would appear in such a mess that Jo didn't dare ask. Late for the first two, missed the third - there were many reasons to be doubtful about today.

A deer broke cover from the trees and stopped for a heartbeat then disappeared, melting back into the copse. Her eyes travelled along the treeline up to the horizon where a thin mist was forming. The damp air was beginning to penetrate her coat. Tara was due at three o'clock and she needed her head to be clear well before then. If she turned up, it might be her last session.

Turning down the hill towards home, she considered the tragedy of modern times, that everything was governed either by money or the lack of it. Where, exactly, was the philanthropy in all of this - help refused more often than given. General love for, or benevolence towards, the whole of humankind was the dictionary definition of philanthropy. At least she'd had the sense to quit the counselling service. Targets for how many clients you can see in a day can cut your general love for humankind right out from under you. It still made her blood run cold. But this girl might be it. She might be the one who can make it, prove that with the right approach, that real change was possible. Jo was always optimistic. Her clients needed her to be; every time she hit that moment, the moment when their life locked on to yours and somewhere inside you knew you'd got enough strength to give to another, hope would be resurrected again. And that was the trouble with her. She was pleased to find she still cared.

The woods lay behind her as she barrelled down the side of the hill, off towards the broad grassy margin on the edge of the field. Standing in the lee of the trees on the soft green corridor above the field, she turned to face into the wind driving straight across the solid brown furrows she had left behind her. The farmers were good around there at keeping the borders wide on cultivated land. How many centuries had it taken before someone recognised there was wildlife on the borderlands, and that we depend on that as much as the cropped fields, like stitches in a tapestry.

She couldn't lighten her mood today, like a river that had burst its banks, the ribbon of its identity spreading out across the plains. Whichever way she looked at it, there had to be a sense that something improved for them, for all the Taras of this world, otherwise what was the actual point of it all? Her life plan, to find something meaningful, was more like two stops short of anything: no money, no meaning.

Walking back, the sun came out and she arrived home warmed through and calm. The smell of lavender greeted her from the open door of her consulting room, putting her instantly at ease. Her mind began to engage the old pathways before a session: feel well, think well, and act well. It was a small touch the lavender, but it brought comfort. She hoped it worked for her clients.

When the doorbell chimed bang on time, she was surprised. It was impressive that Tara made it at all, what with a long journey by bus and everything on her plate. I'm not late again am I? she asked as soon as she was through the door. Jo could see immediately that the week had not been kind. Tara avoided eye contact, brushing past into the room.

No, you're fine. Come on in.

21

Settling into their regular chairs Tara relaxed a little, despite a habit of being guarded. She was soon able to pick up where she'd left off the week before, something she had been good at from the outset. This was a healthy sign, some obvious commitment to the process.

I know I promised last week to tell you about Dylan and everything, she said looking up briefly, I've thought about how to do it a bit more now. She paused.

Jo sensed her hesitation. Only if you feel ready to tell me, Tara, it's up to you. If it would make it easier, we could talk all around him.

No it's okay. I can do it I think, but I might cry, I warn you. She shifted in her seat.

I want to do it now you know, she went on, I've got to start somewhere. I suppose you know it's the real reason I'm here? They're not going to get me on that one, I can say what I like in here can't I? She looked up, fear watching from the secret of her face. Jo nodded, You can, Tara. I won't tell them everything you've said, but you remember what the deal was?

Oh, I know, I know, she said nodding her head from side to side.

I have to tell the court that you've been coming, if I'm asked; give them a rough outline of what we've talked about. But you told me we should go ahead when I explained it to you. Is it still okay?

Yes. Tara studied her phone, frowning.

Are you sure?

Well it's like this, I tell you about my shit life and then I get better, she said without looking up, and they let me have Dylan back.

The person Jo had met on the first appointment was here

again. Defensive, brittle, her shop all shut up with the closed sign right out front.

Is that what you want to talk about today?

No, I want to talk about Dylan, but that's not what I keep being told by the social worker. She says to me, *oh you've got to do it for yourself Tara*, she says, *not so that you get Dylan back.*

I suppose it's hard not to think about getting Dylan back?

Yes, that's what I live for don't I.

It wasn't a question. Jo knew it would insult her intelligence to answer as if it was. I can imagine how you must feel about that, she said truthfully.

I doubt it, she said.

Do you think the social worker understands?

Well, call me stupid but no. That social worker, Carol's her name, doesn't know jack shit.

Why do you feel that, Tara?

Because she keeps on saying it, doesn't she. *Oh Tara, you've got to work with us*, she says, and *oh we know what you must be feeling, Tara.* Well, does she? I don't think so.

Snap. Shut. The sound patterned in her words, while Tara's fingers twisted around the handle of her bag.

But it was your choice to come here; we were right about that weren't we? You are doing this because you've decided to.

Yeah, and that's because I'm not as stupid as they think I am. I know I've had a shit life, but that doesn't mean I can't come here and do something about it. I am going to win you know, I'm going to show them. She put her hands in her pockets.

What would you like to show them?

That I can be a good mum. That maybe, well okay I'm not afraid to admit I *was* in a very dark place in my life back then, but I'm coming through it. I can get through it.

Tell me about being a good mum, what does that mean to you?

It's not like my mum for a start. I know that much. Everything she did I do the opposite, then I can be sure I'm getting it right.

What did she do wrong?

What didn't she do wrong? How about love? Let's say that you have to love children, *Mum*, have you ever heard of that? she said, looking into the middle distance. Yeah, mum, that's why I know you got it wrong because you didn't love me and that's why I'm in this shit. Thank you very much for that little lesson in life. Tara hauled her bag up on to her knees and started rummaging through it as though her life depended on finding something.

What else would you want to say to her, Tara?

I don't want to say anything to her. Tara's head was still in her bag. I would, she said, pushing her hand down further as if she could feel whatever she was searching for, like to say to her… She looked up and raised her head until their eyes met. *Fuck Off.* That's what I would like to say to her.

Jo did not flinch.

And what else?

Well, how about she didn't stay at home for us.

Do you remember that? How old were you then?

I remember when I was like five. I had my brother and my little sister under the bed because I thought the baddies would get them when we were home alone. I looked after them when she was out every night. She laughed. I did quite a good job too, but I wasn't much good at the cooking. That's when I burnt the kitchen down, well a bit anyway.

Did anyone help you then?

Not the social workers. They were all over us like a rash that night and what did they do? They took my brother and sister away to one place and me to another and I didn't see them for the next two years. *Oh but you've become parentified*, they said, *you have to be a child again*. Thank. You. Very. Much. She rubbed her hand up and down on her nose vigorously. I didn't see them for two years, but I got them back. I kept on and on and on until they let me see them.

Was that hard for you?

It was. Her face flinched as if something had passed close to her eye. But they don't care about that. *It's all in the child's interests*, she said in a sing song, and they go on and on and on about it as if they know.

Do you blame them for it?

Course I do. They're supposed to be helping us, not breaking families up. Why should I have to lose my brother and sister? She was angry, her voice had begun to crack and rage was seeping out through the gaps in her armoury. Why should I have had to lose them? Tears started to roll slowly down her cheeks. I don't care about that woman. And that was all they ever asked about. What contact would you like, Tara? they'd ask me. They only ever meant with that woman or that bastard. He didn't even want to know, except for five minutes when we went to court. She was shaking now, soundlessly, her shoulders heaving as she pushed a tissue into her eyes, that young girl again, trembling.

They were all I had, she exploded in a sob, and they took it all away, cos it was never the same after that. Great waves convulsed her. She could hardly speak. My brother has never spoken to me about that time cos he was told that I wasn't his mother and he shouldn't... he shouldn't come to me for stuff.

Jo stayed with it, her anguish, letting it settle deep into her reserves, sensing the damage in each word.

...And he never did, not ever again.

The sense of loss widened like a crater. Jo stayed still, in that place with her, whilst across in the other chair Tara attempted to stifle her sobs. It was not the first time she'd ever spoken about it, but it was the first time Jo had ever seen it raw, like a livid welt across her life.

There was much to comfort her over, so Jo offered what she could – empathy, love even. Tara allowed herself to be the little girl after that, defences down. For the whole of the remaining hour it was as if a small girl was putting her hands out in front until someone picked her up. The flowering tree outside the window framed her hair as she spoke, imagining the play she would have had with her sister and brother; and the basket of fruit on the side table became a toy basket of her own making that nested her stories tight into beds of safety. Tucked in, each apple lay beside each pear as if they would never be apart. She pictured it for Tara as she spoke, asking how she would be now, if her brother and sister were there.

I would tuck them up every night, Jo. That's what I would do. Even if they was grown up, I would tuck them up every night for the whole of their lives.

3

The Old Friend

Carol came out of the office late. Dylan's case was back in court that week and there was a deadline for the paperwork she probably couldn't meet. But what the hell, she couldn't do everything. Bob had increased her caseload tenfold and she was maxed out.

Hen had been gone less than a month and wasn't answering calls. The idea of going round had crossed her mind several times during the weeks, but Hen's parents had never liked her. Hen always changed the subject whenever she asked, said they were shy, that was all. They took a long time to get to know people. Carol wasn't convinced.

Outside the building the wind was up. Clouds raced across the sky. It had been a cold grey spring so far, but a flash of sun last weekend had released the frost and shaken everything out, so that all the shades of grey were tumbled about in a bright blue sky.

She'd called her car The Orange Crate, owing to its dubious hue and pedigree. It stuck out like a sore thumb on every street, a creaking Citroen that had somehow managed to hold up long enough to get her round on visits. She'd have to talk to Bob about it though because it was an old banger. As of yesterday, the latest fault had arrived in the form of a blow hole in the exhaust. It wouldn't last the month.

Without Hen, all the rent was on her shoulders and the outgoings had doubled. She checked her phone, but there was nothing there – no familiar voice saying it had all been a mistake. Two days of messages had gone unanswered. Furniture and bills were hardly the stuff of reconciliation, but she'd abandoned all attempts at making up. Hen hadn't replied to those emails either. She threw her bag into the boot. The car smelt of old lunches and the paperwork which was piled up in the back. The passenger door didn't open at all. Everything she took around with her pounded into the boot along with wellies and a ragged Barbour coat.

She sighed and tugged on her hair, too tired to even think. Her plan was to get shot of the office and see if she could finish something tonight at home. She was only twenty-nine and so far in life the words 'short and sweet' had brought her a long way. That was her epithet, on account of how she was full of bounce and only five foot two with wiry red hair. It suited, but in the sombre state she now found herself it didn't belong any more. She turned the key in the ignition and the engine started up with a growl. She glanced in the mirror, sighed again and thought well, maybe this face needs a rest, and headed for home.

She was weaving her way across town, her head telling her this wasn't like any kind of life she wanted any more. Her block of flats on the Poundyard Estate had been Thatcherized during the eighties, when everyone tried to buy up flats like there was no tomorrow. Now there was tension between neighbouring blocks, enough to make her nervous and jumpy. She had seen her fair share of pitched battles on the stairs or in the car park between owner-occupiers and housing association tenants. It was the owner-occupiers who made all the trouble, leaving rubbish on the stairs as if an underling would come and clear it all up after them.

Today was no exception. The first thing that greeted her at the entrance was an open black bin bag at the bottom of the concrete stairwell. It had happened before. She wondered if there was some deliberate intimidation going on. It made her not want to go down the stairs anytime at night, the bins always had to wait till the morning. She used to nag Hen about taking the rubbish bags down. Then, becoming scared herself, she would put them out in the corridor, lined up along one wall, the contents stinking the place out. Hen was convinced the neighbours were targeting them. She used to come into the kitchen in the daytime to get away from the shouting matches coming through the living room wall. Once, after she'd said something to them about the rubbish in the stairwell, she'd heard them shouting through the wall: *don't you go thinking you'll fucking give us any trouble.* No one could ever be sure if she and Hen were the intended targets. The bloke next door was always shouting being well into his drink. Out front it was always littered with boxes and bags of empties. Fosters FourX or Strongbow.

Hen would say, look Carol I can't be trying to think about the finer points of why Virginia Woolf tried to write the way she did if I've got screaming lager man in my ear all day. Carol didn't like to say that she didn't know about Virginia Woolf and was more likely to know about the bottom of a lager tin, but Hen was sensitive. It would have offended her. She had once said she didn't like books much and Hen wouldn't speak to her for three days.

She picked her way around the bag and headed up the stairs. She wasn't expecting to meet anyone because she always came home later than the neighbours, but today she was home before five, her heart in her mouth right up to the front door. Before her key was even in the lock, she sensed there might be trouble brewing. Next door was slightly ajar, which was unusual. She could smell the smoke and drink even at a distance.

Searching for her keys, Carol didn't notice new scuff marks at the bottom of her own door. She'd made so many complaints to the council and the police that she'd lost count of the issues. It had become impossible to maintain the outside in a clean state any more. Instead, she cultivated a deliberate blind spot to avoid seeing the dirt and decay.

As soon as she stepped through the front door, she sensed something was not right.

Hen? her first thought was that Hen had come back. She called again, Hen, are you there? Paper was strewn all over the hall floor: bills, newspapers, pages of something crumpled into what looked like rubbish. Was this revenge? Rooted to the spot she listened for any creak of sound, then called Hen? Are you there? Nothing came back at her except the ringing in her ears.

She had been trying to get some order in the place after Hen left and had piled newspapers and letters into neat stacks lined up along the wall nearest to the front door. These were now strewn like litter across the floor.

She picked her way through, along the corridor, heart pounding in the wall of her chest. They might still be in the flat. Her fear of burglary and stolen possessions was nothing to the fear of a burglar running out at her.

She rounded the door frame into the living room, paralysed with fear. And there it was in front of her, the aftermath of a hurricane. Every single thing turned upside down, the furniture spattered with her clothes and her paperwork. Straight away her eyes registered the up ended vase in the middle of the table. It wasn't a very nice vase - all blousy green and blue glass - but it had been something they'd bought together in Camden market. It had come to symbolise that special day so had been installed as the centrepiece of their dining table. Still centre stage, it now stood on its head surrounded by screwed up paper and dirt. On the floor a trail of her shoes led into the kitchen where she could see immediately that the orange Le Creuset saucepans were missing from the stand. Panicking, her eyes scanned the room for her laptop. It was on the kitchen counter with the lid closed – she never closed the lid – a sheet of paper was poking out from beneath the lid with Hen's writing on it.

Dear Carol,

I've been to collect my stuff so that we don't have to keep messaging about it. This is the painful part but like Virginia Woolf said 'it's far harder to kill a phantom than reality'. We have loved each other, Carol, but the life we've been living together has lost its fire. You have your life and your job and I don't belong in that world and I have my writing and my literature which is like a plant dying in this environment. It's my passion and I cannot see how we can go forward if you can't share that with me. It's not a criticism of you, you are a lovely person, but I can't go on living here any more, it's stifling my creativity. We both need to move on.

I'll drop the key round next week when I collect my clothes spinner which I couldn't fit into the car.

Hen

That was it then. No burglar but a woman far too self-absorbed to care. Tears began to fill Carol's eyes as she surveyed the stricken chaos. Nobody could have done this without intending to cause her pain.

She picked up the phone.

Jez, she said, I need you to come round.

Five minutes later and he was at her door, cigarette in one hand and a carrier bag from the off licence in the other. Jez was a bit of a wastrel, but the only friend she could call on right now.

Hello babe, I brought some gear, he said waggling the bag and tilting his head to one side

She smiled wanly and stared at him, wondering if this was something she wanted to do or whether it was going to turn out to be a giant mistake. I'm glad you're here, she said pushing her chin forward for a kiss, come in. He smiled a lopsided smile and sauntered into the hallway, giving her a peck on the cheek as he brushed past.

She was too numb to feel anything much about the mess except that she wanted out: out of her life, out of this flat, out of her shitty overworked helping everyone life.

She *was* pleased to see him despite it all and in some part of herself was a kind of devilish relish that he was such a waster she wouldn't have to put on any pretences.

What is it, babe? Something's wrong.

It's Hen, we've split up

Oh babe, that's a bummer.

And she's taken half my stuff. Carol was fighting tears.

Definitely a bummer then. And all this time I thought you were sorted.

He carried on through into the living room. Well blow me, look at the state of the place, he said. Was this your bird did this? he shouted, then muttered to himself, oh sorry, that's probably not what you call them.

She wasn't very happy about something was she? he shouted.

I'll get glasses. How many have you brought?

Four and a couple of beers. He chuckled, then came the sound of the double click and hiss of a can being opened.

You've had some shit going on then Carol? Jez was sprawled on her sofa with a can in one hand, the other waving at the room.

Well, let's drown our sorrows then, eh? He pointed across at the table, not getting up, I've put yours up there, darlin.

Yeah, make it a big one, Carol had a can open in her hand already and was rummaging in the drawer for the corkscrew ready for the wine.

I thought you two were out there putting the world to rights? Jez said, working for the social? He wiped the back of his hand across his mouth and looked up at her grinning as she handed him the corkscrew.

Yeah, I am Jez, but you know what, I might give that up as well. What the hell, there's so much shit going on in my life I don't know what I'm doing anymore. Do you want a wine yet?

I thought you liked all that stuff, trying to help *poor* families and that.

I did, no wait do. But you know what, without Hen it's like I don't see why I should even stay here now. I can't see the point anymore. She sat down in the chair with a thud. Perhaps I should travel. She put her can on the floor and attacked the wine bottle with the corkscrew. You see, I don't know if I am helping families, or whether I make it worse for them, she said twisting the corkscrew. Anyway, you never liked what I did, so maybe I don't either. Not deep down.

You pulling out then or is this fighting talk the start of some kind of payback?

Well you can talk. What about your life, Jez.

Since she was a kid Jez had been coming in and out of her life like a bad penny. When he started at college soon after her, they kept up their friendship, but he dropped out by the end of the second term and they lost touch for a while. He was single then and as far as she could tell, ever since.

Two years ago, when she was struggling with coming out, she'd bumped into him at the local Spar. Turned out he lived a couple of streets away. They'd been on a couple of benders, worked their way through far too many bottles of wine which had not made her feel better but had kept her away from desperation at the time. Once she became a social worker she tried to stay away from him.

Anyway, look I didn't get you round here to argue about all this stuff. You're my mate and all I want is to kick back a bit if that's okay?

She pushed the thought of what she had to do to the back of her mind. There was no way a statement was going to get

34

written tonight. She would have to say she'd been burgled, Bob would understand.

You'll be alright there, Carol. I'm your man for that. He smiled a crooked smile Come over here then and let's get stuck in.

This feeling it gave her was not entirely new; a kind of sunken joy as if she was free but not free. And it *was* seductive - oh yes, and wholly destructive too but she greeted it like an old jacket, all moth eaten, that had been hauled out from under the bed – call it a kind of comfort eating. Moving over to the sofa with a beer in one hand and a tumbler of red in the other, seemed about right. Tonight was not the night to worry about where her ethics lay.

At exactly seventeen minutes past eight the next morning, she woke on the floor of the bathroom rigid with cold. Her shoulder was keening with pain and she was wedged between the bath and the pedestal washbasin. Staggering to her feet she found that the same clothes she'd been wearing yesterday still clung to her. She made her way to the living room but Jez was nowhere to be seen. The detritus of the night lay strewn amongst the havoc of her flat; on the coffee table leftover pizza lay half eaten, abandoned next to her laptop which was emitting an unhealthy whirring sound.

She teetered towards the table and switched it off without even glancing at the screen. She didn't want to know, aware of one thing only: her head hurt monumentally and her mouth was foul. She picked her way around the shoes and went into her kitchen where the empties were lying about like a bombed skittle alley; she found no coffee where she expected it to be, except for a pile of grains on the counter next to an empty jar and some dregged cups. One mug seemed to have survived clean and with her hand she to scooped the small mound of coffee grains off the counter into it, rubbing her hands on the front of her trousers.

She had a sickness in her belly and the voice in her head was telling her she had done more than booze. Jez was bad news, bad news and bad news and not only was this written all over her flat but she also had a creeping sense of guilt that was making her sick to the stomach. The kettle boiled and with a slight tremor in her hand she filled the mug, watching brown foam rise up to the rim. Her legs hurt on both calves but she didn't know why and since she'd been moving around there was also an ache in her lower back as well, probably the result of having spent the last few hours squeezed into the bathroom where the base of the pedestal hand basin had imprinted itself into her lumbar region.

So I'm now supposed to feel good, am I? Taking a sip of coffee, she set the mug down between the debris on the coffee table, but something caught her eye amongst the cluster of objects. Two slender tubes rolled from ten-pound notes were beginning to unfurl themselves amongst the litter. A lurch of self-disgust hit her. Oh god, no, not that. Please let it not be that. Reaching over her cup she snatched both notes up in her hands and crumpled them as if they had no value and threw them to the floor. She glanced at the clock on the wall; it was eight forty-five, giving her only fifteen minutes to get ready if she was going to make it on time. Today was a court day and the flat was at least an hour away from Stanford Mags. No statement and no care plan was bad enough, but late as well would take some explaining. Bob would cover for her, but it wouldn't be the first time she'd shown up late - there might be repercussions in court.

No kids, no problem, that's what Carol had always thought about herself when she was younger and she had been no stranger to a couple of lines of coke once in a while, until the eureka moment which had taken her into social work training. Pride didn't come into it. In the end it was more like shame. There was never a good reason to do it and there were plenty of reasons not to.

Her mind fogged up when she tried to think what to do, remorse hanging around her like a sick vapour. Staring despondently into the dregs of her coffee, nausea was hitting her in waves, whilst something like gravel in water was moving through her intestines. Words like irresponsible floated to the surface of her mind and all she could think was that she'd let someone down. Nobody knows and they mustn't know, she said out loud checking the time on her watch which was still on her wrist from last night. It was nine o'clock. She scrambled to find her phone.

Hello, Daphne? Yes, it's Carol. Is Bob in? she paused expecting a negative, only I'm supposed to be in court in an hour and I've been ill all night. She waited, listening while the receptionist said something sympathetic on the other end of the phone. Yes, I know… I feel bad, she said, trying to make herself sound ill.

He's not answering his phone Carol, do you want me to go and see if I can find someone? He may have already left for court I'm guessing.

She didn't speak for a second, Hello? Are you there, Carol?

Yeah, sorry Daphne, she said weakening her voice, I thought I was going to be sick again. Look, can you get Bob to ring me and tell him I'm a bit unwell, but I will be coming to court, only I might be a bit late.

Are you sure, Carol, you don't sound great?

Yeah, no it's fine, but I won't have been able to put in the statement he asked for that's the only thing. Can you try and ring him on his mobile and let him know?

Yes of course, but only if you're sure. Daphne was beginning to sound as if she was starting to have some doubts, so she said her goodbyes and put the receiver down.

It was a set piece after all - pulling a sickie; and now she had to get this show on the road, pressure off. They were going for removal, but she'd have to wing it; anyway, Dylan's situation was no mystery.

4

The Barrister

You're not going to get him back today, Tara. It's a non-starter, I'm afraid. Harriet Fairwell was being firm. Number one she reckoned that with this particular woman there could be no beating about the bush and number two it might be a kindness of sorts. She had studied the evidence, including the photographs of the squalid flat, all of which signalled Work Needs Doing Here. Within the first few minutes of sitting opposite Tara in the lobby of Stanford County Court she had taken in the details of the woman who was to be her client for the day: young, dressed smartly suggesting she had made an effort, with fingers like birds that fluttered to her forehead whenever she spoke. Harriet was keeping an eye on the clock above them because she had no more than thirty minutes to extract the essentials for the hearing that lay ahead. She already had a page and a half of notes: about the difficulties Tara had faced when Dylan was at home, her attempts to get hold of the social worker, her habits, as well as the positives, like volunteering for her local charity shop on Wednesday and Thursdays.

The wind was whining outside, blowing leaves and coats sideways and out through the window she caught sight of a woman fighting to gain control of an umbrella which threatened to blow inside out.

Harriet didn't believe in giving her clients false hope when the outcome was as open and shut as this case appeared to be. Even if they had only met for the first time that morning, Harriet had already worked out that asking for the child back today would be a lost cause. Tara Downley had high expectations, but getting the strategy right from the start meant you might have a chance – not a phoney effort full of bluff and bluster, but a real solid opportunity to get everything working again to fix the problems. They might give you a second shot if you were lucky. But it would have to be realistic, with vital support put in on the ground. For Tara's sake, Harriet was setting her sights on the end goal – to get Dylan back at the end of the case. It would probably be twenty-six weeks before they reached that stage and it was unlikely they could stretch this case outside of that deadline. Only if they set it up properly from the beginning, on reassessment the department might give her the thumbs up. There was no way Tara would come round to giving up on today easily though, Harriet thought. She wouldn't be able to see that far ahead, couldn't see that there was a long road to travel first; she was still trapped in the wreckage of the day social services came calling.

Look, I know I won't get him back today, Tara said. Surprised, Harriet hesitated before she said anything, remarking to herself how seldom she'd ever heard those words from a parent. From the outset she'd spotted that Tara was quick: her opening words had been *glad you're here to speak as I know what needs to be said but don't think I'd make a very good job of it*. It was an impressive start. Here was a woman who talked straight.

It's not that I don't think we can make out reasons for him coming straight home, Tara, it's that people are going to be wary because you've had a care history. She sat back in her chair. Those photographs tell their own story, Tara, you have to accept that. I think perhaps you know there's some work you have to do? she asked as gently as she could.

Tara's mouth was working under pressure from her emotions, her hand tugging at a strand of hair, pulling it straight and flattening it down behind her ear. Eventually she nodded, but her eyes were filled with tears.

Tara, don't worry, it's clear what I have to do, but I had to talk it over with you first. It's tough to hear and you are being very brave about it. I think you knew that you've got work to do. It wasn't a question this time. So we need to think about how to approach today and that's why you've got me here. She smiled, hoping Tara understood she wasn't alone in all this, that she had a strong ally.

Dylan had already been taken by the police, Harriet knew. The bundle of case papers she'd picked up from chambers the night before included photographs of the flat in every damning detail, the cooker, the bathroom, even the state of the front garden. But it was the newspapers on the bedroom floor with the dog faeces that crowned it. The entire case would end up focused on the pictures because the magistrates would seize on them. Any whiff of the slums and middle

England, who occupied the magistrates' benches, would give it a well-manicured thumbs down.

Has the social worker said anything to you, Tara, about where all this is heading? Has she told you what you need to do to get him back?

Nothing, that's what she's told me. Nothing, she said, wringing a piece of ragged tissue between her fingers.

But have they been round to talk to you about today and the next few months? Has she been around to your place? Tara shook her head.

Something might have been said, a lifeline thrown to her like: *take part in this assessment and you'll stand a better chance of your child being returned.* But Harriet was long in the tooth. Sometimes it had been said and somehow they couldn't hear it. When children had been removed all the mums heard was: *your child is being taken away.*

No, they haven't been round. They haven't called me neither. And I've got bloody voicemail. If she'd have tried to call me once, I'd have got back to her in a flash. Like, hullo? I want to know about Dylan, don't I? They think I can't do it, but they're wrong about that, like they were wrong about everything when I was in care myself.

Tara had not taken off her jacket. She was sitting with her hands folded on her handbag. From the tone of her voice, it struck Harriet that Tara wasn't angry despite the rhetoric. She made a mental note in case it mattered later. She was still trying to get her measure, understand her limitations, her strengths - all a necessary part of the process. You couldn't just rock up and open your mouth. You had to let them get under your skin, *become* their voice. And so far she had the impression of a woman with reserves of strength and a wry intelligence beneath a brittle exterior. But it was clear she was inexperienced in life, more like a bird careering out of the nest, sorely in need of some navigation.

A rudimentary working plan was taking shape in her head. Proposals would inevitably be hurled her way – assessments, contact meetings, the lot. She couldn't second guess how Tara might fare in any of them. More often than not it was the ones you least suspected who would go the distance in the end, surprising everyone.

A *working relationship.* That's what they called it in social services quarters. To be able to cope with social services putting your child into foster care was one thing. Then seeing him only a couple of times a week at best was another. But to be cooperative on top of it all, or better still *keen* to work with them, well that took the biscuit. The working relationship was the most difficult part, the hurdle at which so many fell. But you can never say never, and perhaps they had all been mistaken about Tara. It wouldn't be the first time a client had walked in through the door on the wrong end of a social worker's judgment.

When you get out of there, Tara said, you don't ever want to go back. Oh, yeah they want to look after you they say, to get a good start in life, but you know what? It's a lie, cos you've already started your life by the time you got there, and it's usually shit.

Harriet nodded. I know, she said, thinking how much better it would be if the people in the system could learn something from the kids in care once they'd grown up.

I've thought about all this before I got here though, Tara said. I reckon I could teach them a thing or two about what to change, whatever they say about me. I even thought of becoming a social worker myself.

I bet that's true, but they'll still want you to have assessments, Tara.

Meaning?

Meaning that they want to understand what went wrong, at home I mean, with you and Dylan.

Nothing ever *went wrong*, she screwed her face up with disgust.

The obligatory sizing up, each of them appraising the other, was still underway. And it *was* a big ask to expect a stranger you only clapped eyes on five minutes ago to know what you want, to understand it inside of half an hour. It's not as if *we've* ever had to do it: meet a person and tell them everything intimate about yourself in the first ten minutes; all those secret things in your life, even the bad stuff. But Tara was not diffident like others, no doubt the result of endless social work visits during her childhood; every six weeks listening to them trying to answer when they asked you about your wishes and feelings. Underneath that tough exterior there just might be an understanding of how she got herself into this situation.

Have you done any work on the flat yet?

Of course I have. You wouldn't recognise it! And I've got the pictures to prove it. She dived into her big purple bag and pulled out a packet, twenty glossy photos, each taken in milky light showing a spotless house, the kitchen, the bathroom, a bedroom with two beds in it that had not been there before. The contrast to the pictures she had studied overnight was stark, unrecognisable - even the garden had been cleared.

You've done a great job there, Tara, well done.

Harriet meant what she said. The belief that this girl could pull herself out of trouble was gaining ground. Do you think you can keep it that way? Even if Dylan returns? Waiting for the answer, she scanned the faces of assorted people scattered throughout the lobby, checking there was no one listening to her conversation. Small groups filled the available seats, each with a black suited advocate scribbling notes like a worker ant. She could see from the tension and held-back tears that what brought them all here was common suffering. A place of unease, a cathedral of argument. She was satisfied no one was eavesdropping. Once she'd caught a journalist taking notes of a conversation between a lawyer and his client, without them being aware he was snooping behind.

Listen, said Tara, I'm not going to let that happen to me and Dylan again, not ever. This is learning the hard way, isn't it?

Until there was a sign it was sustainable with everything in place, they must hold off an attack. If Dylan was returned too early and the wheels came off, it would be another disaster, especially if they had to pull him out again. There would be no going back; no second chances in this game. Tara said, you want assessments? I can give you enough assessments to keep you lot talking for a week. She sat back, smiling triumphantly. I've had them all.

New ones I mean, Harriet ventured.

What for? So that they can say it all over again?

Harriet had been here many times before: the Bumpy Start she called it. At the first hearing, sometimes there was everything to play for if the children were still in the home. You could try to hang on to them, but if they'd already been taken out, then getting them back was a long haul. Not that she was against removing them when there was no other option. She'd seen plenty where she would have driven round there herself, cases where you wondered what had taken social services so long. But then some clients could tell you what happens to kids in care too, the ones who'd been there themselves. It was a crying shame. All those little ones let down, shoved into unseen corners.

The court bundle was three lever arch files, some of it Tara's childhood from fifteen years back when they'd taken her away from her own mother. Taken out and returned, taken out, returned and then taken out again, each time sent to a different foster carer, torn from her sister and brother, a mother with partners who usually left via a revolving door. Neglect and violence, in front of their young eyes. The only lesson they ever had from their mother about love was that you stuck fast to a man who left you with the black clouds of inadequacy printed on the side of your face, so bad your eye closes up.

It was obvious there would have to be assessments. There was too much at stake. The social workers wouldn't risk returning Dylan until they could prove it wouldn't happen again. Ignore the drip drip of neglect at your peril, they said. And then they had their own backs to cover, higher up the chain of command they would stop you dead if you came up with a care plan that was anything less than a cast iron guarantee of safety.

She said, it's so that they can see you as you are now, understand how you would cope if things got difficult again, you know, whether you'd let it slide back without realising.

There would be issues about contact too today. Whether Tara had been allowed to see him at all since he was taken was a question that needed asking. Have you seen Dylan, Tara? Have they let you see him?

Twice. Tara snapped back. Only twice and for an hour and

that's not enough. It's a bloody joke that is, he's my son. He doesn't have his blanket with him and I know what that does to him.

His blanket?

Yeah, it's a shitty bit of cloth and it stinks but he loves it and he goes mad when he doesn't have it. They wouldn't let me give it him cos they wanted to wash it. Well, it wouldn't stink then would it, and then it wouldn't be his stinky any more would it?

We'll have to see what we can do about that, she said, thinking that time was running out. They needed to reach a decision. Tara, we need to think about what to do at this hearing. Is there anyone who can move in with you? Help you care for him, like an auntie, or granny, or even a friend? Someone they'd think could, well, protect Dylan making sure you're doing the right things?

Tara scowled. Nope.

Help you to keep the place in shape?

I'm doing that already.

What about your mum? Would she help?

She's not much cop, but yes she would help sort of. We don't get on that well.

Has she seen Dylan? Oh yes, she's seen him and she's paid for some things for him. She keeps on at me too, but I get the hump with her.

Is there someone you have any contact with in the family who could help, like an auntie?

Tara shook her head. I've never had much contact with them, they're a useless lot.

The answer didn't surprise her, but she had to ask anyway in case there was someone who could make a difference, and fast. She'd had clients who went off somewhere and found people, capable people who could help. Once she had a girl who came to court with a different person from the church every time, and though not one of them understood the scale of her problems, they came to help. But that girl had had Alone written all over her. The chintz clad ladies from the church were all she had left, but they couldn't take on the kids.

If you can accept that we're in it for the long haul here, Tara, which I know is difficult, I think it's the best approach. She was giving advice now: you don't have to agree to Dylan remaining where he is for now, in foster care, while they do their assessments, but it might prove better for you in the long run. But we can contest it if that is what you want – I would give it my best. Tara had been listening intently to every word, her face impassive. What about the pictures? Don't they make a difference? Won't the judge see I've done what I need to do?

You're right, they are important, but it's more than a clear up that's needed. It would hurt to say it, but Harriet knew she had to and went on. …It's about the risk that it could happen again. That's what they will be thinking. Look you've done a brilliant job this far and it shows you *can* do it, but unless someone can figure out what led to everything getting that bad…. She trailed off, waiting for the words to sink in. I don't think we would succeed Tara, if we fight it out today and it risks them thinking you still don't get it. It is your shout though.

I was depressed, that's what happened. I do get it, Tara said, isn't someone allowed to get depressed once in a while? Is that it? No one gets depressed, is that what you're telling me?

She's right, Harriet thought, but Tara needed to recognise this thing was different, because her son was suffering, *had* suffered. Living in that place may well have affected him, especially if mum was there, but at the same time absent emotionally. It was a fine line, but modern-day standards demanded domestic competence and more. You could get away with it if you were an artist from the middle classes parading bohemian values, but not if you were poor. Being a *good enough* parent, they called it.

A social worker once said to her: *when they ask why they came on to social services radar, tell them they were simply unlucky.* But what Tara said was true: people get depressed. Bad things happen. And they can happen to everyone. She wasn't about to spin the lie that everyone else here was doing Perfect Parent. You know what, Tara, you're right, but I don't think the magistrates will buy it. And there may be something even you think you need to do to make Dylan's life better. But if that's what you want me to say to the court today, I will. It's not that you haven't done a brilliant job - you have, but this is only the start, isn't it?

She waited, watching Tara's emotions rise and fall. At first her jaw set and she got her phone out and stared at it for a few minutes swiping, but when she looked up, her face had softened and she asked, will I still be able to see him, if we lose I mean?

Of course, that won't change and might even improve if you can work with them, show you can do it over the next few weeks. It will help at the final hearing.

Work with them? They don't come and see me. Believe me, I don't count for nothing now they've got Dylan, she said. They don't come and see me. I already told you that.

I know, but do you think you can do it? Work with them I mean, show them you can get stuck in with whatever they ask you to do, for Dylan's sake.

I'll do whatever I have to. She was glued to the screen, but when she looked up and their eyes met there was a shine in her eye. Of course I can, she said.

I knew you would. She admired her for that. It was far from easy, but a battle at this stage was doomed to fail and might stand against her in the long run if she couldn't see that she'd have to work on herself, work with them. *No insight* they would say and scale down their plans for returning Dylan even further. *She doesn't realise she has to change if she wants her son back,* they would say, and condemn her at the starting blocks.

I know I'll lose. I have heard what you said, she said, but I still want to try. At least I want the magistrates to know I haven't sat on my arse and done nothing.

Right, well, I will give it my best shot. Meanwhile I need to go and see what I can do on the contact front then, in case we don't succeed, she said and smiled. You stay here, I'll see what I can do.

Harriet set off in search of the other side. There were only two consultation rooms at Stanford. It was an old building, all panelled oak and stone staircases built when dock briefs were still around.

She found the social workers with their brief in one of the rooms. They'd turned out in force: the social worker, her manager. She could tell immediately who held the power. The manager nodded politely staying aloof, but the social worker, Carol, decked out in a big scarf, big coat, asymmetrical haircut was odd socked yet breezily energetic – perhaps too keen to get involved. Harriet knew straight away she had been the one Tara had crossed paths with. She wondered about that keenness. It seemed forced in the choking claustrophobia of the consultation room, and she avoided eye contact whenever Harriet looked at her. In the head chair was a woman with red hair coiled neatly at the nape of her neck– their barrister – next to a man in pin stripe who had old school written all over him.

Case of Dylan Downley? she asked, addressing the red head.

The woman looked up from her notebook, a smile slowly tightening her face. Florence Uppart, she said. Are you for the mother? Harriet had clocked the heels and the starched shirt the minute she entered the room, but the acid smile gave it all away - nervous, confuses passion and commitment with ruthlessness, oh and not married yet but probably dating another barrister somewhere. She returned the smile.

Cruel to judge this early in the process, but then sizing up the opposition is what happens. Harriet Fairwell for mother. Who else do we have here? she said to those in the room generally. The pin stripe was definitely the child's solicitor, elderly and long in the tooth. He'd get his instructions from the guardian if there was one, but the court advisory system was in a mess and there'd be no way he could have jumped the queue. The courts appoint a solicitor for every child, no matter what their age, whose job it is, on instruction from a guardian, to try and get above the melee and see where the child's best interests lie. It didn't always work that way. Much depended on individuals, when it shouldn't.

I'm representing the child, he said.

No Guardian yet I suppose?

Not yet, I'm neutral of course.

Neutral, my arse, she thought. Of course you are - that's why you're sat in here with the local authority. Her client would

51

never believe the guardian was independent if their actual rep was cozied up in the same room with social workers. Trouble was it would be vital for Tara to put her best foot forward with the guardian. It would be their recommendations to the judge as court adviser that would more than likely carry the day and if Tara took against such a key player, then she might lose everything.

It was impossible to avoid the meet and greet, the socialising chit chat that went on at court. Lord knows she was guilty of it herself, but early in the case when feelings were running high it wasn't cricket for the guardian's rep to sit with the local authority like this. It stuck in her throat to see how little others thought about that. Couldn't they see themselves, she wondered, professionals forgetting how to keep their noses clean of bias?

I'll tell my client that, she said crisply and hesitated for a nano second before letting loose a small shot across the bows: and have you spoken to her at all? She gazed innocently at the child's solicitor. To let her know Dylan's being separately represented I mean? Her eyes returned to her notebook as she waited in the ensuing silence for the torpedo to hit its target.

Well no, I don't think I need to today, not without a guardian present anyway.

Typical! He hadn't even noticed the attack. It had obviously missed its mark. She wasn't surprised; he didn't have the look of a grafter.

And what is your position, Florence? Both smiles were frozen, hers and the red head's. False friendliness.

We want an order, Harriet.

The easy familiarity, first name terms from the off had her thinking Florence would be savage if crossed. We need to keep Dylan where he is whilst assessments are done. Oh, and we want a psychological assessment of your client.

I have some pictures of the flat, she said.

We've seen them thanks, Florence said, the corner of her mouth lifting slightly, and we will be relying on them. Look, is your client going to oppose, I mean what *is* her case exactly? She smiled at her little group, we don't want to give her a hard time, she turned back to Harriet, but honestly....

Yes, we are opposing. She thrust out her hand holding the photos, I meant pictures of how it looks now. Her hand holding the wodge of shiny prints hovered there for a second whilst a flicker of eyes criss-crossed the room; no one reached for them and she was left with her hand outstretched. Suddenly it became obvious that Tara *had* been telling the truth when she said no one had visited from Social Services. Nobody wanted to see the pictures because they knew full well what they would show - the flat in a pristine state. Then where would their case be? Maybe it wouldn't see off an interim order, but it might look like she'd made a good start.

Has your social worker visited at all? she asked aiming the question at Florence, but all the while watching the social worker from the corner of her eye, sitting right next to where she stood. Of course, she already knew the answer but strategy mattered here. She wanted them to *know* that she was aware. She was beginning to realise Tara was dead right: they hadn't been there for weeks. It was another shot across the bows. After an age in which nobody spoke, the social worker slowly reached up and took the photos.

She leafed through them without pausing on any one image, I've not been able to visit for a while, and, she said thumbing through the last few, I've been concentrating on getting Dylan settled in at the foster carers. She looked up and turned towards the red head. But I have made a couple of calls and no-one's picked up. She tucked her chin under and examined the toes of her boots where both her feet were pushed together.

Improbable sun slanted through the window and touched the edge of the witness box where the patina in the wood glowed deep chestnut brown. Carol's hands were resting on the edge of the box and Harriet could see that her fingers were grimy, a detail noted, then stored away. She had been giving evidence for the past ten minutes, describing the state of Tara's flat in February. Harriet was on her feet questioning her.

Can you tell me what meetings you have had with the mother since February, when Dylan was removed?

Well, I have tried to keep her informed of what is happening with Dylan. There've been some problems with him settling in. Harriet noticed the social worker was studying her hands on the edge of the witness box.

Yes, I'll come back to that in a moment, but what arrangements have you made to engage with my client?

I've tried to meet her several times, she said, turning to face the magistrates who were listening carefully. Of the three, Harriet thought the chairwoman seemed the most engaged, a good sign, but the winger on the right, a grey-haired middle-aged woman wearing purple was stony faced.

When did you try and meet with her?

I went out to the flat, but there was no one in, she said shifting her weight from one foot to the other, and I've tried calling her several times, but her phone, well, there's never been a reply.

Voicemail was one of the first things Harriet had asked Tara about. If she was going to find out if the version of events Tara had given her was true - that they had taken Dylan and not said a word to her since - then she needed to know that Tara's phone could register missed calls or keep messages.

Can you tell me when last you tried to phone?

I don't have the precise dates without my diary, but it was very soon after Dylan was removed and then I made another couple of calls over the last few weeks.

You say a couple of calls. How many was it?

Oh, I don't remember.

Was it two? Or more than two?

More than two, definitely. Yes, she said and pulled her hands in behind the wooden stand.

Was it three or more than three?

Yes, three.

You say none of them were answered?

That's right.

Why didn't you leave a message?

I did I believe. Yes, I did. But Tara has never got back to me.

She glanced at the magistrates who were writing.

Only my client has voicemail and a missed call register. She says that you have not called her once since Dylan was removed.

I believe that's wrong. I can get my diary?

But you haven't written to her either. I mean, if your calls failed to get through, you'd have taken other steps, to make an appointment as soon as possible wouldn't you? To discuss her son's welfare?

Yes, of course I would, that's exactly why I tried to phone.

But if you failed to get any answer by phone, you would surely have written to her. Did you write to her? The social worker tugged at her hair and cleared her throat. ...Or drop a letter round if your calls hadn't been answered?

No, I didn't.

Why not?

I have had a very busy case load. Yes, I suppose I should have written.

Do you remember which days of the week you called?

No, I don't but it would have been in the morning, probably.

Might it have been on a Wednesday or Thursday?

Yes, quite possibly.

Your worships, might the social worker be permitted to fetch her diary?

All three magistrates were blank canvasses, not a shadow of expression across any of their faces, only the merest nod from the chairman. She could not tell what was going through their heads, or whether they were grasping the picture as it emerged. The woman in the purple cardigan, however, was becoming irritated.

The social worker disappeared down behind the stand and fetched up a diary.

Yes, I think I have phoned, let me see...oh dear, I am sorry. She turned towards the magistrates. It seems I haven't diarised it, but I do remember it would have been a Wednesday or Thursday.

My client is a volunteer at the local charity shop on a Wednesday and a Thursday. You knew that, I think?

Oh, yes, I might have forgotten. The social worker was looking uncomfortable now, leaning heavily on the wooden ledge of the witness box.

Perhaps you can see that she might be very worried that she hasn't heard from you. You didn't leave a note when you called round either, did you?

No, she said, her voice quieter, I didn't.

And you should have made every effort Ms. Leadbeater, shouldn't you? You have the care of my client's son. Surely your responsibility is to make every effort to meet and talk with the mother about what she needs to do to get her son back, is it not?

Yes, well as I said I did try. She turned to the magistrates. I have been working on this case the last couple of days and I wanted to bring a statement to court this morning about what we want to do, but, well … I've been ill. She hung her head submissively awaiting the next question. She wore the look of someone being questioned unfairly. Harriet knew to watch her step; if the atmosphere became too tense, with deferred discomfort spreading from the witness box, the magistrates would be unable to handle it. You could lose the day if they thought you were being mean.

I realise you may have been unwell, Ms Leadbeater, but we are talking of a time before the last couple of weeks.

Yes, of course. I'm sorry, but what was the question again?

Well, perhaps you can help us with the date you last visited and found my client absent?

I was conscious that I needed to speak to her before this hearing, to tell her our plans, so I called on her yesterday evening but got no reply.

At this Tara could not help herself and blurted out, that's not true, from behind Harriet.

Ms. Leadbeater, I suggest that you didn't visit my client yesterday evening at all. She was in all evening.

I did make the visit, but there was no reply at the door.

At this point, the social worker cleared her throat, then coughed lightly behind her hand. With studied patience, she waited for the next question.

The magistrate in purple whispered to the chairman, who nodded, then said: Mrs. Fairwell, we are wondering, in view of the fact that you have said your client may consent to Dylan remaining where he is in the interim, what the point is of all these questions?

I don't have very many more questions for this witness, Sir, she said realising immediately she was up against their limited tolerance for detail. It rankled with her though. Plainly, it had not occurred to any one of them that they might need to scrutinize social services' plans to make sure they were sound. After all, no decent plan equalled no return of Dylan. It was all too easy once the juggernaut of care proceedings was hurtling down the hill for a parent to see a child slip from their grasp. Before you knew it, some nice middle-class family would have a new baby. Social engineering by default, Harriet called it. Only the courts could keep them on their toes, hold them to account.

Perhaps they needed more of a steer. *A magistrate is not a qualified lawyer* she would explain to her clients. Times like this amply demonstrated why you had to map it out as best you could.

Hoping to win some extra time, she turned fully towards the bench. It is important, she said, that the Local Authority works with my client to ensure that she is placed in the best position to understand what is happening with her son. Your Worships will want to know if this has taken place.

The chairman was fidgeting. Was he taking it in? He looked

right and left at his colleagues and Harriet pressed on, aware her window of opportunity might be rapidly closing. My client wants to work with the Local Authority and take all necessary steps to bring about the reconciliation of her son back into her care. To do that, she needs to know, is *entitled* to know, how Dylan is faring and what the Local Authority's plans for him are.

Yes, but do we need to hear any more of these questions? It was the woman in purple. Unusual move that, to speak out of turn when you're not the chair, Harriet thought. The chairman started with surprise, but then followed purple woman's lead, Mrs. Fairwell, the witness has answered your question. She *has* been to visit and your client was not in.

Sir, my client does not accept that those attempts were made.

He was riled now. Yes, thank you Ms. Fairwell, we have heard what your client has to say.

It was useless to go on. The tide had turned. She finished there and then. Thank you Ms. Leadbeater, I have no further questions.

Stepping out onto the High Street, into the freezing rain which had not let up all morning, Harriet summed up the morning's events to herself: she could be brave, but it hadn't been there for the winning. What she had said to Tara at the start was exactly what had happened. In the end they got what they wanted, a chance to be assessed, to work with them on an agreed path, or at least everything in place for Tara to have a good crack at it. A psychological assessment would not be done inside of three months; there'd be a parenting assessment based on notes taken whilst she was on contact visits, which might help Tara in the long run.

The psychologist, Margie Harrison, was unknown to her, a risk she didn't like taking, using an unknown expert, but her hands were tied. A junior at the solicitor's office had already agreed to the choice. The CV was impressive, but you could never tell on paper. They might be anti-parent, especially if they worked part time in an adoption agency. There was that old robing room banter about the reports, especially the cut and paste ones, where some stray name from a previous case has crept in: *we could write the reports ourselves.*

The rain was a downpour. She was making ready for a quick dash to the station when she heard a voice behind her. Want to share my umbrella if you're going to the station? It was Florence Uppart.

Your lady seems nice, Florence said as they were settling into their seats on the half empty train. She propped her umbrella open on the floor where it could drip, there was always plenty of room on the one o'clock fast train back into London. Do you think she'll come through? she asked.

Harriet didn't want to get into a debrief with her oppo. I hope so, she said firmly. I'm not giving anything away, else it comes back to bite me later. Best find out what might be in store from the expert. What about Dr. H? she asked, have you used her before?

Oh, I have, Florence said. The enthusiasm was a little worrying. When local authorities fastened on to a particular expert, it was all too often a sign that they were accustomed to getting what they wanted from them.

She's always on time with her reports, Florence explained, and she comes across well in oral evidence. I like her.

It all sounded innocent enough.

Do you use her a lot?' Harriet asked, pushing her damp hair back off her face and sliding her trolley bag under the seat.

Yes, we do and I've seen her in action. Doesn't beat about the bush and always sticks to her recommendations under cross examination.

And that always makes them popular with you guys, she said. Let's hope she gets it right then. My lady is determined, and I don't think she'll only go half measures to straighten herself out either. I hope whoever it is has the nous to see that.

Florence smiled, clearly measuring her up. What chambers are you from?

Two Middle Square. You?

Ferris Chambers.

Ah, the basement set. James, her senior clerk, complained bitterly about Ferris Chambers, because they always undercut the bidding process when there were tenders out for local authority work. They would be the cheapest in the bidding process, it was as predictable as night follows day that cash strapped Local Authorities would send all the work their way, good or not.

Carol had an electronic key to the office. Dropping in and out late in the day or even at night was part of what they did as social workers. No one would question her if she turned up after court. That late night check on a child new in foster care, an emergency removal when the police needed you, all of that stuff, plus those long days in court meant a late night stop off at the office was pretty standard. She touched her fob to the electronic gate, confident enough to ease her conscience.

All those bloody questions. What did they think she was trying to do, abduct the child for god's sake?

Hi Carol.

Nnamdi the night caretaker looked up from his paper as she swung through the lobby. His was a familiar, comforting presence on the desk at night. For the late women workers he would make sure they had a safe ride home. They knew he had their back.

Hi Nnamdi. This time she did not stop to chat.

No one was in, thank god. She cleared a space at one of the hot desks and tapped her password into the waiting computer. It was too easy to add documents to files after the event. It had to be, because some days were a chaos of visits in and out of houses, too many to count, when you were too worried about the children who would look at you hoping for something. File notes, part of the job since she didn't remember when, but drummed into her every time the tragedy of a child death hit the papers. Waiting for the file to load, she wondered how she had looked, sat there in the witness box, like a fool being baited. And there it was, Dylan Downley's case file. Her tongue touched the edge of her lip as she typed…

/file note, visit… and she started to tap out yesterday's date not pausing to look at it.

It was too easy to do…. *visit to the property, 7.20, no reply at door. Waiting 15 minutes and checking letterbox, but no response. Plan had been to discuss with mother the court hearing tomorrow and let her know what I would be saying and obtain her view and general update on Dylan ready for court tomorrow.*

She tabbed back through the file, looking for any other evening visits to check how she'd written them. She'd just add two, enough to cover it if anyone checked up. If management wanted to see, she would be in the clear. It hadn't looked good in that hearing, as if she hadn't given it enough thought. Sloppy, that's what that barrister said at the end.

/file note, telephone call to update mother, Wednesday, no response.../

A few minutes and the job was done. Bye Nnamdi, Carol called swiping her fob out. A hit of clear air and she felt a thousand percent lighter. Job done. The child needed to be removed and they had to make that happen. To protect it. She shook her head a little as she put her key into the Orange Crate and checked behind her, just to make sure.

5

The Mother

Tara was sitting by the window, taking the last of her cigarette. There wasn't much to see outside, truth to tell, except the pigeons on the roof of the petrol station opposite. She began to warm up as the sun broke through the bank of grey cloud above the skyline. There had been no rain for over a week and on the trees in the park, where she used to take Dylan, the buds were swollen and sticky. No one had visited her all through the beginning of spring, not even Carol who'd been a right Mrs Bossy Boots about everything. *We want to work with you* she'd kept on saying endlessly, but then faded away and didn't make contact. Every time Tara phoned Carol herself, she would get a different social worker, sometimes the duty worker, and they would look at notes on the file and tell her some stuff about what she had to do. But it was general stuff, like clean up the flat, get some help with her issues. Nothing more specific than that.

It's true she was relieved not to have to answer endless questions, but now she needed to know what was going on. The social workers repeatedly used the same phrase *work with us* but it was unclear what they meant by it. She had to phone to ask about Dylan, but all they'd say was he was fine. It wasn't enough to know he was *fine*. What about what he'd eaten for lunch, or whether he'd pointed at something? She was a mother who needed to know, like any other mother who needs to know. Was he talking more, or putting out his bottom lip like he used to do? That cracked her up every time. She was the one, the only one that cared about it.

Her keys lay in the nest of her lap, the plastic photo fob underneath her hand. It carried a picture of Dylan. She could run her thumb up and down it whenever she had to think. Her mum had paid for that fob right before Dylan was taken into care. She'd been a fat lot of use since, but then it was nice she paid for it like a proper nan should. He had that 'I'm going to be a tough guy' look on his face. No one ever believed he was only three because he looked like a proper little man. She dug herself further into the cushions of her chair. He was like her, he was, and everyone saw that.

It would be twelve weeks today since he'd gone. She was waiting for her friend Steph to come up the street with her boyfriend. He was bad weather waiting to happen that one, but she couldn't have Steph without him bringing that lump of meat along and she didn't want to be alone – not today.

Living without Dylan had made her cave all in. Whenever that happened, she was a mad dog, like as if she couldn't breathe. That's what it was like anyway, she told Steph the first time it happened. It's like I can't breathe at all, Steph, and I'm going to die of it without him. She'd been shut up behind that black door a few times since and she couldn't go near it anymore. There's only one thing your mind turns to on your own then, but that would be a dead rain on everybody's parade.

Nobody wants to know any more. The leaves on the trees beside the garage were coming out. They looked like ears and nobody was listening to her either. He was stuck there, she was stuck here; a million of his heartbeats she'd missed, and he cried every time she left him after contact. No-one took any bloody notice, sat there taking notes, telling her he didn't want her food because he'd already eaten his lunch at the foster carer's.

The doorbell rang. She stubbed out her cigarette on a saucer and got up to answer it. Steph would have some money; her mum was soft on giving over her money even though it all went on the drink mostly, but at least they'd get a good night out of it.

C'mon Tara, open the bloody door.

I'm coming Steph, keep your hair on. It was a double lock and sometimes sounded like more than it was getting open. A right faff. There they were: her standing, him looking the other way. Come on in then, she laughed at them.

She hadn't done it in ages, had a binge that is, not since when she was expecting Dylan, which was the first time the social made a big fuss. Some nosey gobshite had told them.

You all right? Steph asked matter-of-factly as she stepped inside.

Yeah, waiting for you. Are we going out then, Lee? He moved past her across the room, throwing himself in the chair with his legs stuck right out, his head sunk so low that his chin was nearly on his chest.

66

Alright, he said not looking up, put telly on then.

TV watching position. Steph sat down nearer.

Do you remember that night we went out and got wasted, Steph? she paused, expecting Lee to say something nasty. He didn't, only because he'd turned on the TV and was flicking channels.

It was when I was pregnant Steph, and that nurse in the hospital the next day went mental about it and told social?

Steph was looking at her phone, she was always on her phone. Yeah, that was when you had to go in because you thought you were in labour.

Lee still didn't say anything. The football was on and he pretty much ignored Steph most of the time anyway. He wasn't that nice to her, but she put up with it because he was quite loyal in a funny way.

Where should we go then, Lee? Steph got up and went over to him, said it right in front of him, which looked stupid because Steph was big and when Lee was sitting down, he looked skinny. They looked like those people in the circus, the hundred pound woman and the ten pound man. Steph had bigger thighs even than when Tara was pregnant. She looked nice though because she wore a lot of black which suited her white skin. Steph had a tattoo on her wrist now; *Lee* with red roses. He didn't know about it till afterwards, but was sort of pleased and got drunk that night.

He drank White Lightning a lot, which made him drunk really, really quickly. Steph didn't mind though because he was so funny when he was drunk. He'd be all over her then and telling her she's his red rose, except when she asked him if he loved her. That pissed him off. Then he could be a right nasty bastard and hit her. Now Steph said shall we go down

The Brickmakers?

It was cold outside. Maybe Dylan was still wearing that old coat they'd put him in. She wanted to take hers off right there and then, put it round him now in this stupid blind street. They were ambling along the main road, beside faded terraced houses where hardened rocky old trees survived the relentless haul of traffic in the front gardens. She was dawdling behind Steph and Lee, hoping that Steph would let him go on ahead. He hadn't said much Lee hadn't, because he could be a grumpy bastard sometimes.

Steph, do you remember that coat I bought Dylan that I saved up for? She probably couldn't hear. The traffic was too loud. Steph! she called. Steph shouted over her shoulder, yeah what is it mate? Steph always called her mate which was funny. You know that coat with the little motorcycles all over it that I bought for Dylan?

Steph turned round and was walking backwards with her hands in the pockets of her big button coat. It was so cute, he looked like little motorcycle man, a proper little hard man. What about it?

Well the foster carers won't let him wear it anymore. They say it's too small for him. Fuck them. I know they're lying because I only got it a day before they took him, didn't I?

He can't be much bigger, Tara? Steph shook her head. When we saw him together, I'd say he wasn't any bigger. That's their bullshit that is. They don't want you giving him stuff in case he thinks like, this is from mum.

I know it, Steph, but they won't let me get his clothes anymore. Anyway they've got money. I keep being told not to bring him stuff anymore, because the contact workers are telling me that I bring too much stuff. Suddenly, she had a picture of him at her breast. She could feel the suck of his tiny mouth and the flower of her pain was a blood red rose until she couldn't bear it any more. She stopped at the garage and bought him a big bag of all colours jelly beans to take to contact. He would count out his days till the next contact. It didn't matter even if he couldn't count.

The warm air of The Bricklayers greeted them with a waft of beer as they pushed the door open. Lee wasn't that popular in this pub and she didn't know if they'd let him stay, so they snuck over to a corner seat behind the machines near the back door. Nobody seemed to mind. Steph stood them all a round of cider and Tara downed hers in one. This was going to be her good time, whatever kind of a night it might turn out to be.

She didn't have any cigarettes left and cadged off Steph who was generous like that when she had money.

Get us both a packet Tara, Steph said, and get three more pints out of it too.

Three tenners, just like that. Tara didn't like not having money, but she never did at the end of the week. She had helped Steph once anyway, when her mum stopped giving her money after a falling out. Steph's mum was quite rich and didn't like Lee because he was a waster who, in her opinion, wouldn't ever change. Steph said her mum thought he was like her dad, but her dad didn't know when to stop and Lee did. Lee had that romantic streak too which Steph was mad for, even when he was being a right nasty bastard. He would sometimes cry afterwards and tell her that she was his angel.

She looked through the amber of her glass and could see his little face, Dylan's, shining at her from the picture on her key fob. What you waiting for then? she said to Lee. He drank his in one, but she was looking at her tawny angel all the way to the bottom of the glass and didn't answer him when he said go on then what about you? He said he was going to get the next one for Dylan, which meant he was alright really was Lee, which was how they had to have another one. Steph had to get them though because they wouldn't serve Lee. He paid this time then said he'd buy some down the shops if they wanted and they could take them home.

They didn't get home. Lee stopped at the shops for three bottles of White Lightening. It was so funny they couldn't stop laughing, because he goes in the shop and asks for Light Whitenings. Steph nearly wet herself. They cried all the way back to the park and Lee had the hump they laughed that much. In the park by the bridge Tara thought okay then, here we go, because nobody's going to care now, will they? They don't ring and they don't want her food and she don't want their stupid messages anymore. Steph, she said, did you know that they sent me a message last week at contact where they said I'm not to take photos any more in contact? It was that contact worker who's the nice one, but she said she had been given a message by the social worker that I mustn't take any pictures of Dylan.

Oh, she says, let's take some pictures now, Tara, and she took some on her phone that made them cry even more. She even took some of Lee with the hump which he didn't like much. Tara was a bit worried he'd be at her for it when they got back, but he didn't. When Tara put her finger up to the camera, she said send them that. Even Lee thought that was funny.

She couldn't remember what happened after that except Steph said she shouted a lot at someone, like one of those crazy women. Some scabby old man passed by and tutted at her. She shouted, what the fuck do you know? And you don't know why I'm doing this either, right at him. Steph told her to stop, but she shouted, this one's for all you stuck up bastards, like you, who think they know. That's when she started *really* drinking. Steph said Tara wanted to jump the bridge, and she remembered that. She wanted to jump the bridge, she really did, on the life of her boy, she really did. She wanted to jump the bridge and Steph said that she took the paracetamol in her bag, the whole packet washed back on the booze. She didn't remember that, but did remember looking in the bottle trying to see her tawny angel. He wasn't there. That's what made her want to take all the pills.

Tara said it was a goodbye sort of day anyway. She was going to climb the walls on the bridge. It was Lee who went to get an ambulance, even though he was drunk. He was out in the street, she said, stopping people and they wouldn't talk to him. He was too drunk, but then there was this one woman who made the call when she saw Tara. I didn't know about any of that, she said to Steph. She was holding her hand and saying, it's alright mate. It was her afterwards who told Tara what happened. I wanted Dylan, Tara said, and couldn't stop crying.

That's it Steph, that fucking great black door. It's gone and fairly closed on me this time. She said she didn't know about that, but that Lee had been good. That's why he got some help, she said. Tara was still crying then, but said to her, you were right about him Steph, because Lee *has* got a romantic streak like you said. Tell him thank you for me. I know if he hadn't been there, I'd have been looking for angels at the bottom of the river.

6

The Therapist

Jo Juniper was not well. The illness had crept up on her, with some days worse than others. This week had been no exception. Her bones ached in every part of her body until it had become a constant hum in the background. Sometimes her joints ached so much that she could not bear to sit, or tolerate standing for long periods. Doctor's visits and tests had followed and after predictable questions about stress and overwork it was decided that to run a gamut of endocrine or neurological tests was not necessary. A blood test brought no discernible result. Warm baths and Pilates had become her only allies against the constant sense that her body was creaking and groaning. It was her scaffolding shifting in the weather, she liked to say, and fortified herself with a large dose of stoicism. At least she could gain a sense of perspective when her clients appeared one after the other bearing scars. The legacy of the human condition. It helped to keep it all in perspective.

There had been a gap since she had last seen Tara. She was at her desk waiting for the doorbell whilst reviewing Tara's notes. Although poor health aggravated by long periods of sitting had forced her to reduce her case load, still the clients she kept on were those on the cusp of meaningful change. Tara's motivation had outstripped others on every level, showing reserves of energy that could fuel her recovery.

Five sessions into her treatment back at the beginning of April, Tara told her she was running out of money. There was nothing unusual about that. People did it all the time, but Tara had told her in a way that pulled her up short. *I'm going to find the money to carry on.* Jo was more accustomed to the kind of client whose entry into therapy was at best hesitant, who wanted to get through it, which injected a subtle resistance into the process. Running short of money cropped up regularly and was a convenient exit strategy for those who could not face the challenge of meeting their shadow side. With Tara it was a different story. Nobody was going to stop her doing this, she'd said, and with that she promptly went away to fix it.

To Jo's mind it was inevitable that a gap in their regular meetings would follow. Finding a way to fund expensive therapy would defeat even someone on a modest income. Tara only had welfare benefits to make ends meet. Since Dylan had left her care, she spent most of it on presents for him and travelling to and from contact. So it was with some surprise that after a lull of a few weeks, she requested an appointment.

She sat back in her chair and sighed. The weather had been unforgiving for the last few weeks, with no let-up in the rain throughout July. This coupled with the pain in her joints, reduced to a slender collection any brighter moments, punctuating the long hours spent in her consulting room. The woods and fields at the back of her house were bleary with sodden leaves. She walked every day to keep her spirits up, but the damp crept around the trees like a wraith.

She'd had a client once, Geoffrey, whose life had deteriorated to such a degree that like a leaf shed from a tree he had quite simply fallen to earth and slept rough on the streets. She was a young therapist then, naïve about the pitfalls. It was years before she recognised that some of her own insecurity came from him. Park bench syndrome, she called it. To her it was as if a deep crack in the life of her client had opened up, sometimes because of illness – something which she now feared – but in others their lives had simply chasmed open when the pressure of living bore down upon them. Hours would be spent exploring what had gone wrong, testing the strength of a piece of fabric, looking for the loose weave, gently pulling and stretching till the threads broke loose and the rent was clear.

A ring on the doorbell interrupted her thoughts. Tara looked different in some way she could not put her finger on; it was instant, some kind of hollowness in her face. There was less vitality there. How are you, she asked as she led up the narrow stairs to her consulting room. We've had quite a change of season since you were last here.

I'm okay, I suppose, the answer when it came was diffident, restrained.

Have a seat, Tara, make yourself comfortable. It is good to see you again.

She didn't take her coat off as she would have on previous sessions, a routine never precisely set, but one she had grown into over the weeks. She sat with her feet neatly crossed, arms folded upon a large grey handbag on her lap, silence imprisoning her.

We've had a long gap, she smiled at Tara, reluctant to lead. Where would you like to pick up from? The room was heavy with the unsaid. Or maybe we'll simply start afresh?

When I came before, I think I wanted to learn how to control myself. She spoke slowly, carefully punching out every word, staring ahead.

Yes, I remember, you wanted to stop being angry, she said as gently as she could.

It was a joke though, that was.

Why do you say that, Tara? Is it because you still feel angry? Is that why?

I'm so angry it's eaten me up. I'm dead inside now.

Jo noted the flat tone, the lack of movement, the air was rigid with emotion; she had a sense of unease. The sound of wood pigeons cooing in the trees beyond drifted in through an open window.

What has happened since I saw you last, to Dylan I mean?

He's not my son anymore.

And then the tears brimmed over and rolled down Tara's face. She had not moved, her feet still crossed, her arms strapped across her bag.

He is still in foster care?

He's attached.

What do you mean, Tara? Is that something you want to talk about?

It means that's what the bitch social worker said in her statement. Tara put on a sing song voice *he's become attached to the foster carer* that's what she said.

That must hurt terribly.

You're dead right there, she sighed and stretched her legs out in front of her. But I'm here, aren't I? I've not given up.

The next hour passed rapidly without much let up in the strain. Reaching for her in every way she knew how, throwing a life line to try and shore her up, protect her for the weeks to come. It was one of those sessions where, right before the end, beneath the heavy clouds, a glimmer of light shone through.

I'm glad I'm here, even though it's hell, Tara said unexpectedly. A ghost of a smile hovered around her mouth, gone as soon as it appeared.

I'm glad you're here too, Tara, she returned warmly.

And I'm going to take your advice and ring that social worker.

Well, it's not advice, but I'm sure she'd welcome your call. You *do* matter Tara, to her as well, I'm certain of it.

I feel I have to prove something. And you know what, I am proving it, but she's too blind.

I see you, Tara. *I* see you, and you are a good woman who cares about and loves her boy deeply. It shines from you.

Thank you. That means a lot.

She was crying again. This time her head was steady and she rose to arrange herself to leave.

I'll put that on my mirror for next week, she said. One last thing, I've got to see a psychologist. The court says I have to do it and my barrister says I must too. I wondered...if you knew her?

She wanted a good word put in probably, which couldn't happen. They have to go in blind otherwise it would be a disaster for the court. The ethics were tight. But Jo knew she *would* put in a good word, not for any other reason than because within the limitations of what she could say Tara had shown openness, consistency, and genuine insight. The words were there to be said – not made up, but real words about this girl who was standing up to it all, who had the strength of ten to hold herself upright. Of course, it all depends on who the psychologist was. Some of them, the lazy ones, were there for the money. They churn them out too; you could write the conclusions yourself, most of them. The trouble was, the bad ones liked to think that people whom they consider to have had shoddy lives will only ever do shoddy. Past behaviour is the best predictor of future behaviour, they will say, as if they were packages to be neatly unwrapped, not human beings who achieve that glorious, electrifying moment when everything changes.

She closed the door softly after Tara. What she could say that would help her step into a different pathway?

Four hours later Jo sat with her head resting on the back of the chair in her living room. She was flat as mud, blown out. Tara had gone, but something else had arrived to haunt her. Her own baby.

It was not as if she even knew her. Barely seen even, she was just a baby needing a home. How could she ever have done it on her own? She pictured herself, young, frail, two steps away from being described as 'too serious'. So she had hit back with too much sex and drink. It was what you did if they said you weren't fun. It was what you did if they said you were frigid. Oh, not that they'd say it to your face, not those young red-bloods. If you even tried to fall in with the other girls, watching the rhythm and swing of their hips to learn it, they'd call you a prick tease if you refused to go round the back of the café for a blow job.

Was that why she'd become a therapist? No wounded healer ever made it out the door of the training room without knowing something about their own hurt. And what a joke it was, her mind picturing Tara for a second, to say that you had to be a 'good enough' parent which sometimes missed the obvious ones who were trying to make it. Only the poor get on the radar. Middle England, we are indeed, protected from the social engineers who think they can improve us. We are so good at covering up our own dirty laundry, then pontificating about what the poor need help with.

Sighing, paced around tidying cushions with restless hands, her mind curling around the memory of the tiny, tiny hand that wrapped itself around her fingers over eleven years ago for those precious few weeks. That cry came to mind, as it always did. Even after all these years it still had the power to make her feel a tug in her breast, ready for the milk.

Her own mother was long since dead but always, as night follows day, her mind turned to unforgiveness. It wasn't as if she could even try to forgive, it simply wasn't there: in its place was an unsaid, unforgiven hurt that forever kept them apart. It wasn't the adoption. No, she had long since learnt to reconcile herself to that. But the brutality of it all, which her mother passed off as kindness, she could neither forget nor forgive.

Eleven years ago, she had been standing by an open window at the home of the adoption society, holding Anna, her tiny fingers opened and curled. She was sleeping that blessed sleep which knows no enemy. Jo straightened her skirt, brushed her hair aside with one hand, her other arm heavy with the weight of her baby. She could not care for her yet. She had scarcely left her own childhood behind. Pregnancy had blown her world apart. You can come here, her mother had said. Wait out the pregnancy and then we can quietly deal with it. The same rage rose within again. How could she have done that to me? How could she have done that to Anna?

She had needed the toilet while they waited. To at least do her hair, so nobody could ever say that Anna's mother had been no good. That would mean the baby would be no good.

There had been a sense of relief when they told her a family had come forward already, good people with a nice home; he was a civil servant. It was what she wanted, a good home for Anna, two parents with a steady job. Anna growing up in a house with carpets, sitting by a fireside whilst a kind mother read her stories. It was a fine picture to reconcile with. Can you hold Anna a while Ma, she said and passed her over, folding the knitted white blanket close over her feet and tucking it neatly beneath her tiny sleeping arm. I want to look my best for when they come. Her ma's lips tightened into a small smile. I'll not be gone long, she said over her shoulder. The toilet was down a corridor. It smelt of antiseptic, bare of furniture, all doors closed save for the small cubicle at the end. It was important to be in a fit state – not too nervy, so that when she gave up Anna she could do it as a mother would: proudly, with a proper goodbye kiss. Mummy knows you'll be safe, she'd say. She smoothed her hair in the mirror and pulled her coat around her, to look respectable, not smart, or clever or pretty, but decent.

A decent woman.

Jo sat down, drink in hand. She pictured it all over again: pushing open the door, I'll have her back now ma, looking at her watch. Stupid, being worried about the time. Ma? Her mother stood there empty handed, one hand to her throat. Where is she? What have you done?

In truth, the second her hand touched the wood of the door, her fingers pressed onto the cool satin paint, she knew. A lurch in her stomach as it turned over, the breath stopped in her chest. Her own mother, empty handed as the dead.

Her mouth opened and closed again, the shape of that howl. Jo got to her feet and went straight to the fridge searching for the bottle of wine. She wasn't a big drinker but it was one of the only things that worked. Her breath came short as she gathered drink, glass, biscuit, tray. She stood and looked at the tray, silence gathered as the light shifted from twilight to darkness outside and the night closed in.

She would be eleven and a half now. And then the vision, a tall black haired young girl, sometimes happy, sometimes not. Those other dreadful moments, imagining her sobbing and alone. But it was never going to be a true picture, nothing less than the heart instructing the mind could create such images, conjuring something back to life from the bare sticks of a dead fire. Yet she had always believed in that black hair, that dark bloom around her face, so soft it took her breath away. She would be tall perhaps, as I am tall and *he* was tall. But she did not want to remember him; her desperate belief that her daughter must be alive and living a good life bloomed once more in her mind, the touch of that hair a whisper she could still feel on her hand. With exquisite pain she lived again that last gasp of mothering, breathed it in, nurturing it as it nurtured her.

She could search. Put it out there, see what comes back, even if it was a grimy envelope which takes three months to

80

find its way home. She shucked back the last of her drink and set the glass down with a sigh. No amount of search would return her to her baby's warmth on her hands. Nothing could give her the soft treasure of her tiny fingers or stem the flow of a mind's milk that gives and gives again, but asks nothing.

Twisting out of the field of her memories came another dark spectre: a girl grown into a woman she does not know. Hostile. Not wanting contact with a stranger. All those mothers who had sat in the therapy room, aching with fear or guilt, was she no different then? She kicked off her shoes and let her eyes fall, shuttering out the day. Sleep at least was a place that did not know her.

7

The Social Worker

The Orange Crate was sick. Carol had been walking every-where. Everywhere. The final evidence on Dylan Downley's case had to be pulled together. She did not even want to think about what she was going to write. So far as she could tell he seemed to be doing okay with the Shirleys. She was a pretty experienced foster carer and knew how to manage these difficult little toddlers once they came to her. They'd be toddling around with their toys quiet as lambs in no time.

Carol had not seen anything of Hen since the letter. Her life had closed down. She didn't even want to write back. She wrote to Jez instead and popped the note through his door. *WTF Jez you should've seen the state of the place. C.* In her mind, the fact that he was out there on the Poundyard Estate did nothing to make her feel better about anything. It was toxic and best left well alone. If she was a bit shabby round the edges of late, well okay, Bob was probably right – give herself a bit of an MOT like the orange crate. What did he mean with that? When she'd been late to the looked after child review about Dylan, the chairman had proper glared at her, especially since Tara had been sitting there awhile and looked in good shape. She'd done her hair up and was wearing makeup, even a skirt. She was sitting looking relaxed as if she was used to meetings, but I mean *used* to them like a professional who's there all the time. She was going on about the report, saying it was unfair.

And what did you mean by this, Carol, and what did you mean by that, Carol, and then Tara was reading *.. and we have had a police report relating to an anonymous call from the public that indicated that Tara was seen in a public place in a concerning state with possible mental health issues.* It was her report. How could that not have been a fair way to put it? Tara was always going to make a big deal out of it in some way because she still didn't get it.

You're painting me in a bad light, Carol, and you know it because you haven't been to see me since the day you took Dylan off me and you know it. I've been doing therapy and I've been sorting my place out and you wouldn't know that either because you haven't been to see.

Then the chair asking her. Is that right Ms Leadbeater? The mother here is saying you've not been out to visit. Of course, this meeting is not about criticizing anyone but we *do* need to get the facts right.

I haven't no, but I've had some difficulty in getting hold of you Tara. You know, we need to meet and I can fix a date to come after the meeting?

Well, she'd only bloody well brought some more colour photos with her hadn't she. That wasn't expected. Shimmied them right across the table straight towards the chairman when she was talking. He picks them up and suddenly Carol has to explain why she hadn't seen the photos and why she hadn't been out to visit. It ended with a grilling about what she was planning to do to reassess Tara. It wasn't good. Well *of course* I'll be assessing her, she'd said, but we have to get the psychological assessment first because that will inform the parenting assessment. She wasn't wrong to say that either. Well fuck knows, they're always going to give the social worker a hard time at those meetings aren't they, so it looks like they're being fair. It would have to be a visit to Tara's later in the week, even though she'd no idea how she was going to get there. Nobody cared about that though, did they.

Then, when writing up the report, Bob came right around the back of her chair.

How's it going Carol? Getting your reports out?

Hi Bob, yeah this one's not due for a while but you know….

Are you getting your stuff in on time? Because, you know, it's about how we're functioning as a department?

Yeah Bob, I'm on it. Really. Don't worry.

She had to say the parenting assessment would be done, and that they were waiting for the psychological assessment. Then it occurred to her she should best check the date for it all. Well, god knows, maybe it was that time already, she had no idea.

Margie Harrison rang in to her assistant. She was supposed to be coming at one o'clock, Dawn, but she knew what they were like, always late. Can you be sure to make a note of the time for me please? she paused, one eye on the grey skies above the house opposite. The paving man was due to arrive for the patio any minute, but so far he was a no show. I'll be setting off in under an hour, but I'd like it to be ready for me, in case I'm cutting it fine on time. The new garden was her pride and joy. A postage stamp maybe, but an award winning one at that. Stephen Laker was as likely to exhibit at Chelsea, as to convert her tiny postage stamp and the kudos was worth it. She had resisted applying for the open gardens scheme because frankly, the paving let it down. Hence her plan. Indian stone, no less. Cost an arm and a leg, but oh so worth it.

Is it only Tara Downley you're doing today Margie? Only we've still got to reschedule Jason Carter who failed to turn up last week.

Okay can you try and put him in for 3.30? She was tight on time, but could at least try and squeeze a day into the remains of the half she had left. I can always see if he shows and reschedule a second if need be, she said.

The traffic to her clinic offered no favours at all, practically gridlocked all the way down the Fairway crawling at no more than five miles an hour. Worse, the weather was bucketing down.

Pushing through the doors of her clinic, she spotted a smartly dressed young woman in a black skirt, the solicitor waiting for Tara probably.

The assistant handed her the papers on her way through, Hi Dawn, is she already upstairs? Can you get her solicitor a drink if she needs it. It was more annoying that they were on time, no wait, early! She'd have to phone the paving man before getting started anyway because there'd be no chance tomorrow if the weather didn't improve. She took the back stairs to her office which had an adjoining door to a conference room where the

85

assessments were done.

And here we are, she beamed broadly as she came through the door, I am so sorry you've been kept waiting. Surprisingly, it was a woman in a suit sitting at the table. She hadn't met the solicitor before, so she apologised, realising the woman downstairs must have been someone else. I'm sorry, I thought you would be Tara, anyway pleased you could make it. Is she here?

If you mean am I the solicitor, then no.

Her wires were crossed, but all she could think of was, you must be Tara, then?

Well, if that's who you're expecting then yes, I am me. One o'clock, your office said.

Okay, well pleased to meet you. Can you tell me why you're here, she said a little annoyed to have made a poor start. First impressions mattered; it was important to gain their trust before a test, then the answers were more open.

I'd have thought that was your job? the young woman said, clearly defensive.

Well, you're right in a way, she laughed, but I have to also check that you know why you're here. It's part of getting your consent for the assessment.

Oh, okay well, I want my son back and they told me I had to have this assessment. The young woman looked down at the table when she said this. You know I've done it all, what they wanted. All of it. She didn't look up.

I'm not here to assess you in that way Tara, she said, I'm here to find out how you function and if there's anything about the way you function that led to Dylan being taken away. Tara fiddled with her bag, exploring the grain in the conference table wood with her finger. It was going to be difficult to coax this woman to engage, Margie thought, but then as if on cue, Tara let out a heavy sigh, tilting her head back as far as it could go and then levelled it with a direct stare at Margie.

Alright then, let's get on with it, she said. Blunt but not overtly hostile, Margie noted.

She had prepared a raft of inventories for Tara to undertake: the Parental Stress Index, the Child Abuse Potential inventory, a standard personality test and a couple of others. She expected it to take about forty-five minutes, time she badly needed to phone the paving man. He must be there by now, unless he'd been rained off.

I'll set you up with my assistant Tara, if that's okay? she got up and showed her the way into the next room. She will help you go through the first part of the assessment.

I thought you were doing it? This is so not what they told me it would be.

Yes of course, this is only the first part. It's the technical part if you like. Are you okay? she smiled not waiting for an answer. Don't worry this bit won't take long.

Dawn, this is Tara. Help her through the first part then give me a buzz when you're finished?

You know I'm not going to be good at this, she said. You do know that it's not for me, this kind of computer thing? She looked stressed, I can't do it if you are going to make me write stuff down. Margie could see that Tara was panicking as she dumped herself in the nearest chair.

It's fine Tara, Margie said, nodding at her assistant. Dawn will take you through it and you don't have to be good at writing because the computer will write it down for you.

Margie straightened her skirt as she walked across to her desk. At least this part would give her the chance to sort things out. She jotted down a couple of notes: nervous, unhappy with the testing, suggests disguised compliance for desired outcome (return of child).

Hanging on the end of the phone which was ringing out, it struck her that it was probably a given she'd have to give evidence on this one. It was a hunch, nothing certain, but a lot of the care parents unfortunately don't get it and why should they. Being assessed was nowhere like anything they would ever want to be subjected to in a million years! It was always about compliance for them because there was no other option. Nervous was the name of the game for most of them.

The afternoon wore on. When Margie popped her head round the door, Dawn seemed to have done some wonders because they had got through the tests in record time.

The paver had arrived at her neighbour's house moments after she left and he was already stuck into the work, despite the deluge which showed no signs of letting up. Thank god for good neighbours. A glass of wine in the courtyard, yes, that's what it deserves to be called, The Courtyard.

Tara was sitting in front of her again, looking more hopeful than earlier. Have I passed then? she asked.

Oh, it's not like that I'm afraid.

But some of those questions got me to thinking though, you know. It's like, who doesn't feel stressed when they're a single mum. You tell me? Who doesn't. I tell you what, anyone that says they're not is a liar.

Can I ask about your childhood now? Margie ventured. It shouldn't take too long.

Well, it was shit if that's what you mean, I was sexually abused, but then you'd know that already because those social workers, they want to bring that up they do, every single time.

But my mum bought me this you know, she held up her key ring, and that's Dylan, that there, and whatever you may want to say about her she's a good nana.

Was she a good mum?

I'm not saying that. She's been a good nana she has.

But what about when you were little? Tell me about it.

Tara didn't want to at first. It was stop start, then she wanted the toilet. She was understandably on the defensive, questioning why she should have to say what had happened to her and why her mum should come into this. She said it wasn't bloody fair. No way had she done the same to Dylan. He'd always lived at home with his mummy and she would never...

Did your mother believe you when you told her about the sexual abuse?

No. It was apparent she was angry now. I don't want to talk about that, she said, I've told you. He was her bloke. He was a dirty old man and he came after me, but she got rid of him and she's nana now. We don't talk about that stuff.

She made sure some of her notes recorded verbatim what Tara was saying, with a mental note to annotate observations later.

And I have never, ever said to Dylan I don't believe him about anything you know. I wouldn't do that. I'm doing it different for him.

What do you think the concerns are then, Tara? She had asked this question once already but got nowhere. Why do you think social services had to take him away?

I know someone's given you what social have said, so I expect you know about all that already. She was defiant, but it seemed to Margie this could be her default setting for a stream of endless professionals asking her questions.

Yes, but it would help me to do this assessment if you could tell me what you think the concerns are.

Well, there aren't any now because I cleaned my place up and I can show you the pictures. She rifled in her bag and pulled out the stack of glossy images of her flat.

I cleaned it and I've been to every single contact and don't let them tell you I haven't because they'll lie about everything, they will. And I'm on time. Look, I'm not going to make that mistake again. I've had therapy and that has changed the way I think about stuff and there's no way I'd go back to that.

But do you accept there was neglect? Of Dylan I mean.

No, I don't. Dylan was never ever neglected. He always had food and he always had clothes. I'm not saying I was perfect, and I know he shouldn't have Chinese and stuff like that because it's not healthy, but I never neglected him. You can ask my friends.

Margie tried again, tell me what you say was wrong Tara. What is it you wouldn't do again?

I know it was dirty. It was in a state, but so was I. I know that when I get in that place in my head, I don't want to clean up or do things properly. It was in a state, I'm not lying. Anyway, they took pictures. But I was never not there for Dylan and he's little, he's not been hurt. I would never hurt my son. She looked down at the table, then back at Margie and her face looked worn, the skin beneath her eyes crumpled. Are we nearly finished with all this?

Margie wanted to get the report at least half done that night, key phrases in her notes helped make short work of it. Lacks insight.

Yes, it has been helpful to meet you, she said, offering her best smile. I'll be able to do a good write up.

Does that mean it's a good report?

It was always tricky when they asked this. Well, it will say some good things about you Tara, yes it will, but I can't tell you how it will be overall until I've thought about it.

The way down the stairs to the front office was for clients, but Margie followed Tara down. Closing the door behind her she checked her phone. No missed calls, only a message Cocktails in the courtyard yet? The body of the report she could lift from last week's assessment, then it would be a quick fix to knock out most of the rest and write the individual sections before her friends descended for drinks. She glanced up at the window, but the rain was still coming down. Inside then for drinks.

8

The Barrister

Harriet was not looking for glory in what she did. She told her friends it wasn't like that, especially when that old chestnut was thrown at her: 'how do you defend someone who you know is guilty?' (That's not how it works). Then they always move onto how wealthy you are because all barristers are wealthy. (They're not). If ever a window of opportunity came along and it seldom came, she'd bend their ears about the grannies, the aunties, all the decent ones she'd represented. She'd tell them that no, if your grandchildren are being taken into care, they won't automatically be given to you. At least not without some kind of *assessment*. Grim. She'd tell them how, if they admitted to the dope they smoked in the seventies (those who can remember the seventies weren't really there), or the bottle of wine they kill some nights, they might even fail the assessment and never get the grandkids anyway. The clincher was always when she told them how they'd have to go to court without being represented and cross examine loads of witnesses and no, they wouldn't get legal aid. Not anymore.

It was sad that few people realised the worth of the job. Not because she wanted to be hailed as a hero, and that for her was the point- not to be, but because it *was* bloody heroic. It simply was. Oh, the ones she could talk about, the ones who kept you awake at night. And no, it wasn't always the *poor little mites* as her mother would likely have it, but it was the poor parents, the ones who'd tried their best and still couldn't get anywhere. The ones who showed their love in the face of great adversity.

Sometimes in court, when the world conspired against them, they had to demonstrate that they'd faced not just any old adversity, but the right kind of adversity. Harriet could remember hearing parents, often women, talking about how they'd managed in their life after they had been sexually abused; how they'd picked themselves up day after day and got on with life. But sometimes even that would bring with it some sanctimonious criticism of how they'd *not dealt with their issues*. But if, instead, they said they'd got a job after putting themselves through university or night school, then it sounded acceptable, and they might stand a chance. The odds were stacked against them, because it had to be the right kind of adversity to score brownie points with the middle classes. Judge Tyron had said to her, when she was still training: the local authority is like a naval warship with all its guns ready, but the parents are in a rowing boat with a couple of oars. Remember that, Harriet.

Which brought her to Tara. Tara was one of those without a paddle.

Harriet slung her bag in the boot of the car and left the

house before the frost had time to bite, getting the red eye into chambers.

Hi Greg, she called through the open door of the clerk's room. He was always first in and last to go. He would get the graveyard stories, from those who had slunk away after a beating from some regular bully on the bench, or the mighty victories wrenched from the jaws of defeat in some far-flung mags court.

You're early as ever Greg.

Got stuck with the billing catch up this month, Miss, and since we're on target in the first quarter it's worth getting it out. You're on the Downley case final hearing today, Miss. We've got the local authority brief in chambers too, so you'll have the pleasure of Mr Bestfield.

George? Oh Christ, thanks for the warning! And I'm saying nothing Greg about the fact that if it's George we'll probably still be going next week. Greg, you didn't hear me say that.

No Miss, I didn't hear you say that, and will await the outcome with interest.

Oh Tara, Tara, Tara, she was working her way through the updating statements, why did you have to get yourself involved in a barney in the park? She would get a different explanation from Tara the minute she asked her, but the fact that she'd been reported by anyone at all, most of all a member of the public for some shouting in a public place didn't help her case one iota.

Arriving at Stanford Mags, she spotted Tara sitting by the courtroom door as she went through security. She'd clearly made an effort to dress smartly, but looked thin and pale.

You're early, Tara, it's good to see you. The anxiety was in her eyes which flitted from place to place.

Hello. I was ready pretty much nine months ago for this day and it's no better now it's here, she said.

Once Harriet had found a room, she got straight to the point: we won't waste time beating around the bush Tara, it's not all lined up in your favour. If it was, the local authority would have caved long ago. Tell me about what happened in the park.

Nothing happened in the bloody park. Nothing. I was not going to jump and I was not abusive either. They're making up lies because you know from the day they took Dylan that social worker has not bothered with me and she doesn't care that I've done everything right that she asked me to do.

It says that the police were called and that you'd been drunk, shouting at passersby and that you'd taken pills and it all finished up with an ambulance? The trouble is, Tara, the witnesses seem to have been unconnected members of the public and one of them rang the police. It's hard to argue that it's made up.

I don't care if it's bloody hard to argue. It's been made more than it is. It was twelve weeks after, Harriet. Twelve weeks! And they'd told me I couldn't have a photograph of my own boy. They told me that I couldn't see my boy and take a picture of him in contact. Well why shouldn't I do that, he's still my son.

So what do you want me to say about it? I can tell you I was shouting. Alright I was shouting. There. She looked at the floor, then jumped up from her seat and lunged for the door. I've got to get out of this place. I'm not being funny, but this is so much shit.

Tara please don't go yet. There are some things…. But she had already disappeared and was half way out through the lobby. Harriet sighed, and wrote contact, no pictures in the margin of her blue book.

The courtroom was cold when they trooped in, the clock a few minutes shy of lunchtime. George Bestfield had spent a deal of the morning telling her everything they would be doing after the order was made, as if it was a given. Tara was back in the building, as tense as an animal in the slaughterhouse.

It was Margie Harrison giving evidence that afternoon and it would be a dealbreaker. The report was long enough, but the boilerplate passages gave little room for manoeuvre, given that they'd practically been rehearsed and perfected over years. Her conclusions occupied a page and a half. She had fixed Tara with a diagnosis of depression, anxiety and some symptoms consistent with borderline personality disorder, though she didn't go the whole hog, saying there were insufficient symptoms to make a definitive diagnosis. Perhaps that was where the wriggle room would be. She recommended therapy but said it would have to be for two years and had squarely placed it outside Dylan's timescales. More wriggle room, thought Harriet, given what she's done already.

Since the family courts had come under the twenty-six week rule, there could be no delay in finalising the case by the twenty sixth week. Harriet had seen it go downhill since the start – but it's good for children, ran the argument. The great and the good who never had to face being given another set of parents, bleated on about how the children 'deserved' a decision to finalize where they would go. Ship them off to another family and that was that, but since it was all done with unseemly haste, little Johnnie is not going to lie around in foster care wondering what the fuck has happened to him.

Two women and a man were on the bench. The woman in the centre looked younger than the other two. The wingers were plainly uncomfortable, and Harriet wondered again whether three days' training could ever be enough. Did it even sink in? God knows what they were told about how they should go about the task ahead of them.

Margie Harrison's evidence took most of the afternoon. She was a consummate player and before she got to her feet Harriet had studied the professional techniques on display answering George's tame questions. Turn and face the judge or mags when you're speaking. That was a classic. Designed to make it easier on the witness, it always gave the expert witnesses an air of detachment. If you can't take the heat, get out of the kitchen, was Professor Tim's rubric on how to behave as an expert, but many of them were in the junior league compared to him. Harriet didn't think experts should be detached. The better ones had real feelings, but this one was a cold fish.

She'd been on her feet with Ms. Harrison for the best part of two hours.

Ms. Harrison, the mother was nervous at your assessment, wasn't she?

She was. But that is not unusual.

But Miss Downley was particularly nervous about the computers, wasn't she, and in fact said to you that she wouldn't be good at it? Do you remember that?

I do and she was reassured by myself and my assistant who is very experienced.

Miss Downley is dyslexic, isn't she?

Yes.

And being told she was going to have an assessment and seeing the computers could have been very challenging for her. Particularly challenging wouldn't you agree?

Oh, they're all a bit like that, these parents in care cases. Many of the people I assess, Margie Harrison said resolutely facing the magistrates, have not always had the best start in life and they can often be nervous, find the process challenging and even be uncooperative. But our tests are designed to factor in those aspects and weigh our findings to ensure they are not unfairly treated in that respect. It doesn't invalidate my findings.

Harriet thought the winger on the right, the man, looked bored. She cracked on.

Your findings include two mental health conditions: a depressive disorder and anxiety.

Yes.

These are not uncommon in the population as a whole, are they?

They are not, but here we are dealing with how it impacts on Ms. Downley's parenting. I think we can see from the circumstances that led to these proceedings that they have the capacity to have a very great impact on Ms. Downley's ability as a parent, such that she is not able to parent to a good enough standard. Still facing the magistrates she went on, I also found that her behaviour and functioning show some characteristics consistent with a borderline personality disorder....

But you did not feel able to say with any certainty that she has it?

No, Your Worships.

That thing again, she had her face turned away from the court towards the magistrates who were lapping it up. None of them would ever dare to disagree.

Margie Harrison went on: I could not say with certainty

that she has this disorder, but we found that she displayed sufficient characteristics for me to conclude that she may have. And certainly, over time, if life develops in such a way that she has negative life experiences, then this may compound her difficulties.

Out in the lobby she tried to keep the ship steady. It's alright Tara, but try not to show how you feel about the evidence because the magistrates are watching you like a hawk.

But that fucking psychologist only saw me for less than an hour and she's up there on her hind legs telling them I haven't changed. It's bullshit Harriet, you know it is. She was banging the chair next to her on every word. They. Just. Don't. Know. It's. All. Lies.

Back in court Harriet could see the bench were tiring.

You would agree that she is very competent in contact, Ms. Harrison? Have you read the contact notes?

I can see she tries, but has spent time on her phone in contact and is not able to prioritize Dylan in contact.

Tara was whispering behind Harriet, but at a volume that could be heard: she wasn't in contact though! Harriet could tell the whole courtroom had picked it up. Tara, tell me quietly please.

Ms. Harrison, you will have heard my client saying that you haven't observed contact?

No, but I was sent a large bundle of contact notes and I have read them. It appears in the notes that contact supervisors have noted on several occasions that Ms. Downley spends time on her phone whilst in contact with Dylan.

I had my phone out to take a picture, but they wouldn't let me, urgency in her voice raising the volume.

But you would agree – and for the record Your Worships,

this point is not in dispute – that the quality of contact is good?

It appears to be adequate at the stage Dylan is at now, bearing in mind his young age, but as he matures and develops it is not clear whether Ms. Downley would have sufficient resources to stimulate him.

Harriet was becoming annoyed. Ms. Harrison, I am sure that if you have not observed contact and the local authority accept it is of good quality, you would agree with their opinion?

Yes, but I am simply recording that as a part of my instructions I am asked to consider the likely capacity of a parent to provide good enough parenting in the future and in my opinion Ms. Downley would struggle as Dylan gets older.

You would agree, however, she has shown a good commitment to therapy?

She has been to some therapy, I understand, but I have not seen a report and cannot vouch for whether the therapist undertaking the work is qualified to address the issues.

Ms Juniper is a qualified psychotherapist Ms. Harrison. You will be aware of that?

I am aware that she is, but there are different approaches. Certainly Ms. Downley was showing disguised compliance when she saw me and seemed to think her assessment was *so that she could get her son back*, to use her words. It may be that the therapy she has undertaken has not been sufficiently challenging. If it was based on her self-report, it would be less effective if Ms. Downley lacks insight into her difficulties which, in my opinion, she does.

Harriet could see she was getting nowhere fast. The more questions she put, the more entrenched Margie Harrison was becoming. The questions were giving her views too much oxygen, so Harriet began to close her down. She brought it to a swift end putting the last gasp question: that Tara loved her son and surely Ms. Harrison could agree with that? It was never enough, but there were precious few experts who'd disagree.

Harriet was horrified when Margie Harrison turned to the magistrates and said, no, your worships, I am not certain I could agree with that. I know she thinks she loves Dylan dearly and that has always been her difficulty, because she sadly lacks insight into the broader aspects of love and what is needed to meet a child's needs.

That woman is an automaton, she said to no one in particular outside court. She was walking towards Tara who was sitting rigid in a chair, staring straight ahead.

I'm sorry, Tara, that was hard for you to listen to. We can still do our best to make a case out of it with the Guardian though, but I'm sorry that you had to hear such a negative opinion from that woman.

I knew it would be like this. I knew no one would give me shit in this place. You know what? I'm done, I know what they're going to do.

You're not leaving, Tara, please don't leave. If the magistrates see that it will all be over.

It's over anyway, you know that. I'm not going to go. I *will* sit there and they are going to have to look me in my face when they take my son away. And they won't ever forget the look I am going to give them. She stared ahead, her hands clasped around each other in her lap, the knuckles white and sharp.

II

Part Two

Two Children

9

Anna

Anna Ainscott was not going to give in. Two years down the line from her first brush with adulthood - the only name she could give it - she washed up on a beach in Valle Gran Rey, broke. It wasn't exactly washed up, but beached like a driftwood orphan. At twenty-three the prospect of going back to some kind of new millennial world would throw her off. Saturated by Facebook, Instagram, the endless swooping vultures of corporate education, ready to snatch her freedom like a juicy rabbit's foot, 'Grow your career at Fulford Uni' 'The world is yours if you come to ...' An endless drone of debt laden advice had driven her to the margins. Her friends had shipped out, grown a debt, drunk a lot, shagged a lot then three years later all boomeranged back in with their parents. Courses naming some unknown professions like Events Management sent them out in their hundreds looking for work at Tesco.

She threw her dreads back over her shoulder and gazed at the silver ring on her toe. It was five years since she left the cosy bungalowed world in which her parents had hunkered down for the home run. Retirement for them. For Anna it had been five years of sofa surfing with the odd shared house in between which had left her restless. Now out here by the sea, she was not exactly anybody's, but if Gomera could give her a mate or two with the same hurt and love and a free swipe at the murky corporates then it would be home for a while.

Her phone buzzed.

U coming down for drumming?

Am already here, where u?

On my way, c u there.

Jack was her best mate so far. He wanted to be a circus performer to escape violence which had been his parents' pastime when they were not drinking. He was a beautiful man, tall, thin with white blond hair that hung below his collar. Two years round Australia and Thailand in a beaten-up van had given him the taste for wild living and he'd set up camp in a yurt in Normandy living on mushrooms and fishing for a decade. He could have stayed, but love had fled in the footsteps of his girlfriend who voted with her feet in favour of regular baths and a career in journalism, so he took to the road once more. La Gomera had been a chance discovery, after meeting some Germans who had friends down there. Those in the know believed in the poetry of its landscape: that it had the power to rejuvenate.

Jack wanted everything she didn't. His mission was to shed his family, every link, number, likeness, message, even his DNA if he could. His taste for the bohemian was a stand up and look at me slap in the face message to the small-minded

106

xenophobia of his parents. As he saw it, they sucked up fear of everything foreign as if their lives depended on it, from every anti-immigrant toting tabloid on the high street. Travelling was his answer to their small mindedness. He delighted in curating his appearance to be as far from that Tory cliché, the 'hard working British family', as he could possibly make it. Not that Jack wasn't willing to graft – he could be industrious if the mood took him. But that was his problem: his life was chronically scuppered by mood swings. If he wasn't reaching for the next new idea he'd be sleeping in the van, unable to get out of bed for days.

The wind was ceaseless in Gomera and today was no exception. Standing up to look for Jack, she faced into it, sounding a constant drone broken only by the sound of the waves crashing on the beach.

Down by the beach she met Jack. Let's tuck in here out of the wind babe, he said, and she folded her limbs under her, tight into the curve of the seawall. The drummers were setting up and, as the sun dipped below the clouds, the last rays caught them in brilliant silhouette.

Anna's journey was a counterflow to Jack's. She was searching for family, not trying to rid herself of one. To look in the mirror and examine her own face, features never recognised in any other living being, brought loneliness right to the centre of her life. Even though hers had been, by the standards of the average overworked social worker, a perfect adoption, Anna had always been that misplaced girl- a refugee who didn't belong.

No nature/nurture argument spouted from the mouth of some modernist social commentator could change those deeper feelings. She would always be the outsider. It was the song of her DNA which would get to her sometimes - a desperate need to see likeness in the faces surrounding her. Growing up she had tried to come to terms with life, to find gratitude. But it wasn't like something that could be fixed, that displacement. Sure, her parents had been okay. They could tick every middle-class box to work up a desirable profile, but they were like all the others: two sad people whose IVF journey ended in adoption. It wasn't a choice; it was the no-choice option.

Jack was lost in the music, but Anna's mind wandered away to the sea as it rolled in and crashed on the corner of the short café street. She had told Jack before about her adoption story and how she meant to trace her family and he had always been supportive, but today when every online search led back to the same dead end, she needed his support more than ever.

She tugged on his sleeve, but had to shout because of the wind. Sorry Jack I know you're into it, but I've been thinking all day about making that trip you know? Do you think my plan would work, Jack? It's like I've scraped the surface online and without shelling out more money every time, I'm stumped.

Jack turned his jacket collar up against the wind, Yeah, but why don't you write to them Anna, I mean isn't it the easiest way?

She turned the ring on her toe, contemplating. Write to who? I mean they're social workers, Jack. I can't for the life of me think why I would want them in my life. All those patronising bloody visits. *Oh yes we know how you must feel.* The fuck they do. I was even ready to do what they wanted then and write some kind of soppy letter 'Hi here is me, I like origami' or some such crap.

I know, babe, they're shite, the lot of them, but they might set up the meeting real quick you know? It'd save you hours and hours of this searching. I mean you know already it's likely to be that woman you found, because every search brings you back to her yeah? She had the same name as on your file and everything.

I know but what if it isn't and she looks like something else and I hate her. I honestly don't know. She might say she doesn't want to see me. If it is that woman, what do I know about her? Nothing at all. It's so fucked. She's gonna know she hurt me and then what? I'll have to deal with her baggage as well as my parents' crap about what they think they should have done to make it better. Well, no one can make it better. I'm the ugly fucking duckling and I know it.

Jack shuffled up close to her and put his arm round her shoulders. Let's listen to the drumming for a bit, babe. Let the sun go down and take your anxiety with it?

She smiled at him. Thanks Jack, you're good to me. She was glad to shelter in his friendship, for now, but everything was screaming I've got to get out of here, move on. It's never going to work, this meditate on the meaning of life thing, at least not till I can finish it properly.

The drummers were six now and as the sun began to reappear beneath the blanket of cloud that had kept the weather cool, the final rays shot across the black volcanic sand of the beach. The drumming picked up pace, held a steady rhythm as the last of the heat reached the small band of people sat on the rocks. Everyone was chatting and the cafes along the beach hummed gently with the early evening clink of glasses. Valle Gran Rey was still a village despite the inpouring of the new hippies searching for a better life.

Back in the campervan, she sat on the bed with her hands wrapped around a mug while Jack cooked. She loved his van, with its crazy collection of badges from his travels. Even the cups were a mad mixture of oddball souvenirs picked up along the way bearing the legends of the place: Crete, Berlin, Las Canarias.

Thing is Jack, I can't get away from it. I can't get near it and I can't escape either.

It's your life calling, Anna. Whatever it turns out to be, you've got to go for it. If it eats you up this much and it does, you've got to travel that road to the end of the line whatever you might find there.

I know, but it's like following a thread and sometimes you can pick it up and run with it, other times it drops out and you're all over the shop.

What I want is to get to that place where someone out there wants to claim me, you know? She laughed to herself. Oh yeah, and I know I'm that sad old stray. There's my parents for sure, but what do they know? Roused now, the old arguments were tuning up like noisy instruments inside her head. I mean, they *say* they love me and I'm like their daughter totally. They even say that I frigging walk like Uncle Anthony, or talk like auntie Sue for christ's sake! But then they want to change everything I am, from the way my hair is down to the things I want to do with my life. All of it is shit to them Jack.

But that sounds like my life totally, Anna. You say it's all your own adoption story but hey some of us don't even have that excuse. He smiled at her apologetically, but you know I don't mean *excuse* excuse?

He was laying out plates moving at speed while he spoke like a chef. … salt, pepper, a bit of chilli.

110

Anna curled both feet under her on the bed. I can't get into this now Jack. I've run with it and run with it and I'm tired. I guess I've got to go and find out for myself.

He spun around two plates in hand. You're right and dinner's up, my darling.

Dinner was a stir fry full of beans and garlic which was Jack's speciality. He tossed himself onto the bed afterwards and pulled her into his body which smelt of cooking and garlic.

I can't even.. You can, you don't need to think now babe. Be here with me. He ran his hand down her arm as it lay across his chest. I only want to sleep you know? Yeah that's cool with me babe, whatever. You can sleep here you know? If I sleep here anymore, Jack, they'll chuck me out of the hostel you know.

She didn't want to stay with Jack, but he was kind and although the sex was ordinary it was undemanding. But another day with you is another day I am not going to where I need to be. And where is that... where is that?

When Anna woke up Jack had gone to chase the surf. The van smelt of sea and garlic and as she pulled on her leggings she wondered about Jack's quietness. This, his cave carried only a few books: Kahlil Gibran, John Berger, Thich Nat Hanh, but all of them stood on the shelves like evidence of the beauty of his aim: to find himself as a quiet man. But he seemed to have no real desire to go anywhere did Jack. I'm too restless, running from this and that. She could smell the sex on her and was sleepily planning a cold dip when her phone pinged.

Come down, we've got stuff to learn about! J x

Jack never locked the van, so she closed the door on it without a thought for the contents which were too poor to be of interest to anyone else. She was grateful to Jack for many

111

things, but having a sometime home in the Jack's Straw Castle, as he'd named his van, gave her a place to go when the hurt was too great.

The corner café was already busy, trekkers in twos and threes, speaking mostly in German at tables inside and out. Jack was inside with a girl and two men who were clearly fresh off some boat, with backpacks propped beside their tables.

Berlin Anna! Listen to these guys! Oh, by the way this is Anna, he announced to the table, she's a good friend of mine. One of the guys went to get up which was sweet. No please don't get up, but thanks anyway. Where are you guys from, I've not seen you around.

We arrived here this morning but we're on our way back to Berlin by a long route. Jack's been telling us about you and your travels. The speaker smiled at her and she wondered about the girl with them, who did not seem as friendly. Rudi, the one who had spoken, introduced everyone. She looked across at Jack with a little shake of the head and a quizzical smile. Rudi spoke before Jack could. Well in Berlin there's the coffee which is good and the art that is even better. He laughed expansively and Anna noticed his teeth were white and even. We don't know much about Gomera he went on, but we do need people to come to Berlin to help with a festival we're gonna be doing there, if you're interested?

Hey, that sounds like a good gig, what kind of festival? The girl, Marta, who had said nothing was sipping her coffee and watching Jack. Oh c'mon Rudi, the other guy interjected, you can't say that without saying a bit more. His name was Seb and he was fiddling with his sandal which was broken. His clothes carried a lot of dust as if he'd been travelling a long time. He ran his hand through his thick black hair. We'd be lying if we didn't say that the festival hasn't yet happened, Anna, he smiled apologetically. Rudi's pretty fired up about it – we plan that it will be a kind of art fair festival with world music and hopefully bringing in travellers like yourself. We all used to work in a hostel in Berlin before we travelled together.

Rudi pushed his chair back from the table, yeah it's the world-wide travelling community that we hope to entertain, he said, people like you and Jack. He put his arm around Marta, and you my girl are the person to get us there I'd say? Marta smiled across at Anna, he wants me because I know people in the music business, but it's not world music Rudi, so I'm not sure how useful I'm going to be, she said ducking out from under his arm and turning towards him.

Well it's a plan, that's all, Seb offered, still concentrating on his sandal strap. Jack who had been quiet throughout looked relaxed in their company. They're pretty cool, but what do I know about them? Marta seemed to sense her reservation. You've only met us today Anna, she said, so you must be thinking what are these crazy Germans going to do with me, if I get back to Berlin and there's nothing there, huh? Anna laughed relaxing a little, yeah well, I was a bit unsure, but….

But you could come with us? Rudi put his hand out across the table to Anna, palm open and looked at her intently waiting, the question open in his face.

It was mad crazy. Okaay… she smiled, this Rudi was a bit of a gem, but wicked she sensed. Jack? He was grinning and shaking his head up towards the ceiling. He said, we could you know Anna, he brought his head down level with hers until their eyes met: we could just fucking do it, for no other reason than we can.

Rudi's hand was waiting, Seb and Marta had both stopped whatever they were doing and all eyes were focused on her. Marta was smiling shyly. It would be nice if there were some other girls, Anna, besides only me, she said.

Okay done. She reached across and took Rudi's hand which was warm. He curled his fingers around hers and did not let go, making her wonder what else he might want from her.

10

Berlin

Anna woke up to see the sun leaking through a bamboo blind. She did not recognise her surroundings but with the memory of last night came a rush of shame. Rudi was nowhere to be seen, but this was his room. It was small and messy but his sheets and bedding had the feel of having once adorned the very grandest of hotel bedrooms. He had pursued her since they first met in Gomera, but it was Jack who was on her mind now as her body told her about the night before. Her head was aching and her nose was blocked. She ached in every limb.

She pulled on her jeans and a hoodie and peeped out through the door of the room into the apartment. Rudi had been dancing expansively around the room he shared with Seb and Marta, but she couldn't remember them in last night's hazy pictures. Rudi larging it up with too much wine filtered back to her as she cast her eyes round the dimly lit furniture. There were beer cans on the floor as well and she noticed her socks by the front door. Nobody appeared to be there so she grabbed what she could and started to dress, back in Rudi's room. As she searched for her bag, voices were coming from outside. She recognised Rudi's immediately. She didn't know where Jack had gone the night before and felt bad for him. It was going nowhere, but... Jack was her help-mate in a way and she didn't want to hurt him. And Rudi, well he had charm in spades. Her head ached and she remembered how he'd swept her up in his arms and carried her off to the bedroom. She'd laughed and laughed, but hadn't put up a fight.

Hello, my girl. Rudi came through the door with brown paper bags in his arms, Seb and Marta following behind. They seemed absorbed in a conversation which sounded like it had something to do with Marta's parents and was a problem. They barely acknowledged her.

Hi, where's Jack? Sorry but I don't remember him leaving last night, I probably should, he's my friend. Oh, god, that sounds all wrong. Sorry Rudi.

Marta said, Hey, hey, don't worry about it Anna. Rudi also seemed preoccupied, but he wasn't involved in the conversation with Marta and Seb. Anna wondered why Marta appeared to be speaking for him. Oh yeah, he did leave. He went to the hostel, I think it's where your bags are right? He's coming over though, why don't you text him. He's cool with it.

Thanks. Anna went back into the bedroom and pulled her phone out of her bag. There were three messages from Jack.

Hey babe, hope you're cool and had a good night. Rudi seems an interesting guy. I'm here if you need me.

Babe, will u be coming back tonight, or... no don't worry you don't need to answer that. Lol x

Hi babe, text me when you want your stuff, or to meet up? J

x

The guilt swept over her. What a cruel fuck I have been. She didn't even know... now what? She wanted to see Jack and get out of there.

Anna, Rudi burst into the room and threw himself past her onto the bed. You don't even want to go now, my little lady, you want to come over to daddy, I think? He lay back on the bed with one arm under his head.

Rudi, I... You're going to tell Rudi that you want to be bad again, all over again aren't you. He sat up on the bed and reached for her arm. Rudi, no I'm sorry, I've gotta go.

What? And you just got here. We've not even started all the fun yet.

I know, and you've been great. Thanks, but I've got to go. She grabbed her bag and headed for the front door, passing Seb and Marta on the way - sorry guys, gotta go and she was out before they could even reply. She shut the door behind her, relieved. Setting off at a pace down the street she was weaving this way and that, through the crowds until she was too far away from the flat to be brought back. She stood still for a moment, grabbed her phone from her bag and texted with shaking fingers.

Sorry, Jack, I'm so sorry, mate. I'm coming back, I'm on my way. Pls wait for me, pls don't go.

11

Dylan

Did you not hear me? Get your boots on. The cars won't clean themselves.

Dylan rubbed his hands together to see if he could bring warmth into his dead fingers. His hands ached along the bottom of his thumbs where he'd scrolled himself senseless into the night looking at every conceivable spelling of Tara Downley available online. With the e, without the e, with an h, without an h. He'd managed to find more than he bargained for- fifteenth century mill workers, a place name, but none of them seemed to lead anywhere. He could have looked at census records, but none online without coughing up money first.

Sid the owner stomped into the freezing hut they called his office. I'll have two out of here by lunchtime, but not if the pigeon shitters breakfast is still laying across the bonnets, lad. Can you not get out there and see to them?

Sorry Sid, yeah mate, I'm there.

The work was freezing. It was December and the pigeon shit had hardened in the frost. He wasn't allowed to scrape it off, because it brought the paint off with it, in sheets. His first day in the job he'd pissed the owner off so badly he nearly got the sack before he'd even started. A ten-year-old Skoda estate with pigeon shit all over the bonnet was his first car cleaning job since he'd started at the garage and he'd gone at it with the gritty side of a kitchen sponge, found on the side of the dirty sink in the toilet block. He thought his hard work would see him in with the boss, till he realised the black crust on the sponge was paint and not pigeon droppings. The garage owner had been kind about it, scratched his head, didn't say anything till he was about to pack his bag. You'll have learned that lesson then, was all he said. He didn't know what the car went for in the end. It sat on the forecourt with the metal shaving on the bonnet for weeks until one day it was gone.

The garage gig was the worst imaginable job he could have chosen in some ways. When he applied, he'd already ruled out being any kind of office man, but then what line of work would fit? His parents thought he'd wasted his life by the time he was fourteen, so any advice had been shunted away by a constant slew of criticism. You look cheap dressed like that. You don't like school, so why would you want to do A levels? You could have been brought up in a filthy hovel, you should be grateful. Is it drugs you're doing out there every night? I suppose its dirty sex you're up to with those girls. Left to himself he'd practiced how to set his clothes out at night for the day ahead, how to lay his breakfast. A spoon, a knife, laid side by side. Plate, dish, small green teapot he'd picked up in a junk shop. Milk jug. He'd taught himself how to be decent enough.

He lived in a one room bedsit at the top of town. The attic slopes on the ceiling made him feel safe, despite having to duck his head whenever he reached across to fetch the remote. Buying a TV had been the first thing he'd done when he took on the room. Before he moved in, he wondered briefly about the microwave above the sink in the corner, if it was enough to make dinner on.

Everyone else in the house kept to themselves. Miggy and Alan across the landing were odd to be in one room when they had two wages coming in. Alan was stick thin and never spoke. Miggy told him she wrote stories for Jackie magazine in her spare time, cribbing the plots off soaps on the telly. The girl opposite was too beautiful to be here and he predicted she'd not last long. She had a cat which he borrowed one night when a mouse got in and ate all his cornflakes. It only took one night; he woke to hear the cat growling followed by, a little later the sound of it crunching through bony parts. He'd wondered briefly if cats ate cornflakes before he realised the truth of it. Downstairs were some Mormons who kept leaving leaflets in the bathroom and another couple who were into medieval reenactments and who seemed to have the best flat.

But the little attic room at the top was his alone, made to feel safe and with a mattress and quilt he salvaged from the no-sale cast offs left outside the second-hand auction rooms down at the bottom of town near the old town.

He fancied himself as a bit of a writer, but there wasn't any kind of work where they'd look at him at seventeen, and say, yes, a writer for our team. He was no scrounger and would do whatever it took to pay his rent on time and if that meant garage hand, then so be it. The cheapest rent he could find, at the top of a Victorian house, brought him an attic with shared facilities, but he was glad to have it. It was home.

Dylan's friends from school were still there, in school that is. Not one of them looked for him after he left. When he'd come off Insta and all of the other social media crap after one of his mates posted a picture of his new car bought by his parents, he made the decision to leave. On that day. And the prick wasn't even old enough to drive. What a joke. So he'd walked out of school, because one thing he knew was that he didn't have to be there anymore, didn't have to be like them.

Part of the garage job idea was that maybe the owner would teach him to drive. For the same reason he'd hung around the piano at his local catholic church every Sunday when he was thirteen, hoping somebody would notice that what he truly wanted was to play the piano. No offer to teach him ever came. I'm not having that racket in the house, there's nothing worse than someone learning an instrument, his mother had said. I'm not listening to that all day, when he begged to learn to play music. He tried after that to make a flute out of the little cardboard tray that Bounty bars came in. Round and around went the Sellotape till it was like a plastic tin whistle and then he gouged holes out with a pair of scissors. His father, like his flute, stayed mute. He had always been silent, an abstainer from life.

Dylan's one single desire in life was to find his mother. He'd spend hours on his phone, searching all possible variations of spelling. He wanted to be with her, whatever that meant. His belief was that it meant she would be someone who would want him. Really want him. It was probably a cosy myth, one told often enough to put you off, like a doomed fairy tale where the granny turns out to be a wolf. But Dylan wasn't going that way, he knew enough inside himself. That was why he wanted to make something of himself, not become rich, but be a decent enough man. He wanted his mother to meet a decent man when she met him.

Once he caught a train to London to go to St Catherine's House because he'd read you can spend a whole day in there browsing. On the platform at Birmingham New Street, he worked out all of the lateral searches he could do to find links. He'd start geographically, look at the towns where they'd told him she had once lived. High Wycombe, Milton Keynes, Wroxeter. It couldn't be that hard to find a person in this day and age if you got the dates right.

A pigeon flew past his head and landed on the iron girders above the rails, cooing and preening. The train, when it came, was a fast one all the way to London with few stops. He crooned his neck out of the window at Milton Keynes and had to stop himself getting out to wander around. With no idea where to start he would most likely get cold and then end up having to spend more money on trains. The woman steward with the trolley called him love when he bought crisps, which he liked.

Queensway was a bright, busy marching street. Wide enough for horses, yet gridlocked with cars and criss-crossed with people who all had Important Places to Go. He was in no hurry now knowing St Catherine's house was halfway down, having scoped it before he set off. Standing outside, he thought someone had made a joke. The sign read St **Catherine's House closed as a Public Reading Room.** A body blow straight out of the how not to manual. No fucking chance, it said.

When he got back to his room that night, all of his money

wasted on train fares and cheap sandwiches, he was bloated and cold. Nobody at all apart from the trolley lady had spoken to him all day. He didn't miss the fools from his school, jabbering about blow jobs and Special K. Two types of people had become interesting so far in his seventeen years: anyone by the name of Tara and anybody who was adopted. But there weren't many of the second type.

Hi, Maeve. He texted his friend.
   Hi what's up. It's late for you lol.
   I went all the way to London. Just got back
   Hey fab, was it?
   No it was shite.
   Remember the place I was going to go to/ the records office.
   Yeah, the big trip, it's your mother you're after finding? As in, The One.
   Yeah that trip.
   What did you find out? I'm excited for you, you should've told me you were going.
   We could've met I suppose but anyway. Nothing.
   ?
   It was shut, the Records Office.
   OMG, what a waste, so are you going again?
   No shut as in shut.
   WHAAAT?!
   Yeah for ever. I couldn't believe it.
   Not sure what I'm supposed to do now.
   What about that SW you told me about? Can't she get the stuff for you?
   Yeah she did. But I wanted to find where Tara is now.
   Oh right. So sorry mate. It must hurt.

Yeah it does a bit. You good?

Yeah, writing my dissertation, got to get it in next week.

What was it on again?

Human rightsey shit.

Good for you, keep going.

BFN

The social worker had given him some papers but not all. He didn't know why. She said she needed to *read the whole file first* because of Data Protection. He didn't understand when she told him he was not allowed to read the names of his adopted parents.

Social worker: I'm sorry Dylan, but I have to go through it to protect third party rights.

What third parties, do you mean my mum?

Well if you mean your adoptive mum, then yes. I haven't got their consent you see to release papers with their names in it to you.

But wait, I lived with them...

I know but it's data protection, Dylan, you see. I can't release anything that mentions them.

Hang on, why not?

Because it's their data protection rights, Dylan, you see.

What rights?

I can hear you're angry about it and I'm sorry about that.

I'm not angry. Just so I get this right: the people you placed me with, my adopted family who I know and live with, well lived with... you're saying you can't tell me who they are?

That's it, I can't release papers to you that have their names in them without their permission.

That's fucked that is, s'cuse my language, but that is totally

124

fucking fucked.

He didn't hear from her again and had to chase and chase to get any papers at all, until a grey plastic envelope arrived by post one day. It wasn't a file in his book, it was too thin, just a handful of papers. Nothing much about Tara that he didn't already know. He knew she tried to keep him, that was it. And that was enough. There was one thing new though: she had been to therapy during the court case. It was part of his Birth Records Report, one line that said she had borrowed money from relatives to help pay for it.

I want to talk about my son. She must have said that to the therapist.

He stayed at the garage for a year before travelling. In Bristol, he stayed for a bit because he met a girl who taught him how to play ukulele. She would tell him he needed to live up to his name, and not for the first time wondered if that was why Tara chose it.

On his 21st he rang home, but no one said much. How are you, Dylan, his adoptive mother asked, we've not heard from you in a while. I'm good. Travelling, you know. Dad? Is he okay? Oh yes, we're very happy in the new house. We go on regular trips away by coach you know, see plays, opera, all sorts… There was a long pause while he tried to think of what to say. Then, I'm in a quilting group, she said.

He wondered when she was going to say something about him being 21. It didn't come so he figured 18 must have been it.

On his 18th he had still been in the bedsit with the sloping ceiling, and they'd sent him a card and a small silver box like the ones she collected, set out on her dressing table. He supposed it was what you did in their world. Give people Victorian boxes. He stored his plectrum in it for a while but then gave it to a charity shop.

12

Tara

Nobody explained what would happen at 18, or 21 or on any of the birthdays since Tara lost Dylan. Nobody told her that she'd have to get time off work, that her guts would hurt, that some years she would be unable to get out of her bed. Oh but didn't you have therapy? her mates would sometimes say if ever she talked about it. Like a magic pill that was supposed to wipe it all out.

The best they could give her was to say she should put herself on the Adoption Register. Put her name out there like an advert, only it was like an advert in a secret hidey hole under the back stairs, because no one had heard of it or knew where to find it. Like, write it up in neon fucking headlights and then stick them behind the lift repair room at the back of a concrete multi story in the middle of Walsall. Yeah, sure. But she filled in the form anyway. For her it was a dedication of riches, the more times she put her thoughts and actions out there, the more and more would be the signals he could pick up on. As if her breath could breathe into the air a code, like What Three Words that would bring him home to her: *Always here, Mum x*

Tara went back to her old street often. Even though the houses had become gentrified since she lived there and were now the homes of Ruperts and Tabithas. It was part of the same dedication, as if one day simply being there might bring him in from the cold. She could see his little legs running down the street, the red socks gathered at his ankles with the blue stripe around the top. She would stand on the street and walk back along the pavement past the house imagining the next young man to turn the corner at the end of the street would be Dylan, his brown hair with that small curl in it sitting at the nape of his neck.

On his 18th birthday she sent a card and mini celebration cupcake from the bakery where she worked to the social services post adoption team who were supposed to forward letters. It probably wouldn't reach him, but she wanted him to know she'd done it, to find out one day. But it was useless. She may as well shout into an echo chamber. Blow kisses on the wind.

Tumbleweed.

No one ever wrote back, and she would wonder what had happened to the cake. She pictured nuns eating it, their mouths covered in cream icing as they pushed it into their gaping holes.

The morning after his 21st she went in to work thinking she would probably eat too much and feel sick. Daphne who she worked with was kind and left her a tea by the till when she went to hang her coat up. No worries pet, she said. Tara's job had been the one constant in her life, secured by the chance that bread and cake would always be wanted, so the shop could not make her redundant. This made her feel wanted. Even the Spires family, whose bakeries adorned the high streets of the county towns, knew her name by now which made her proud and was a smack in the eye to her past.

On the day she decided to make a payment to a search organisation, a man in a beret came into the shop and asked for six iced buns. He was not your usual iced bun customer, but was skinny with suede desert boots and long hair. After she'd boxed them up and tied the green ribbon tape, he said: What a lovely job you have, but if it was me, I'd be fat. I love an iced bun, me.

She smiled at the skinny man and wondered what his mum was like. No, you're right, she said, we have to watch ourselves in case we bump into an old friend and they don't recognise us. He laughed as he went out the door and she wondered about the curl of his hair and whether if it was shorter it would sit on the neck the way Dylan's had done. It was brown, but hair darkens with age.

The bakery had kept her in work for the past six years, even though she had been through a rocky patch after his 21st. Endless sick days put the job on the line, paid her less money too, but Daphne had always watched her back with the Spire personnel people, so she kept her job. She'd moved to a different flat too, cleaned her act up and ditched Steph and Lee. Well to be fair, Steph had already ditched her because of what happened with Lee, and when she ditched Lee, the decision she was making was a much bigger one than changing a few friends. She had it in her to become someone decent. Her therapist had shown her that all those years ago.

The search organisation was one single social worker with an official looking website. She was nice on the phone and said she wanted to help Tara. I don't think we'll run into trouble with this one, but of course I can't guarantee the outcome. No, no of course, Tara said, I know you can't make promises. And then she'd thought about what promises she'd made Dylan, and how she'd broken them even though it wasn't her fault. She'd closed the curtains in the hall for a while after that phone call, because outside the window the ash tree, which had a low twisted branch, reminded her of when she'd told Dylan she would teach him to climb trees.

The social worker asked when she last saw him, and she cried when she said he was three, wearing the red socks with the blue line around the top. You'll think I'm stupid, but I think about his socks a lot. She twisted her hands together. It's whether the new people thought they were cheap, but he always used to pull those ones out of the drawer first because I was teaching him to dress himself, you see. I know, the social worker said, these small things stick in your mind for years. It's easier that it's you coming forward, because often the children are desperate, and the mothers don't want to be contacted. It might break up their new life, you see, if they've not told anybody.

Tara thought afterwards about breaking up her life, how she would do it in a heartbeat to find Dylan. Not that there was very much to break up. After Dylan was taken, she fell apart for a few years, then dossed around getting drunk a lot. She used to see a lot of Steph even after she had a bit of a thing with Lee. Tara hated herself for what she did with Lee, because he was such a player. It made Steph mad. But after The Bricklayers threw them out one night, she got wasted and they had a shouting match and ending up having sex on the way home to her place behind a park wall. He came round a lot for a while after that. Nobody was going to help her. And Lee, well, he had fucked off at the first sign of trouble.

She went to make the payment at the bank after skinny desert boot guy had left the shop with his buns. Her world was better for it. It was more money than she'd spent on herself, but she'd saved the money specially for this. The social worker told her work would begin as soon as the money arrived in the bank.

It was three months before she heard anything. Not that they hadn't been in touch; a few emails saying they were working on it, nothing much. There was something about a prize at school. A list of names in a newspaper that had been photocopied and there he was: Dylan. The surname had been blacked out with thick pen, so it didn't look very nice on her wall, but she put it up anyway. Dylan, her boy so clever, he had won a prize for being in a team that came up with a new invention for a bicycle helmet. It put her in mind of him at the playground, always climbing.

13

The CEO

Eleven years later

Goldspiers Inc were big players in machine cast small metal parts manufacture. Dylan's entry into it had been sideways from a job he hated. After the garage laid him off, his only options had been make or sell. The idea of factory work- the monotony, the assembly line, all filled him with horror. So he told himself selling had to be top dog over factory work and if that was a way into a wage, he'd do it. Just for a while.

En route to the interview with one of the big hitters in photocopy manufacture he had wanted to run in the opposite direction, sick to his stomach, as if he had lost something precious. His mind was telling him he would not be selling so much as selling out. The interview was everything he hated: shallow, male and heavy hitting. Selling his soul to the devil he took the job. It was commission mostly with virtually no security.

On the train to Manchester, he remembered his younger self and how the idea of putting himself out there had made him shrink to start with. Anxiety floated his nights into a twilit world of self-doubt, punctuated with peanut butter toast. Before the end of his first month, he knew he would get fired.

The day before the final tally, he was called back by a customer. You sold us the wrong machine, she said, we wanted one that enlarged as well as sorted. His heart rate went up as he listened to her complain, realising that it was his own miserable mistake, until he remembered that the old manager there, Brian, had left the firm. It was Brian who asked for this particular model, he told her. The old fool, she said, sounding suddenly ashamed for complaining. He must've made an error on the order, no wonder he left soon after.

So he offered them discounted rates on photocopying paper for six months in compensation. Grateful to hear no more, the company believed they'd done well out of it, never mind that he'd signed them up for a rate easily available to pushy clients. He slammed into the end of the month with commission to show. He kept his job.

The gig as an after-dinner speaker was small change. He did it mainly because he could. An accelerated rise through the company from salesman to CEO at 29 had brought him global attention, because it coincided with the year that Goldspiers floated on the stock exchange. The front cover of Business Today carried his picture and with it the offers rolled in: talk to us, help our company, tell us what we're doing wrong, how does the future look. He was always being head hunted. From a shy start, he'd become an accomplished man of the decade. If you don't come out of your shell no one knows you're in it, he would tell young acolytes, and they'll crush you under their boot. It had become his favourite saying.

Most gigs earned him enough to take off for a skiing holiday. Not that he ever did. Once had been enough. His girlfriend of eight years told him she was leaving him on the last day of his only adventure on the snowy slopes after his skiing prowess failed to materialize. A luxury no one needs, he would say when board members blathered on about their upcoming jaunts up the mountains.

Dylan arrived at the conference half an hour before it kicked off, as he always did. Latifa from Indexa Conferences met him at the door as friendly and welcoming as you could wish. He was genuinely grateful to meet someone else who hadn't lost their human touch. She briefed him on the audience: they are mostly here to get your take on the energy crisis to be honest, Dylan... Can I call you that? Yeah, sure, go on. I mean, that's the major concern out there at the moment, and you've got this year's vote for being the man with his finger on the pulse. Thanks, yeah I'm sure they think I've got a magic wand, no one ever wants to believe it's plain old hard work. He laughed and she looked up from her notes. She had very white teeth. He liked that, and invited her for a bite to eat after.

It wasn't pleasant, he knew that, girls in different towns. A night here, a night there. It made him feel cheap, because it never came to anything. Moving on was his thing, he decided. His parents didn't fit much into his life either. No one did anymore since Emma left him on the ski slopes of France. The parents didn't seem to want to know about his life and it was mutual. Everything he'd loved as a teenager, all the music, the gigs, the bands, the outrageous clothes, had been trashed. It was, they said, a doomed world. The young had made it so. And nothing since had raised their interest or pride, despite his success, so he let them lie. Old before their time became them, and their friends were strangers.

He had, he discovered, what the psychologists referred to as thwarted belongingness. It was a fine term, but one that didn't make perfect sense in a world where everyone seemed to want his contact details. But shallow gets what shallow is, he knew that and didn't make friends at work. He thought about his mother often, but had given up the endless searching. Once in a while he'd put her name into google, but too many Tara's depressed him and he moved away to hover over the icons of his business success.

That was nice, Latifa said, her naked back beautiful in the half-light. Yeah, he meant it, though he didn't look up from the idle scroll he'd gotten into on his phone. It had replaced the post coital cigarette, the phone, sharing stupid pictures from Instagram. I've got to go, she said, getting up and moving towards the door, draped half in his shirt. Sorry, he looked up, sorry yeah it was fun. He smiled but his phone buzzed and he didn't say any more.

Hi

You don't know me, but I am looking for a Dylan Downley who is a relative. He was born in Slough. Don't know if it's you? Please get in touch if this is you. Tara

He didn't hear Latifa leave, his breathing short and fast, he got up from the bed, leaving his phone lying in amongst a tangle of sheets. His shirt was on the floor of the bathroom where she'd left it, which he snatched up and put on. He had to look at his phone again and clothes suddenly seemed important, he grabbed his boxers from the back of a chair and hopping on one foot thrust his leg in as he grabbed the phone from the bed. The message was still there. On Facebook messenger. So that's it, a simple message. It has to be her.

His mind was spiralling, who does she know, what is she like, is she safe, will she mess up my life. Will she want money, will she want me to be a son and make lots of demands? This was real, but the kind of real that takes over your brain. Will I remember her. Will. I. Remember. Her? That question. Yes that one, only one of the million others that bubbled up in him like froth on a freshly poured beer.

Hi,

Yes I was born in Slough. Can you tell me about yourself, what relation you are to the person you're looking for? Dylan

He didn't know what to say, what do you say to the person who, at this stage, could be his mother, but might also be mad, bad, dangerous or all of the above. Mess up his life? But…. So many buts and it occurred to him that all the wild ideas about what she might be like, might demand from him, did not come from him: it was the vibe that had surrounded his adoption.

Hundreds of hours of search all throughout his teens and into his twenties had never prepared him for this moment, when with a quiet thunder, the first contact with his mother rolls in across the horizon. Everything was blowing through his mind and he knew then that not for one moment would he ever pass this up. *Of course* I am going to meet her, whatever the cost. It wasn't so much a thought, more a kind of effervescent certainty. This. This, the moment I have waited my whole life for.

Ping.

Hi

I think you might be my son, Dylan. He was born on 23 December 1994 in Slough Hospital and then adopted when he was three. My name is Tara, I am Dylan's mum.

He stared at the message for a millisecond before his thumbs flew into action.

Hi again,

That is me. I don't know what to say to be honest. I have spent a lot of time searching for you and now you've found me first. What happens next I'm not sure about but I would like to meet you, if that's okay with you? I am so glad you've got in touch. x

He sat in the chair, barely able to concentrate on anything. Ping. Shit, the client meeting, he stared down at his phone, the calendar reminder told him it was starting in 005 minutes and the counter was ticking off the seconds. 004 003 He raced into the bathroom and began throwing water on his face. Towel, socks, trousers.... Ping. Ping.

He made it to the lift in record time and while he waited...

Yes, I'd love to. Whereabouts would suit you?

I can travel if we are not near. X

His thumbs worked overtime in the lift.

At work will text later but Yes! Will send a suggestion of where to meet. x

Later he would wonder about that x, when had he decided it was right to add it.

14

Tara

The trees outside the kitchen window swayed in the breeze, silver birches, she loved them. Their bare weeping branches so fine they hung like hair, catching every gust. There goes my life, there goes every night I cried, there it goes like the leaves. I am like the tree now, light as threads in the breeze in winter. How like a winter this has been, this absence. It was as if she was swaying, her insides somehow untethered. Since the first text came back, she had not eaten or drunk for hours. Yes, I was born in Slough, it said. Her instinct was to run, run to wherever he is, but she managed to hold herself back, stay polite as she had been told - don't come across as needy. It was like vertigo, as if she was on a tall building looking down on herself. She had waited twenty-six years for this.

I am right. I knew I was right, all these years. He was never lost. My boy knows I am here.

It was her day off, she had planned to do a little shopping, clean up the garden. Gill her friend who lived around the corner had suggested a walk and in all the years she had never turned her down, but this morning she cried off.

Gill knew about it, they'd been friends a long time. Ever since she'd been in what she called her New Life, Gill had supported her in making the right decisions about things. Should she get a dog: no; should she get a boyfriend: not yet; should she carry on trying to find Dylan: yes absolutely. Gill was a good grounder, living alone a quiet, untroubled life, she became a role model. Weekly outings to the garden centre followed by coffee in the eternally rewarding Yurt Café, staffed by gorgeous young farmers of the county, gave them both easy companionship and a sense of fun.

Tara was slow to tell Gill about her history, shame welling up in her like a dirty secret long hidden. When Gill moved into the same street, their friendship grew closer.

She had been married and carried a quiet sadness with her wherever she went. Tara did not like to pry, but in her imagination perhaps Gill had wanted children but been unable to. Her answer to the question had always been, no I don't have children. In time the source of her sadness came out. My son drowned when he was eleven, she said, when they were sitting in Tara's kitchen one day sharing a morning coffee. I think of him every day. My marriage failed in the end. It wasn't strong enough to deal with the pain of his loss every day. Our shared grief: he was the first thing we thought of each day and the last at night, which became all that was between us. It drove us apart in the end. We had to escape from each another. It wasn't that we fell out of love, more that we had become salt to each other's wounds.

When Tara was out walking with Gill down by the river, they

spent a long time watching the water. Gill said, it was sudden, a few kids by the river on a day like this, but somewhere else. We didn't think he was too young, because, well you know, kids go out don't they, even if you try and stop them?

I know that's true, Tara said. She wanted to know it was true, wanted to know what it was like to have an eleven-year old boy or any age of any child growing up.

He was with a group of mates, and they all went in. When they were jumping in the water our Jake must have broken a leg somehow, they don't fully know. He was in trouble and the other kids thought he was hamming it up. By the time they realised, he was too far out. One of them, the biggest one, jumped in but Jake was fighting him – it was the pain, he became hysterical, and so the other lad couldn't drag him out. I feel sorry for that boy, it must have hit him hard because he *had* tried but not succeeded. I don't feel blame at all, you know.

How old would he be now, Gill?

His next birthday he would be twenty-five and my mother, who died the same year, would be eighty-five. In my mind they're both still the same age of course.

Gill, how do you bear it?

Life goes on doesn't it, Tara? But we have to find a way. I try to live life in a good way every day, because that's what Jake would have wanted me to do. I am still his mum and always will be. I still live every day for him in the way he would want me to live.

I can't imagine what your experience has been, but perhaps I have some idea, Tara said shyly, because, well I know it's not the same and all but I lost a son too. It wasn't anything as tragic as what happened to your son though, and it was my fault, every bit of it. Social services took him off me and he was adopted. They said I'd neglected him. Now I believe I didn't deserve to have a boy like him, still don't.

Oh darling, I never knew that. You're wrong to blame yourself though, whatever it is.

Tara told her then, the whole story warts and all. Even about Steph and Lee and the episode in the park, when she'd lost the plot and shouted at everyone. And she told her how there'd been a thing with Lee afterwards, which busted up her friendship with Steph. Everything. It was all my fault you see, she said. The thing is, Gill, I was so young and stupid, I had no support and honestly, I was off my head. You know, my mum was a terrible mum and I grew up in care. I lost my brother and sister to that system. It wasn't long before I got into the wrong company - way too young, which sent me off on one. If I'd had you, or, you know, any kind person who wasn't off the rails I might have been different. I was so, so stupid. I shall live with that regret all the days of my life.

And there hasn't been a day I haven't tried to look for him too.

You should, Tara. Whatever you do, don't give up because your boy is out there, he is not lost to you.

I even paid an agency to help me find him, but in the end, they were not much use. I saved up and everything. I couldn't go back to social, because they would never help me. They hated me. I had this social worker, Carol was her name, who turned up late to every court case. She was the one that told them to take him off me forever. And you know what, she left the job after that. I rang one time to find out if he had settled in and that and they said she'd left straight after the case. I wouldn't be surprised if they hadn't sacked her. I had a bad feeling about her, that she was flaky.

Did the agency help? Surely they should be able to find him in this day and age?

Well it's not easy, they sent me some stuff from when he was at school. I was so proud to see it, he did so well. I knew my boy would be a clever one. He used to say to me *mummy, my socks don't stay up because they are tired* and he was only three when he said that. It was true as well, those red socks, with the blue line – I always remember them – they were from the charity shop. But I got nothing else from them, no idea where he lives, where he works. Nothing. And they said they couldn't help further so that was it. Last year, that was.

But with the internet, maybe you could give it a good go? You've got a phone, there's ways to look out there if you get his surname.

It was blacked out, so I never knew it. That's the trouble, it's not knowing who he is Gill.

Search under your name, Tara. Maybe he uses it sometimes, you never know.

And from that day Gill became her constant support, urging her on. Searching under her own surname, Downley, was a stroke of genius. It had never occurred to her he might use it. Gill said, when you don't have a surname, use what you've got.

Her boy Dylan Downley, was out there living his life and today it would be Gill she would have to thank for finding Dylan. It was Gill's support that gave her the courage to become someone who deserved respect, it was Gill who kept her going when she drew a blank.

Tara looked at the trees and noticed the rain was beginning to fall. It was a clean rain, freshening the air, beginning this new part of her life. If it hadn't been for her, she might have given up a long time ago. She picked up the phone:

Gill?

Hi Tara, I got your message. It is a bit miserable isn't it, let's save it for when it's sunny.

Gill, I've done it. I've found him! That's why I can't come on a walk, I can barely breathe.

Oh my god, Tara, you bloody genius! Tell me how it happened.

Two hours later, they were both sobbing and laughing into their phones, whilst the rain gently misted away the outside world.

15

Dylan

Man up, he said, peering at his reflection in the mirror, the red eyes a giveaway. He was meeting Tara for the first time and felt as if he'd taken a step back all of ten years to a time when he couldn't keep it together emotionally. You know, he told his reflection, it was never an issue in public, all this. It was being shy; I knew it, that's all it was. He smiled at the reflection and looked at his own eyes. They kept on brimming and he couldn't stop, so he said a small prayer to himself: I will remember this day as long as I live and thank you for giving it to me.

More cold water splashing, hair combing hours later, he was sitting with a black coffee in the lobby of the Clayton Hotel, Baker Street waiting for the hour to turn towards midday. He chose the hotel as a venue, but was going to meet her from the tube. Every other kind of imagined scenario had coursed through him, including that it wouldn't happen, she wouldn't come. Since the date had been fixed a tidal wave of feelings had threatened to overwhelm him, but had now receded, leaving him wired, anxious and jumpy. He had been to heaven and hell these last few days, as if on a high for over a week since the message dropped into his inbox. Now, two coffees in, the caffeine wasn't helping to bring him down. A thousand what-ifs occupied his mind as he watched the passers-by: too short, too tall, too old/young/ugly. But in the end, they were all random people, too early, all of them, to be her. It was only eleven.

He was not going to tell his adoptive parents. The last contact he had with them passed with talk about the church, roses, Dad's knee and his mother showing little measurable interest in Dylan's life. Are you still rushing about, she asks. She sighs when he begins to tell her and cuts him off with, you young people are all so busy, I don't know what you think you'll get out of it. A life, a fucking life, is what he wanted to say, a career, some interesting projects, some colour, anything better than what you're doing rotting away in the countryside. But he didn't say any of that.

A breeze blew across the plaza in front of the hotel and the passers-by reacted. He watched as a middle-aged woman in a suit stopped to open her smart work bag to pull out a full-on woolly hat with a large pompom. He laughed to himself, high with delirium. He had no idea if she'd be a nutcase or a career woman or both, or come in a woolly hat.

At 11.45 and he paid and set off, scanning the faces of every passing female. Baker Street station was a short walk away, but he wanted to be there first. Should he buy her flowers? No, stupid, it wasn't a date. He'd left his coat in the hotel so ran back, but by the time he arrived it'd been moved to reception.

Yes, we do have it, wait a second, said the receptionist. John, can you go to the bar and fetch the coat that was handed in? Watching the clock, it was now 7 minutes to 12. I'm in a bit of a hurry…. It shouldn't be long, she said. 4 minutes to 12 and he was running back towards Baker Street, down past the top entrance. He slowed to a walk, fighting to get his breath, his chest heaving. At the end of the street, where Baker Street touches Marylebone Road, the traffic was gridlocked.

He swung left into Station Approach staring intently at every passing face, but there were too many of them, a river of people flowing towards him dodging left and right, holding parcels, bags, umbrellas, all on a mission to get somewhere. His heart was pounding. He crossed the short distance up the incline towards the station, passing the queue of waiting black cabs. In no time he was upon it, slowing his pace even more, glancing at every woman in case it was her; and suddenly a clear view straight ahead broke through the crowd and people were rushing past him.

At first he saw no one, but then there was a woman. There was someone. A woman standing alone there. Right there, where they'd said. She was standing there, a little to the right. There was someone there, but it couldn't be, could it? Yes. No. Was it her? Could it be? She was short and…. Hello, are you Tara? He was speaking to her and she was holding her bag very tightly. Yes, she said, her hand on the bag strap shaking. Hello Dylan and there it was: her voice. He knew her voice. Looking away now, large tears were falling down her face. He was taking her hand, it felt cold and she was shaking, her hand was shaking, but he was hugging her and holding on. All noise ceased. The world stopped too, and every man and every woman and the cars and the buses and the whole world stopped to share this moment with him. This quiet moment which was a sacrament and a beginning.

16

Jo

Jo Juniper lowered her cup firmly into the coaster so that it sat comfortably within the raised rim, then laid her head gently onto the pile of cushions in her tiny single berth. The view the length of the saloon took in her whole world, so far as home went. Single bed, galley, leather armchair, corner placed stove. The stove glinted from behind the glass, giving out enough heat to warm the compact space. Tomorrow looked as if it might rain all day, meaning she had placed a bucket beside the two narrow doors at the entrance to capture the drip drip of water that ran from the door's edge along a ridge in the ceiling, encouraged by the tilt of the tide. This narrowboat had been her home now for two years since she sold up and took to the liveaboard life on the waterways. She had named it Safe Haven when she bought it, as though she had permission at last, to feel at home. Winding down her client list had come with age and a sense that her body might fail her. Her mind turned year upon year to her lost daughter and this small act of naming was an act of reclaiming what had been taken.

The roof had been leaking for a week, a half bucket a day, but she would not pass anyone who could fix it till the boat yard. The noise of the yard, the hustle and bustle, was something she looked forward to nowadays, a rare social event in her limited life.

Boat living had taught her that precision in placing stuff makes for a less eventful life: preventing breakage and unwanted spillage. Rudimentary engineering skills had not come easy. When the engine packed up one day after only ten miles, she peered into it without a clue where to start. There began her realisation that she had to learn if she wanted to survive. Now she could clean out the traps and carry out basic maintenance jobs, enough to keep her afloat.

Her feet hurt today, but it was only a symptom of everything else, the broadband effect, she liked to call it. There was little she could do to prevent it, but it had not stopped her going to every protest against the much-trumpeted roll out of more masts and ever wider broadband coverage.

Living in the south east had become intolerable in the last few years she was there. Her failing health, she believed to be a direct result of the mobile phone signals emitted from every mast. Repeated visits to doctors and private alternative specialists bled her finances dry, and in the case of the former, fell on deaf ears. I am sick because of the radio waves, she insisted, despite repeated diagnoses of a nonspecific somatic illness. When it got bad, she left for Wales in her old Ford Fiesta, taking only enough clothing to get her through the week. It was summer but the beauty passed her by. Even on a bare hill overlooking the Brecon Beacons, the pain still came in waves.

Lupus, one doctor put forward, only later to be disproved by a plethora of blood tests and scans. Not content with their medical interventions, she blamed external toxicity of any kind, meaning she had no choice but to give up the majority of her clients. Being a therapist, she told her friends, you're taking on other people's problems and with that comes every kind of toxicity. You look toxic, Jo, said Sue her osteopath friend, you have to get out of that job.

Desperate for internal reconditioning, she flash-booked a week-long mindfulness getaway in a remote country retreat centre. They had agreed to an 'all mobiles off' policy for retreatants during the day, so she began to look forward to the rest of the week unfolding when she could relish the silence. It wasn't long before her hopes came crashing down. Despite being hidden away in the crook of a winding Welsh lane deep in the heart of the countryside, they did have broadband. By the second day she felt sure that Wi-Fi signals were giving her a migraine, despite the no mobiles policy. The next day's activities being out of the question, she packed a bag and left.

Living on a boat had its advantages, the soothing heave of the water helped her to sleep and musical evenings with motley houseboat dwellers lifted her spirit. Life, as she knew it had started to become more manageable. All her old friends had been left behind in the south east, but she kept Sue in the loop: I've got no clients, Sue, and it feels weird, but a relief. I can finally concentrate on myself, the changes I want to make, how to get my head straight. How are you managing for money? Sue asked. She laughed, having no money seems to follow me around, but for the first time, you know, this is my chance to reclaim my life. I'm done with helping others.

Time for you, at last, Sue replied warmly.

Musical nights had her on the zither, an instrument she'd taught herself during long nights alone in her old house. Hopes of a man had faded with time, it was too far from her emotional home with Anna, to try and become a source of support to someone else.

In the boating community there were many who were living solo. They were not tied to a mortgage, different to the landlubbers who might spend their weekends shopping. It would be a falsehood to say the boaters' world was a step back in time, but she believed they shared values born of the river: friendship, fires and the edge of adventure every day.

Here she could talk about her old life as a therapist with its daily challenge of meeting other people's complex needs. There had been changes to her orientation in more than one way, not only the shift from solid to liquid, land to water, but also an alchemical alteration in the way she thought. Instead of reaching for solution-based positivity, in the service of others, her life had become body-lived, a roundel of weathers and seasons. She was moving from her head into the life of her body.

Many years ago, she resolved she would not search for Anna. It seemed indecent to give a child freely to a new life and then exact a claim upon them because you were sad. The most she could hope for was a reverse search by Anna. But she could not expect it. She filled in the form to add her name to the adoption register, but tried to forget as the years passed without word. Since taking to the waterway, she worried constantly she would miss the post. The post office couldn't help, so in the end she asked Sue, the osteopath, if she could use her address.

She got up to put the kettle on the stove. To save fuel she used the log burner to boil water. Taking a pottery cup from the hook, she wondered whether Sue would mind if she checked again this month for letters. Without the means to ring anyone, friends had faded away. The water was slow to boil; she waited for the whistle. Perhaps she had made herself unreachable on purpose. Something turned in her guts at the thought: I am my own worst enemy.

Writing to Sue for post was her only option, though it seemed so old fashioned. She hesitated before taking pen to paper. Perhaps I should have got a phone. What if she finds me here, on a boat called Safe Haven. Would she understand my life? Such a pointless question.

Dear Sue,

I am sorry to be so distant, she wrote, but Anna is on my mind so much and I don't want to become uncontactable. She must be all of an age now and this might be the time, perhaps, when she may have questions. Has there been any post for me there? Please come and visit, I will let you know when the river brings me your way. Meantime, the shop here will accept post for me if there is anything to forward. I hope you are keeping well.

Love, Jo.

They were nuns who took Anna. That convent, the disinfectant smell of it, rose up in her memory often. All the time she was there with her Ma and the crying after, they neither looked at her nor spoke directly to her. It was to her mother they addressed their grim assessment: it's for the best. And that was it, the point of no return.

17

Anna

Nobody had helped her. Even Jack had left her, after Berlin. He helped her to get home but in the last few nights of travel, when she moved towards him in the night, although he had forgiven her, the trust was gone.

I'll get you back home, Anna, but you know me – I'm not going to stay put and get a job stacking shelves somewhere. And the van, old Jack's Straw Castle, is out there parked up in Gomera, waiting for me to get back to it.

I know, I'm sorry. I don't know where my head was at, with Rudi and all that. I've messed up, Jack.

Yeah, well we're still mates, you know that, Anna. I'm not that kind of guy, you know. I don't dump on women if they get their head in the wrong place. But I'm not gonna lie, it did hurt me.

I didn't mean for that to happen. Honestly, Jack, I am so sorry. I think I lost my way, you know?

They were having a conversation in a brown bar in Antwerp, so called because of the atmospheric polished wood décor which shaded the light and brought back memories, not all of them sober, of British pubs. The weather had put a chill into outside tables, so they were hunkered down inside with a plate of frites and mayonnaise. They had no time limit save for the one their dwindling funds put on them. Originally aiming to hang out in France once they got there, they'd been forced to switch up their plans after Berlin, the twin pressures of transport and cost meant that there was no alternative but to slow down the travel. It would anyway give them a chance to think about what was happening between them – or not.

Jack's Straw Castle, the van, had been left behind in Valle Gran Rey at the time they'd taken off for Berlin. Jack had always planned to go back to Gomera to set up a restaurant on the beach if he could get together enough cash. So hostel by hostel, ride by ride, they made their way down through Germany and were part way across Belgium.

It's just that, well, you know it broke the trust, Anna. I think I want to go it alone, you know. But you'll find another guy, you know? We were good in Gomera, but out here, in the regular world, he looked down, I'm sorry but it isn't what I want. I'm really sorry.

Anna was crying. She shook her head.

It's okay, Jack, I know I messed up. I know it now.

You'll be okay. I promise you, said Jack, and reached out and patted the back of her hand.

I think you've got this all this worry shit going on in your head about your mother and all that. I truly believe if you can find her, your life will change. Give it go? I mean, when you get back?

She couldn't speak and shook her head again, then nodded.

I know, I know. I'm so sorry, I'm so sorry. She could think of nothing else to say.

C'mon girl, let's get you back on the road. If you get home, you can earn some money and get into it properly. I'll help you get back, don't you worry.

Six months later, Anna was asleep in a bus stop in Hull thinking of Jack. The bench she was on was not a proper seat, more of a perch, so during the night she had slept underneath it on the hard ground. Now she had propped herself upright to avoid being asked to move on; she tried to make herself look like a person waiting for a bus with her bag at her feet, but knew the passers-by weren't convinced because of the way they looked at her and then looked away if she met their eye.

Jack came to her mind often as a remembered friend, his kindness, his rebel spirit. Sleeping rough seemed to blank out everything when it was too cold to move: any movement made her colder by letting in the air, so she had learnt to lie still with all of her stuff hugged tightly to her body. Some days, despite the numbness, her mind drifted back revisiting places and friends. Finding new memories helped to keep away shame for the scrag bag life she was living.

It was new, this bus stop life. Not homelessness, she told herself, because sofa surfing doesn't count as homelessness. Well, not if you can use an address to get some benefits it didn't. Getting benefits was such a weird one, she thought. It didn't feel like a benefit when you got it, because your life was so low that nothing registered beyond how to survive the coming night. If it kept you from starving, then that was a benefit to the people who would have to clear your body away, the onlookers who would be ashamed, the relatives who would have to be told how you died.

After getting back to the UK, she had managed to stay at Jack's uncle's house for a month, then surfed her way from London to Hull until her friend whose couch she was sleeping on told her the lease was up. Since then, she had lost her phone contract (no money), her place to stay (no money) and any idea of what to do next (no money).

At night, when the rains came, it was unbearable and it left her wanting her mother, but it was confused, because she didn't know which mother. She didn't know who it was she wanted and perhaps that would always be the way it was: she didn't know, and would never know her.

Around her she had wrapped the sleeping bag she grabbed from Sal's cupboard the day she left. What she didn't use she won't miss, she thought, but deep down was uncomfortable with having taken it, because it was now very dirty after a week outside. The rain slanted across the rigid perspex sides of the shelter, through which she could barely make out the silt brown water of the river Humber across the road. It'd been a month since she was on her period and everything in the particular ache of her body told her she would come on today. What do you do when you're on your period and living in a bus stop. I mean, what the fuck do you actually do?

A man in high viz clothing and dust covered steel boots came into the bus shelter and sat down. He was a dock worker, but you're not supposed say that any more: port operative is what you say now. Nausea was rising in her throat, because she hadn't eaten all day, so she wondered if maybe she was beginning to feel what true hunger felt like. You all right, love, he said, but he was only saying hello not looking for an answer. He lit up a cigarette staring out of the bus shelter and she wondered if she should ask for money, but had not done that yet and didn't want to start. She got up to move around and felt embarrassed when she couldn't fold her sleeping bag properly because her hands were too numb. The man was preoccupied rubbing one of his boots. It was a relief he showed no interest in her, it was like a kind of respect. When the bus came, he stood up, nodded his head and was gone. It made her feel better, as if she was seen. It mattered to be seen.

She set off in search of food, but finding nothing in the bins outside the supermarkets she resorted to sitting in her sleeping bag nearby. A woman with a toddler in tow stopped and puts a cheese sandwich and bottle of coke down on the ground in front of her. For you, she said, her accent possibly Eastern European. Dodging into the public toilets on Nelson Street, she tried to wash her face and hands and tidy her hair. The look in her eyes when she stared in the mirror frightened her and she gave up. Taking her trousers down she discovered her period had started, so she panicked and stuffed her pants with toilet paper, packing more into her bag for later.

Back in the street she headed towards the city centre, hoping to sit in the library for a while. Ever since her life began sliding out of control, she had never stopped searching for her mother. Hull Library gave her an account on her friend's address, so she could use the computers there for free. Searching online had led nowhere, because she didn't know if her mother's name was right - whether she had married, divorced, moved in or out of different names. She was convinced she'd found her at one point, the place matched, the age, everything and even the profile picture made her feel as if she might know her, as if her DNA might somehow click. The hair was the right colour, she had a kind face, but a letter to her resulted in a kindly worded note back saying she was sorry, but it wasn't her. You can never be sure though.

Two hours later she was online at one of the long desks in the library, conscious that her time there was limited: the librarians watched from their desk to make sure you weren't hogging the seats to stay out of the rain, plus she didn't know how long the toilet paper would hold out. After a quick visit to the library toilet, she returned to find her seat had gone and all the computers were taken, so she headed out the door. Today's search produced nothing of note, it looked as though her only lead would be back to the local authority where her mum had lived, see if they could help. She set off down the street towards the city centre.

Hey, Anna? Anna Ainscott? How are you?! Hey, how great to see you!

She didn't see where the voice was coming from at first until a man came into view crossing the street making a beeline towards her. She recognised Surjan immediately, he was an old mate from home. It was too late to run away, although she wanted to, it would look weird. She was suddenly aware she might look dirty.

Oh my god, Surjan, I'm surprised to see you. Here, I mean... wow! I'm sorry, I'm not ... well what do I say.

Ashamed suddenly of how she must look, she became acutely conscious he was clean and she was not. He was so warm and friendly it made her feel like she didn't want him to come too close in case she smelt bad. Pushing her hands down in her pocket so he didn't see her nails, she scanned the street.

Anna, well how strange to bump into you here, I mean do you live here how? Are you working?

Yeah, sure, I'm working, yeah of course. Well not this week, obviously, she laughed nervously, and pushed her hair from out of her eyes wishing she had made more effort in the toilets.

What are you doing, I heard you'd gone travelling and I was so envious. I've fallen into that old trap of doing what my parents wanted, you know how it is. He lifted his hands as if to show he was helpless. So, I'm up here at uni.

Oh, right. It didn't quite work out for me that way, so I'm still between things, you know. What are you studying?

Surjan had a love of music, the cello, then guitar, then piano, any instrument in the music centre he could pick up and master within a few weeks. Back then Anna had been a failing student of the flute, her parents' chosen instrument. What she lacked in enthusiasm wasn't made up for in practice and in the end her parents let her give up after the flute teacher called them in and told them they were wasting their money.

Medicine and I've got a long way to go. But hey Anna, if you're around, come and meet my mates later, we're at the campus bar? It would be good to hang out. I'm sorry I've got to run now, but so lovely to see you again.

He left soon after, weaving his way back into the crowds heading down King Edward's Street. Surjan had once told her that everyone should do whatever her parents told them to, even if they did not want to, because that way they honoured their ancestors. At the time they had all, apart from Surjan, been drinking and talking about what their parents wanted for them. She said her parents wanted her to be like them: a civil servant or a housewife and that she could see no reason on earth to do that. I want to live, Surjan, she had practically shouted at him. He laughed at her and said do what they want Anna, trust me, it will work out. He was the only one in the group who believed that.

She stood on the street looking in the direction he had gone and wondered what her parents would think of her life now. She wondered if maybe what she should be doing is whatever her birth mother wanted her to do. Whatever that was it would have been a happy life, because mothers always give up their babies wanting only that don't they? The stupidity of it is that they don't realise that by giving up their baby to complete strangers they are pretty much guaranteeing the chances of ever being truly happy are screwed.

In two and a half years, she had contacted them only once to say hello. The coldness was there in their voices, the interest in what she was doing hollow, as if they could only expect bad news.

So, have you got a job, Ann? Her mother always dropped the a off her name and called her Ann. Not yet, but you know, I'm going travelling so it's more like I want to work hard, save and then use it to travel. Oh, she had sighed, I see. Nothing else, except a curt 'I see'. But she didn't see. No amount of explanation seemed to reconnect her to Anna or to the passion of her own youth, the desire to see the world. She had dried up and that was the way the conversation went. Well, nice to hear from you, she said, her voice thin. Are you both well, how's Dad, Anna asked hoping he might take the phone, give her some encouragement. We're alright, was all she said and then it petered out. Goodbye then, dear. Anna came away yearning as she always did for some extra words to wish her good luck, to say they wanted to see her perhaps. Friends would hear their mother's say I love you at every call, yet the words never came.

The sun was dipping behind the clouds and the drift of people on the street dispersed into offices and cars. Anna wondered about walking after Surjan, even going to the campus bar, but a dirty sleeping bag was too much of a giveaway. She ducked into Safeways and bought a large bottle of cider. How to keep warm, she told herself.

A few days later she saw him again. This time she wasn't able to hide. He passed her sitting beside her begging cup outside Safeways. She had spent the night in the doorway of a charity shop until she had been moved on in the morning. Bags of clothes which had been dropped off at night in big black bin bags had served as a kind of protection from the wind. It was a cold March and there was a sense that spring was late, with few people out in the evenings.

Anna? Hi mate, I thought it was you. You know what, I'm so glad to see you.

Surjan. Don't tell anyone will you? It's temporary... She tried to get up but her feet were numb which made her slow. Surjan squatted down beside her. No don't get up, Anna, listen I've got an idea. You shouldn't be doing this at all, not you, you're too clever by far. Hey, why not come to my place? You can have a bed there and a shower.

Are you sure? Surjan, it's not how it looks honestly. It was all she could do to stop herself crying. Surjan helped her to her feet supporting both hands tenderly, then bent down to help with the bags.

18

Jo

One year later

They all heard her. Not that any one of them realised they had. Anna's voice setting up the day for the nurses, the patients, the hospital orderlies, the surgeons. Even Mr. Sutherill, the colorectal guy, had joined the ranks and named her as his favourite groove to suture to.

And a good morning to everyone. What a rainy day it is out there, I hope you're all warm and dry indoors. Lovely to be with you all again and today we've some special treats lined up –sounds you may never have heard before, music to lift the spirits.

Before we dive in, I'd like to pass on our huge thanks to Goldspiers for their very generous donation of three cardiac ECG machines which is going to put us top of the list for response time for many many more patients. A big shout out to them and their Chief Exec, Dylan Downley, who is in the building guys! And our sincere thanks to them.

In the women's ward, Jo heard her as she lay recovering from her bilateral mastectomy. It was the sound she had been listening to the night before surgery, and the music had somehow, by some special magic, transported her back to her youth.

Surjan heard her, filled with pride as he carried tiffins stocked with aromatic home cooking for his nan who was mobilising on Ward 9 after a hip replacement.

Dylan heard her as he toured the cardiac unit carrying the new ECG machines Goldspiers had donated, stopping to speak to radiographers, nurses and the tame consultant surgeon who had been sent down to meet and greet.

Tara heard it in the cubby hole office of the League of Friends located behind the hospital coffee shop and staffed entirely by volunteers like herself.

Carol heard it in the hospital's social work office where she was wading through a pile of manila folders on her desk, trying to become acquainted with the new style of social intervention she had signed up to. Against all the odds, she had managed to land herself a job working part time in hospital adult social care.

Jo's body was changed forever. She was trying to come to terms with the news that the tumour had, after all, been more difficult to remove than expected. You never know, until it happens to you, what will be the crooked mile you travel once a cancer diagnosis has caught you in its grip. For Jo, the diagnosis had come late. The temptation to apportion blame didn't come naturally, so deeply entrenched was her training in person centred therapy, so she found herself oddly detached. Until now. To be compassionate to others had become the instinct she leaned in to, forgiving them and herself in the process. Oh, but make no mistake, she used to tell her friends: none of that comes easy. And to her closest friends: try as I might to be compassionate, I cannot, no will not, forgive my mother for that moment when she took my daughter and gave her away. It was a promise. A solemn promise, and she broke it.

So the shock of discovering she had a Stage III tumour in her breast, after her GP failed to recognise the significance of a retracted nipple, didn't edge her towards blame – she didn't fix it on her work, her itinerant life, her sadness, not even her mother. When the final tests in the pre-op process upgraded the tumour to Stage IV, she still held everything in check. But that was then.

Now, lying on a ward surrounded by the ailing, the coughing, the sleepless, minus her breasts, her emotions had risen to the surface like sludge. It was as if she had been hit full in the face with everything sad from her life. The tears came constantly. The nurses kept asking if she was in pain and she wanted to scream Yes! Yes! Yes! but knew they meant physical pain, so she shook her head.

The consultant came to see her on ward rounds. Normally it was a registrar, but it was obvious something was up when it was the consultant who she'd first seen before surgery. The nurse closed the curtains around the cubicle as she left, and Jo thought how funny it was that they did this when everyone could still hear.

Hi Jo, how are you feeling today? I'm okay. I've come to tell you how the surgery went and what we are planning for you. Is that okay? Tell me if you would like me to stop at any point or if you have any questions. She nodded, the words sliding between her thoughts.

His face gave nothing away, the pen in his pocket, resting. I think the nurses in recovery may have mentioned the surgery took a little longer than expected. She nodded. That was because the tumour was more difficult to remove than we had anticipated. Breast cancer is often straightforward, but this depends on whether or not it has spread. I did not think, in your case, that it had. However, we can never be fully certain until the surgical procedure itself. In your case we found that the cancer had metastasized to the chest wall and surrounding tissue.

She waited for him to go on, but he was speaking again. Do you have any questions at this point?

I don't know, why wasn't it seen on the scans?

His smile was sad, that's a very good question, he said. The CT scans are very good, but sometimes it can be challenging with breast tissue, there can be blind spots. We took lymph nodes and the results are not good. I am sorry to say none of them were clear.

I realise you will find this very hard, and so soon after surgery, but I wanted you to know as soon as possible. Is there family we can call?

She thought yes, but shook her head. No, no family, but thank you for telling me so soon. Will I be allowed to go home? I mean, can I go home? Will I have ….

Tears came again and flooded her face.

The consultant reached for the tissue box and put his hand on her arm. There was a gentle pressure from his fingers.

I'll ask a nurse to come in to sit with you. We will talk again about some treatment plans that may make things easier for you, but meanwhile, you can stay with us until you feel able to manage in your home.

Thank you.

Goodbye Jo, I will see you in a few days and we can talk some more.

The nurse came in and held her hand for what seemed like an hour. I'll bring you a cup of tea she said. Would you like the radio on again? The nurses, so tender all of them.

Some of you might be feeling it's a long afternoon out there, what with the sun being so shy today, so I thought I'd bring you this gem of a song in case any of you might prefer to drift off and have an afternoon nap. Let the delightful strains of Sam Sweeney's fiddle carry you away in this wonderful version of the ballad How Long Will I Love You.

Jo let the voice of the radio wrap around her like velvet and thought, I knew this was coming. I just knew. The music washed over her and she let it, uncovering delicate waves of joy hidden beneath her grief. Here am I all alone, and in the end, there has only ever been one person I've ever wanted, truly wanted to spend the rest of my life with.

19

Tara

Gill, you know what's happening down at the hospital is so brilliant. Tara was enjoying a cuppa with her friend from the street. We've already raised a bit of money in the League and not only that, but I've got Dylan onto it and he's been down there now at the hospital.

Tara I'm so proud of you, you know. You've pulled your life around, so tell me what is the burning news you've got for me?

It's Dylan again, but you know Gill now that he's back in my life, what else is there? We've met every month so far this year and you know, we get on like we were always together. But Gill, don't let me go on about it if this is hurting you. I wouldn't want to hurt you. You're my best friend and you are all that's stood between me and… well, you know, a total fuck up for pretty much most of the time we've known each other. You saved me, no question.

Gill laughed a little. It was a quiet soft sound, her eyes downcast, looking at the surface of her tea.

Gill? I'm so sorry my darling, is this a day that's special to you? Oh my god, I am such a stupid woman. How could I not have realised? It was this week, wasn't it?

Yeah, but hey I don't expect you to mark it you know. I do, but what else is there, like you said? We love a long time, don't we? Whether or not there is anyone to receive it.

Your boy is as much with us as Dylan, Gill. There was something I wanted to ask you today anyway. I must have known somehow that it was that time.

Outside her window across the street, the trees swayed in the April breeze. She had put food out on a bird table in the front garden and as winter turned to spring, she would watch the birds swoop in to feed, scrapping and fluttering on the wind.

I've been asked to put together a special playlist. It's for the big summer fundraising day and Anna, the volunteer radio host at the hospital, has put together a whole idea about covering the event as a DJ. So she wants us to contribute our own League playlist. Would you help me with it? I trust you Gill and know you'd be the one with all your strength who could guide me to the right kind of music. We could, well if you agree that is, dedicate a song to each of our boys?

Her friend was looking at her, not stopping to wipe away the tears that came. They came as easily this year as they had every year since she lost her boy.

I'd be glad to Tara. We'll make a grand playlist for the lost boys. A warm smile spread across her face. You're a good friend to me too, Tara.

Over the next few days, the air in Tara's house was laden

with music as she played songs she'd not listened to in years. Gill came round and they sorted through their choices. Together they played, laughed and even danced shyly to their chosen songs. Before long they had an 'in' pile and a 'maybe' pile.

Gill's choice for Jake was Raglan Road, which she could not explain, but it had to be Glen Hansard and Declan O'Rourke singing together. No particular reason, but it's the one I want, she said. Tara said it's in; you don't have to explain and touched her hand. But she also wanted Coldplay and in the end they decided she'd have to have them all.

By nightfall they were exhausted and ordered a takeaway. You've still not chosen yours Tara? Look at this pile, she was laughing now, and not a single one for poor Dylan!

It's in there Gill, it's all of them. But yes, for him the only one it could be is Wild Horses, and without missing a beat, the chorus line poured forth from them both.

20

Anna

Not many weeks after she'd put in a proposal to the League of Friends for their upcoming fundraiser, two things happened to Anna which took her breath away. After the second one she said to herself things always come in threes so let's hope this bloody event goes off well without any giant surprises.

The first was a playlist that dropped into her inbox from Tara at the League who had agreed to organise the event. A playlist was a thing she could do herself, no problem, since she'd become an experienced hand at the microphone, but this was the League's event so she put a shout out for a compilation of their tunes.

The day it arrived was quiet. She took an hour out at lunch time and went down to the lake across the road from the hospital. With her headphones on, not more than one second into the playlist listening to Declan O'Rourke's shudderingly beautiful rendition of Raglan Road with Glen Hansard, her whole body went still. The river of sound pouring out of those men's voices, singing as if their lives depended on it was a waking dream of longing. She was a bird in the hand from then on, all the way until the end of the playlist, which finished on the chorus of Wild Horses. The whole of the selection struck a chord: it was a compilation of longing and lament. The music lasted no more than twenty minutes, but she sat there by the lake for the remainder of the hour and simply wept. At the decks that afternoon she played music for the station as if she could gift the listeners the deepest love and longing; she played the richest, the kindest, the saddest, the most hopeful music she could find. It touched her so deeply it had to be about her mother.

A quick glance at her phone brought a message that announced the second thing that was to take her breathe away that day: Hi Anna, this is Scott Marston the CEO of the hospital. You're doing a great job on the station. I'd like to have a discussion with you about further collaboration within the hospital setting if you'd be interested? Let me know and please could you get in touch with my PA (sorry for the formality), Janet, who can fix up a meeting? Scott

Since Surjan had rescued her off the street, everything had taken an upward turn. Volunteering at the hospital had been his mother's idea: get a volunteer position somewhere, it's what people do nowadays to get on the ladder. Surjan helped her with the application. Her first job was on the tea counter for the League, but not long after, her world began to open up. Real opportunities were being laid before her like a cloth of gold. No money was involved, but these were *life* chances coming her way, dropping into her lap like gifts. The chance to get recognised, Surjan's mother called it, and she was right.

Two o'clock on the 23rd April and Anna was sitting in the waiting area outside Scott Marston's office. Dress code had been a challenge, I mean what do I wear, I sit in a booth most of the day seeing nobody. In the end she was presenting as a slightly smarter version of her daily jeans and hoodie, with an eye to winning some kind of approval from the boss.

Hi Anna, come in. Scott was not what she expected at all, not least because he came out to greet her. He too presented as a slightly smarter version of jeans and a hoodie, well, not jeans exactly but as near as dammit. But perhaps it was unfair to judge, after all what do CEOs of hospitals wear if they're under forty and busy? Take a seat, Anna and welcome to 'the hub' he said laughing a little.

Thanks …. and for inviting me too. Are you a listener?

Me? You bet I am, he replied, clearing papers away from his desk. I can tell you Anna, your work has been so well received, and at all levels within the hospital, it is justly being described as the morale boost we all need, which is why I wanted to talk to you.

Looking around, it was clear this was a man with a job and a half to get through. The papers that were now pushed to the edges on his desk were piled high. Some, she could see, were clearly marked up and tabbed. There was a phone headset with one of those little mouthpieces that curve around the face lying on the desk, socketed into his desk phone, next to a photo of a boy with a football. Although he was dressed casually, there was a jacket on the back of his chair and some smart leather lace ups beside the desk. He was in good shape, his shirt tight, it was easy to picture him out running.

Let me cut to the chase, Anna, I've asked you to come in to see if you're interested in helping us with a project I'm launching within the hospital. In the last four years, since I took over, I have been studying the feedback we get both from staff, usually when they leave, and from patients on the anonymous forms we leave around the place. I need to know, obviously, what kind of ship I'm sailing, it's my job, but more than that I wanted to find out why we are different to any other place.

Sure, she said, comfortable listening while she took in his energy, his shirt sleeves rolled midway up his arms which were tanned. He struck her as an outdoorsy kind of person, so not just running, but definitely a sportsman.

And what I heard back in those first three years wasn't what I'd hoped for, I'll be honest with you. There was a thread of discontent from the staff and higher than average turnovers across several departments, added to which patients weren't putting us as top choice when it came to treatment. I knew it wasn't a gap in expertise, because we've got some of the best surgeons and specialists in the country, so it had to be something else. Then something odd happened and that's where you come in.

She smiled, relaxing a little into the chair. It's not the first time I've been called odd, she said and laughed.

Well, it's not you obviously, he smiled, it was the *effect* you were having. I knew it was something special the first time one of the senior nurses said to me *make sure you keep that girl on who's doing the radio, she's a genius*. The more I heard, the more I asked and, well, what it comes down to is this: you've had a thoroughly positive effect here, because the radio has *become* something. It's like it's more than a hospital radio, because everyone feels as if you're talking to them about *their* lives and that is a rare skill.

173

We have staff here, some voluntary, some on the payroll in the patient liaison service whose job it is to keep track of what patients need beyond the medical care, but I want to set up a project that goes beyond that. If you like, what I'm saying is, if we could bottle what you've got and dispense it regularly throughout all departments, we'd be well on our way to creating the kind of hospital I want to see. So, I am offering you a job, Anna.

Oh. Wow. Suddenly she was taken unawares. She shifted in her seat, this was amazing. Nothing like this had ever come her way, not ever. Keen to rise to the challenge, she started speaking, but her head was exploding…. Scott, I… well I guess I didn't see that coming, but yes! I mean it sounds fascinating. Tell me some more.

We could look at, to begin with, taking you on in a consultancy role, say a two-year contract initially. I'm offering a Band 4 post, we can talk about the specifics later, if you're interested in principle?

In her mind she was thinking, consultancy role… me? Oh my god I did not see this happening to me.

Scott went on, if you're interested of course… Yes definitely, she said, I would be absolutely honoured to take on something like that. I feel already as if the hospital has become a home for me.

Scott could not have known this was a nod to her recent past. The meeting ended with handshakes, something she had been taught well by her adoptive parents. She agreed to come up with some ideas before their next meeting and he would get HR on to the contract and specifics of salary. In the meantime, he hoped she would be on board fully with the upcoming League of Friends fundraiser event.

We've been very lucky you know, he told her, they've done a fantastic job raising funds and one of their members, Tara, has connections with the CEO of Goldspiers who have agreed to triple match all of the fundraising we do, which is how we came to have the new kit in cardio-respiratory.

That's amazing, she said, I'll put some ideas together this week and get them over to you.

Walking out of the Victorian arched door that framed the hospital entrance, the work of the volunteers came to mind. Like hidden scaffolding they beavered away in all corners of the hospital, from the radio down to the team of visitors who come in to hold the hand of the lonely or the dying. Her admiration was genuine. It impressed her that there were others who shared her passion for the hospital. In fact, she had already met Tara, a kind woman in her fifties with a quietly stated ballsy attitude that Anna warmed to straight away. This might be a chance to find out more stories that make up the beating heart of the place. On her way across the carpark towards the bus stops where groups of people waited to be taken to every part of the town she had begun to embrace as home, she rubbed her arms when the evening wind moved across her skin, a reminder of colder nights.

21

Carol

She didn't know when it began, but the night she and Jez went on a bender before court all those years ago had been a tipping point. Not long after, she began to cut corners. Nothing major at first, a bit of cut and pasting - who was going to question that? But then there was another case in court, then another and another, with no line management worth the paper it was written on. Bob, her manager, had left through the revolving door. The new woman couldn't be arsed. All she ever said was *get your paperwork done, folks, and we should be sound* in a Liverpool accent that made Carol feel like she was more of an auntie than a manager. Then there was another case in court with that same barrister, Harriet Fairwell, and it all started to unravel.

The breakup with Hen, which she now called The End of Everything, had been one trigger, of course. That was all the way back at the start, but she had been running from case to case already by then for years, her caseload up through the roof. The last straw had been The Orange Crate packing up. Without wheels, she'd have had no job. Borrowing off Jez had been her great mistake. Him.

Getting ready for that case had been horrendous. It wasn't the family's fault of course. Now that she was here, sitting in a café round the corner from the hospital, and had a job. I. Have. A. Job. Reciting it over made it more real somehow. The cappuccino was frothy to the point of giving her a moustache, but she didn't care, because here she was - *with a job* (yes, I will say it again) - having a lunch break like people do. And oh, how she'd longed for this kind of normality over the years. She could even do with a pension right now. She counted how many years she had to wait: 14 years, 7 months and 8 days, until she could be free of it all.

Carol thought of all the clients she'd assessed over the years as *needs therapy that is likely to be longer than six months given the complexity of the issues*. It was a stupid circus now, where they get you to say the clients are a mess then tell them how to fix it. But the only problem was they couldn't get any therapy, so they took their children off them. Well, not all of them obviously, but it looked that way from where she was in her life now. And she'd done her fair share of the hard-core cases, no doubt about that. The addicts, the alcoholics, well, they were some of the loving parents, but there was so much worse; the neglect. She'd got used to dealing with the hardship, but the parents who didn't seem to care about their kids, those were the ones she couldn't forget. Then there were the full-on nasty cases, the sexual abusers. From those the burden was a heavy one: imagery, random bits of knowledge, all stuff she would rather un-know if such a thing were possible. The best you can do is put it in a deep cupboard somewhere inside and lock it up.

There had been days when she didn't leave her bed, searching for a way to obliterate herself by sleep. It didn't work. Weeks went by, she lost her job in a kind of voluntary falling on her sword before they kicked her out. She'd already abandoned her post in prolonged stress sick leave, so the final goodbye was more of a whimper than a grand showdown. All she did was ring HR and resign over the phone - it was that easy. Nobody came looking for her, not even Jez. The world began to close over her until she didn't exist: no phone calls, no letters. She signed on, got in with Jez's mates and so began the pattern of life that had already nearly destroyed her once before, predating social work. Her career became something that didn't even count any more. She moved to Holland and lived near The Hague for ten years in a toxic relationship which ended only when she left her boyfriend, who was in hospital in a stupor after yet another binge.

There was no coming back to normal life for a while. There'd been odd jobs, three years on a farm outside of the city where they gave her and others cheap accommodation. Whatever they asked of her she would do, to keep a roof over her head. It was like a metamorphosis: she had become as disenfranchised as those she had tried to help. She didn't think about her parents then. Her father was dead – liver failure, and her mother was in a nursing home. Shame kept her away. What she knew, she couldn't forget: her mother had needed help not pity, or worse, disdain.

The years passed until Carol didn't even think of herself as a social worker any more. She was another grey ghost scraping along on the bottom, until one day a redirected letter arrived that was to change everything. Tara's letter. That bloody letter.

Dear Ms. Leadbeater,

We are an agency who offer services to individuals searching for lost relatives...We understand you were the social worker who dealt with our client Tara Downley's case. We would be grateful if you could write back to us, naturally in confidence to at least provide confirmation that we have reached the correct person.

The one case she felt truly guilty about. She would have lost her job over it, if she hadn't left before the guillotine fell. Of all the placements over those years that should have come searching, it had to be this one. Dylan Downley. Tara must be, what, in her forties, no fifties? The memory of Tara, plucky to the end, determined to get her therapy, all of it flooded back to her. The guilt opened an old wound. She could see herself as a young woman, her drive to be a social worker, her sense of pride. The passion that got her up in the morning to change the world.

That instinct in her as a child, to get away, to keep herself together whenever she would see her father lying in his own filth, too drunk to get up or care. Dad's not very well, Carol, let him sleep, from her mother. She who could never say no would stand over him, wooden in her thin dress like a faded print of the person she had once been. It was barely living, an image of her mother which repeated itself on weekends, birthdays, Christmas day before the food was served.

In her teens, she had been so angry she went off kilter, weed, drink, the lot. That was where Jez came into the picture. He'd been a kid with the same species of fucked up family as hers, only his was less safe. They hung out together until she was twenty. Then there'd been a light bulb moment, standing in the noisy darkness of a party at some stranger's house, Jez already off his face, telling some other bloke all the reasons he couldn't work and why it was the government's fault. It was, he said, a conspiracy to keep us down. The words described her; *she* had been kept down. Like her mother. Like her mother's mother. A lightning thought happened inside her head; it was not the government, nor was it this angry drunken man, nor anybody else who was keeping her down; it was Carol herself. If she didn't do anything to change things, she'd end up like her mother.

Her epiphany began. In a string of jobs, Carol worked even harder than the next person because she had to make sure of one thing; to never be anything like her mother. It had come too close, the slide towards a frozen silent woman, who watches a man drink himself into the gutter.

In those early years, she had nothing to her name except the mission. It turned out to be all she needed. Moving into a bedsit, with a shop job part time, she signed up for university. It was that decision which would make her feel whole. Soon home for her became the pub where she worked nights to fund her studies. She hung out not with the drinkers, but with big Dennis whose pub it was, and crazy Michelle who had worked behind the bar since forever. Once she graduated with a social work qualification to her name it wasn't difficult to find a job. They were crying out for social workers in those years. Her first social work team, the faded office headquarters where she'd eat sandwiches of an evening, soon became home for her. She would work late to be with this new extended family.

Wherever she went in the job she'd meet people like her, too flawed to follow any conventional route into work. In those heady early days, it was all about being out there, transforming lives and somehow mending themselves into the bargain. She had been more than a convert, a true believer. They had principles, standards of care, and there was a bigger picture; making a difference in society. She wanted to be a part of that. All that was well before the government smashed the shit out of it with cuts, of course. She took another sip of coffee, watching the lunch timers drift past the window. It all seemed such a long time ago – her belief, her passion in a job which she loved.

The day she finally replied to that letter had been the culmination of four days of binge crying; she had done nothing but eat, sleep and endure raw, blood curdling soul searching. She had to face herself. She had fallen apart, like before she went to university. Jez, his mates, all of it kept her diving back down into a place of no value.

The letter was a painful reminder of what she had once been, all too briefly before her life imploded. I won't fucking do it, she shouted at nobody but the walls and herself. But she *had* written back, not with what they wanted of course, but to tell them no, she couldn't help, was no longer a social worker, couldn't remember the case. But this all led to a guilt pile on, there was no doubting that. Tara Downley's case had been the trigger, the final straw of her breakdown. It was also what had brought her through the door of a therapist, which in time became the singular reason she got out of bed in the mornings. To find a person who listened was all she needed. Not to self-pity, no not that at all, but to listen to her say Yes, I did love my job, I *did* believe in it. And she talked about her father, how frightened she had been night after night.

Did she regret that dishonesty? The visit which had never

happened? Lying that Tara was out? The faked file notes? Not that it made much difference, because the court made the order anyway. But in Carol's mind, it was the lingering doubt that had eaten away at her - did she get it wrong? If she *had* visited Tara, would it have made a difference? If Dylan could have stayed with his mum, then what did that make her, she asked herself. Someone who was never going to respond to a fucking agency decades later asking all those questions, that's what. It wasn't the answer she wanted to give. But that was before now, before this blessed second chance where she had a job as a social worker again.

Carol set down her empty cup checked the time, grabbed her bag and headed back up to the hospital. She enjoyed the hospital workplace, its busy streets and passageways where people's hope and despair lived side by side. It was as if the lost meaning of her job had been gifted back to her in this city of the unwell; help and healing were the everyday bywords of what everyone did here: it was a place with a heart. And she belonged here, yes she did. To get to the hospital's social work department she would regularly pass one of the two hospital cafes and call out a breezy hello to staff. The notice board for the League was another regular stop off and today was no different. With five minutes to spare she could find out what the next fund raiser was. Carol loved the fund raisers, they were her social life and a way of meeting new friends. She was on the up with places to go, people to see. The cliché made her smile inwardly, as if the idea of being a new woman was too much of a joke.

A couple of women were standing beside the League notice-board, papers in hand. Something new was happening. As they parked the papers and pins on a waiting chair, pulling it towards the board, one of the women struck her as familiar. For a moment she struggled to place her, then stopped dead in her tracks. as if she'd had a punch to the guts. The woman chatting away, unrolling a poster and getting pins out, was Tara Downley.

She turned away, shame roiling up in her like a storm, heading blindly back down the corridor as fast as she could. Sick to the stomach, her mind racing, fear rising like vertigo. She could not remain in the building with Tara Downley. By the time she reached the office, her breathing was so shallow she dropped to her chair unable to focus on any task in front of her.

It took two days for her to reach a decision, but once she had she was light headed with relief. This time, Carol, you will not go downhill, she said out loud. She wouldn't quit in shame, but forfeit her job so someone else could thrive. She wept at first, not little tears but great sobs that convulsed her body. No one would ever understand how much she had treasured that job. She rang her therapist, booked a session.

The letter came easily. *... I feel that it is my responsibility to ensure I create and leave improved circumstances for those I work with. With this in mind, I could not sensibly remain in post with a conflict of interest....* There was meaning too in taking the letter in person to the hospital, depositing it on her boss's desk, then out through the double doors for the last time, not looking back.

She may have sacrificed her job, but only so that Tara could live her life and be whatever kind of success she deserved, free of sadness, memories and echoes of past mistakes. Whatever it was, Carol believed in her heart that Tara needed nothing more than not to have a daily reminder in her workplace of the heartache she had once been through.

She wasted no time in sending another letter to the tracing agency. This time, she expressed sorrow that her earlier letter had been unhelpful. Sadly, she said, there was little she could do, but she remembered the case and it was her clear impression that Tara may well manage to get her life on a better footing. She finished it with the words *and it is my sincere hope that Tara and Dylan Downley can be reunited and enjoy a relationship again.* With that she closed down her email and began to job search, typing the words *vacancies social worker, adoption support.*

22

Jo

The water flowed past her small porthole window like silk, taking travelling twigs, leaves and memories downstream and out to sea. Jo was lying in bed waiting for her regular nurse visit. As the days went by, she had weakened to the point where she now spent most of her time in bed, although she could never feel reconciled to what was happening to her. She was dying. When you read that someone has made peace with the world, in what world does that happen? I am not fighting it, I love the world and don't want to leave. This bullshit about 'she lost her battle with cancer' is not me, I am not in a battle with anyone. It is what is happening, whether or not I like it.

The discharge nurse had stalled when she told them her home was a boat. She hadn't thought sailing was going to be right for Jo at this stage of life. Jo had laughed a little at that. It's not sailing, she said, unless you mean sailing away. It's my home and it's permanently moored with all mod cons. The nurse's face was a picture of worry. I'll be okay, honestly, and it's in a very residential mooring where there is parking for nurse visitors even. The nurse smiled at her. Jo wanted to tell her how fortunate she felt, to have been looked after, like having lots of aunties. We can do it, the nurse said, we can set up some support for you at home and from what you've said that should be okay.

A package of visiting support and the promised visit from social care had delivered a carer visit daily and Jo was allowed to go home. Her friend Roy from a neighbouring boat came to collect her. Hello, Jo love, I brought you something for the journey. He took out of his bag a set of new warm socks for her to wear.

Roy, you're a darling, she said gratefully as she swung her legs off the bed. It touched her deeply to realise she had made such good, down-to-earth friends without fanfare. He took her feet and put the socks on before they left, his arm supporting her.

Today, back on board, her thoughts were focused solely on the post. The decision that she must find out if Anna was alive and well had been easy to make. With the help of a friend, she had paid the agent's fee and was waiting for the return letter telling her Anna had been located.

She heard Roy before she saw him. Letters for you Jo, can I come in? And there he was standing in front of her, in his tatty guernsey sweater before she even had time to move. Bless you, my love, what can I be doing for you now I'm here?

I'm being spoilt, Roy, she said, looking straight into his eyes which were so full in ways she could not describe. Her neighbours were better known to her now than when she first came, and she supposed they had chiefly known her as someone they had banded together to help. She felt so stupid, watching Roy set the letters down beside her, not to have listened to her own advice and let herself be better friended than she had been.

Since her discharge from hospital, the carers came every day, more often than not carrying hotpots or stews that had been left outside her door by one of the boat dwelling community. Roy and others had even magicked away the washing up. Each and every time it happened, she sent out messages to thank whichever wonderful soul it was that had given her food and help. The messages that came back made her feel as if she was being stitched gently into the fabric of the community.

Roy, you're a dear, but I think I'm okay today, the carers will be here in a little while and I've got dinner sorted. But it would be lovely if you sit with me a while? If you're not busy...

Course I can, now you have a look at your letters while I get a brew on.

Sitting at the top of the pile she instantly sees the one she has been waiting for.

Handling the envelope, its light, paperweight thinness, quickens her pulse.

Dear Jo,

We are delighted to be able to tell you we have located your daughter Anna. She is still known by this name, but her surname is Ainscott and we can give you her address. Whilst you will be aware that there is no corresponding registration of her name on the Adoption Register, where we understand you placed your details some years ago, we have had initial contact and received approval from her to share with you her details. Please let us know if you would like to make contact. If you wish, you may send us a letter and include a (sealed) letter for us to pass on immediately to your daughter. We will by return give you her address for future correspondence.

In the meantime, please let us know if there are any other intermediary services we can help with. If you do not wish to proceed with the contact, you will hear no further from us. Otherwise, we wish you and your daughter well and hope that you are able to both enjoy future communications should you choose to continue to direct contact.

We would be grateful if you would let us know whether you wish to proceed.

Yours....

Anna Ainscott, Anna. Anna Ainscott.

Jo, love, Roy's voice was filled with concern as he came to stand beside her bed, carrying two mugs of tea, what's happening? Have you had bad news? He set down the cups and sat down beside her on the couch.

She didn't try to stop the large tears which were rolling slowly down her face. Staring at the piece of paper in her hand, she whispered: Anna Ainscott.

Who is that, my love? Have you had some bad news?

She is alive, she is alive, thank god, thank god, was all she could say, the sobbing convulsing her. Roy reached an arm out and took her hand in his. When she looked at him, her eyes were brimming over as she struggled to speak, her voice heaving.

No, it's alright Roy, her voice was sounding unsteady, it's such a relief Roy, it's just such a relief and…. she could not hold back the wave of emotions engulfing her. Gasping now, the words tumbled out

…oh and pain Roy, and joy and, even hope. Today has given me back some hope. This is the day I have waited for all of my life.

Oh sweetheart, that sounds to me like something pretty damned important. Roy put both arms around her and she sobbed into his neck.

He stayed a few hours until he said he was certain she could manage. Jo spent the rest of the evening writing a letter to Anna.

It began,

My dear,

Forgive me if I call you that, but to me you have always been that. To say that not a day has gone by without my thinking of you would be only a small part of my feelings over the many years since I last saw you. I realise that for you, this is more like our first communication, and for that perhaps I have a great deal of apprehension.

May I say that I am so grateful you have said I can contact you. It has been my heart's desire since that day I had to say farewell. I may be wrong to say this to you, but if you are wanting to satisfy your curiosity and that's where it ends, I will completely understand. I have no rights as it is today. I completely recognise that you probably regard your adoptive parents as your parents, because they have loved and brought you up and I have given up all right to expect anything. I hope though that I can fulfil for you whatever curiosity or contact you would like to have.

I am sure you have always had questions relating to your birth, so I can start with telling you that you were conceived in love. Your father and I had a very short relationship, which came to an end not for want of love, but because I fell pregnant and what was unleashed by that fact brought upon us both pressures too great for us to withstand at such a young age. I have not seen him since we ended the relationship at the request of my mother, but I have heard occasionally of him and how his life has gone and believe he has had a quiet, but successful life....

The elephant in the room for Jo was her illness. How could she, at such a late stage, not tell her? There was no ideal way to tackle it other than be as honest as she believed Anna deserved. Nothing less. And how do you say you are ill? Should you say that you are dying?

That afternoon passed like no other, each word weighed carefully in her mind until she had the finished result. On the last page, she added her signature and the words *I love you and will always love you.... Jo, your mother.* With those last few words, her mind gently closed the book of hopes and fears about Anna, the story unfinished, but paused. The envelope addressed and stamped it now waited on the sill for Roy who had promised to come back to take it to the post box.

23

The Hospital Fete

Around the edges of the field, a river of people flowed, eddying
in and out of the gazebos, past the tables laden with cake and
scattered chairs. In the sun's light the day had warmed up,
but with a breeze that was enough to bring out the crowds
for an afternoon stroll. Music interspersed with the gentle
voice of Anna, now a familiar accompaniment to hospital life
for most of the staff, drifted across the top of the marquee
and through the fluttering bunting. The playlist that Tara and
Gill had put together lent an atmosphere of vintage music
festival and the atmosphere sparkled like the best of a long
lazy summer event.

Scott Marsden, on an open-air podium surrounded by a
small crowd, leaned closer to the microphone, working against
the wind which was snatching his words away. He tapped the
steel hood of the mike and the sound carried over the heads
of the gathering people, out into the fields beyond.

Hello and good afternoon everyone. Welcome to our first hospital fete. First of all, I'd like to thank you all for coming, and also to welcome to this wonderful fundraising event Mr. Dylan Downley of Goldspiers. Can we have a big hand to thank the company for their generous ongoing support of our great hospital.

The clapping, sounding like rain on a tin roof, muted the distant drone of the traffic. An enthusiastic burst of sound could be heard from the far edge of the crowd where Tara and Gill were clapping and whooping for all they were worth.

… And if I can now make a couple of important announcements before we hand over to Mr. Downley who shall tell us about an exciting new project.

It's bloody brilliant Tara, said Gill. I can't believe we're here. And all that music, we lived out our whole lives the night we chose it, you and I.

Tara, beaming ear to ear, grabbed the hand of her friend but kept her eyes fixed firmly on the small podium at the front of the crowd. Dylan was standing to the side waiting for his chance to speak.

Look at my boy. He looks so smart there, Gill, doesn't he? I never thought I'd see this day.

It wasn't long before Dylan was invited to come forward. Picking up the microphone with practised familiarity, he stood in front of the podium, near the crowd. There was no doubting his relaxed posture and easy hand movements, all of which gave him the look of an accomplished, yet chilled, communicator. He was speaking to the crowd about a new project, funded by Goldspiers and the hospital.

We will help patients who come to hospital without the support of close family or friends by locating and making contact with someone important to them, he said. My ambition is simple. No longer should those who come to the end of their lives, or their good health, have to go it alone, without a friend or family member by their side to comfort them… and where there is success, it may in turn aid their recovery and link with the Community Loneliness Project which is already up and running.

Tara already knew this was Dylan's pet project. Her pride grew with every new piece of news. But this day, when it was going out into the public, was the highlight.

And we have all known, Dylan was saying, those of us who have visited hospitals even a little, that there are some folks who when they come to the end of their life are sadly alone without close family around them. Well, this is a charitable project close to our hearts at Goldspiers, and with the spearheading of Scott and his incredible team, we want to make this happen. No person should find themselves alone at a time of greatest need.

Scott took over the mic to more clapping. And I'm going ask all those who would like to support the project to dig deep this afternoon to get this one off the ground.

Oh Gill, cried Tara, it's Raglan Road! I can hear it playing. She led her friend out of the crowds by the hand and over towards the source of the music. What a day. They smiled at each other. And what a project, thought Tara.

In a smaller tent behind the main marquee, Anna sat at the controls surrounded by her decks, microphone and laptop, all linked to large speakers mounted tall, sending out the music across the tented marquees and the crowds, Anna's voice now a familiar backdrop for the entire hospital family. The playlist she'd prepared was enough to cover the whole afternoon, including the music she'd received from Tara at the League of Friends. They'd first met in the League's office to discuss the playlist over coffee, the two women taking to each other immediately, though Anna had been surprised by Tara's knowledge of Goldspiers generally.

Now, distant clapping as the announcements and speeches were made reached Anna in her music HQ. Dylan Downley would be speaking today and Anna also expected to see Tara at some point during the day, having invited her to pop in and say hello.

After Raglan Road had finished a head appeared around the cloth entrance. It was Tara with a friend. Hi Anna, is it alright if we come in to say hello? This is my good friend Gill who helped me with the playlist. In fact, the last one, Raglan Road, that was her choice. The two women stepped into the tent. Anna beckoned them to sit as she spoke into the microphone. And didn't we all love that version of Raglan Road, folks? What a song! And now for something a little closer to home, continuing with our vintage vibe, it's those boys from Liverpool.

Ob-La-Di, Ob-La-Da...

Hi girls, she gets up to give them both a hug. I loved loved loved your playlist, what a success. And the last, that was one powerful song, Gill, said Anna. Come, sit down here with me and let's get some more happy sounds on the go.

Tara and Gill spent an hour in the tent with Anna, listening along and applauding her music choices as if they were, all three of them, at their own party. After a time, the canvas parted and Dylan's head appeared around the entrance. Hi,

Mum, he nodded, Gill and you must be Anna?

Gosh, Anna said, how wonderful. I didn't know Tara was your mum. Well, I've heard a lot about you from your mum. She had warmed to him on the instant – his smile so genuine, his handshake warm, lasting.

As have I about you, he laughed, from Scott. He speaks highly of you. So this is where it all happens then, Mum? Gill? You ladies look like you're ready to party!

We are, we are, said Gill, laughing merrily.

Oh we've all been having a great time, said Anna, and your mum's playlist has been awesome. Aw, thanks Anna, Tara was chuffed, she smiled watching Anna and Dylan standing comfortably side by side.

Listen, I can't stop to chat more, Anna waved a hand across her decks, but thanks for what you are doing to raise the profile of the hospital. Goldspiers' input has been amazing. I've heard so many inspiring stories since I've worked here, and it's truly a cause worth supporting.

Well, you too, said Dylan, and I'd be happy to meet and talk more about it if you're up for it? I'll try and catch you later, at the end of the afternoon? Maybe a drink at the local is in order, you'll be thirsty by then, he laughed. Here let me give you my number.

Late into the afternoon, without warning a loud boom cut through the gentle sound of music, swiftly followed by noisy, agitated voices. Anna with her headphones on heard nothing but saw Tara and Gill's faces suddenly frozen with fear. She pulled an earphone aside and heard distant shouting.

Trapped by headphones and wires, Anna called out. Some-

195

thing's happened, I can't leave, can you go find out? Gill, already on her feet, was first to head outside where the air was stiff with fear. She joined the flow of people running, but everywhere was a similar chaos. People were moving in jagged bursts away from the far corner of the field. Where the marquees ended, an active crowd of people were shouting and a plume of black smoke pushed up from the centre.

Gill, with Tara behind her, ran towards the scene. People could be shouting for an ambulance. Many people were trying to get away from the scene, stumbling through the wet grass with children in their arms. Gill and Tara slowed their pace, trying to see over the heads of the crowd to make out what was happening. The smoke was rising from somewhere beyond the farthest marquee.

Gill moved out of the way of a couple making their way towards the far gated exit. What's happened? she called across to them as they drew nearer.

It's an escaped horse, a woman said, it charged at the burger van and something exploded, the man shouted back as he passed. I'd stay away, it's terrible down there and the ambulances need to get through! As he began to speak, the sound of distant sirens broke over the top. Everything seemed to be happening in slow motion. Anna's voice could still be heard in the background, announcing the next record. We need to tell her, Tara shouted at Gill, running back towards the music tent.

Anna, something terrible has happened, Tara shrieked waving her hands up and down, you need to stop the music, the panic obvious. Anna pulled her headphones off, oh my god, what's happened? Has anyone been hurt?

I don't know but I can see a burger van on fire, I think it must have exploded. There are ambulances coming. We couldn't get close enough, it didn't seem safe. Tara was shaking, it's awful Anna, there may need to be an announcement or something. I'm going to go back out there. I'll try and get some information. In the meantime, can you tell everyone maybe to please let the ambulances through?

A wind was blowing through the trees at the edges of the field, fanning the smoke. The air was unsteady. A scattering of people surged towards the gate and the safety of the next field. Two ambulances were bumping across the uneven grass, dousing their sirens as they neared the scene. Somewhere, a horse was whinnying, people were screaming and running everywhere.

In the adjacent field, Tara spotted a horse galloping full tilt down the slope. Those who'd sought shelter there were now scattering in all directions. Close the gate, someone was shouting above the screams. Close the gate! People were streaming right back out of the gate again, a man struggling with the stay holding it open. Before he could free it, the large glossy black mare thundered through the narrow gap heading towards the main marquees. The man shouting to close the gate leapt into the horse's path. It stalled, rearing up at him. He windmilled his arms then ducked as hooves pawed the air above him.

Tara! A hand grabbed her arm. She swung round to find Gill, breathless and agitated. You've got to come, Tara, it's Dylan, he's hurt. Follow me, she shouted and began running. Tara's heart pounded against her chest wall as she ran, instinct hurling her towards the plume of smoke. As they drew near the ambulance men were calling out above the din. Clear the space, please. Can you stand back please, we're bringing a stretcher in. Stand back please.

Tara held her breath. As she peered through the crowd all she could see was a foot on the ground, in a black leather shoe, lying at an odd angle, the rest obscured by onlookers. It was Dylan's foot, of this she had no doubt. She pushed her way to the front of the crowd. Dylan was stretched awkwardly on the grass. She could not tell if he was conscious or not.

Dylan, I'm coming, she shouted. Two policemen with facemasks were taping a cordon around him. Excuse me? Hey, can I get through? One of the policemen tried moving the crowd away from the burning vehicle, smoke belching from a large crater in the side of its bodywork. The other police officer turned to her and said, I'm sorry madam but we've got to get stretchers in here. Can you move back.

But he's my son, I've got to go to him, she was pushing past him now. The policeman held her shoulder; gently at first, then with some force he reached round and grabbed both of her forearms. Wait, he's my son...

Suddenly Gill was on the scene: What are you doing? Officer, this is his mother, can she please be allowed through? Without warning he pulled back, hands in the air to let her pass.

Dylan was muttering incoherently, but on seeing Tara he managed a smile. voice rasping. I've done myself a bit of a mischief, mum, sorry 'bout that. Oh Dylan, don't worry, don't worry, she said stroking his cheek. Someone is coming to help you. Gill, are they coming, she called out, the ambulance men? Where are they?

Two paramedics appeared on cue, setting down a stretcher beside Dylan. We'll take it from here, ma'am.

24

The Horse

Three miles along the canal road out of town due west, the land begins to widen. A canal cuts between green and yellow fields, pigeon-grey water shining with points of reflected light. As the road opens, it passes cattle farms, dotted with barns, silos and scrubby trees scrambling their way towards the distant horizon. It picks up the remains of old market sites – huge flat fields with broader gates where a gather of farmers and horse traders could barter.

For the large black horse and her foal, home is a grass gorged field bordering one of the wide-open cattle treads.

Things have been appearing here in an uproar of shiny metal for days, bringing the noise and clamour of the unfamiliar. On the inbreath, for the horse, all smell has altered. The known scents have scrambled with a miasma of unknown mammal. It would see this as a danger, a scattered threat of rope or maybe fencing. It would watch the unloading of trucks and in the odour of white canvas, catch the rancid breath of mould and enclosure. It would stall if approached, pace the wooden rail back and forth in front of its foal.

In the horse's guarded eyeline, the whiteness on the lower slope billows out, catching the wind, then rears up high to stand tall and square with a wide and empty mouth. The gape fills and empties as people, dogs, rumbling tree legs and flat trees go in, come out. The horse's foal stays away, behind the mother, who is breathing down hard through her nose.

Over the coming days it will see more arrive, its unrest increased by the threat of uncommon sounds, the sudden beep beep beep of something pulling backwards. The horse runs shy at yet another human at the railings, knowing only the smell of hay in its daily encounters till now. It will not be able to tolerate the pungent fumes of fire and meat drifting on the evening breeze. The hot sweat of other mammals will drive the horse to gallop up the slope of the field to the far edge. It will stand hard by the trees, stamp its feet safe in the underhang of old oaks.

By the next morning the mare will be pacing and snorting. It will startle as people approach. There will be the scream of children. It will jerk away from the fence at the sight of them. It will be on high alert, too fretted to stay calm in the face of imminent danger to her foal.

When the sun is high in the sky on the third day, there is a gathering at the gate. The horse will see a gap appear in the boundary, an exit unblocked in the home field. There will come a moment when the people, the clatter, begin streaming through the gap, driving towards the horse and her foal. The horse can smell danger on the air. The scramble of sweat and bodies, the whistle of non-living sounds, something choking the air. She is not used to this smell of searing flesh, fire. It is acrid, burning in her nostrils. Her nerves are charged. She paces the field in front of the foal, snorting. The foal too is nervous.

There comes a moment when grey cloud eclipses the sun for one transient moment, the noise climbing to an unbearable pitch. A loud boom shatters the air. The horse bolts, thundering towards the people surging upwards across the grass, blinded by fear, rearing and stampeding into the field with the great white shape until her path is blocked by a man waving his arms. She rears up, pawing the air. Veering to the right she gallops towards the clearing where gawdy patches of colour cover the field. Flashing blue lights move between the blocks of colour and the air splits with a sound coming towards her. She swerves, taking the hedge in one high, silent leap.

The screech of brakes would be heard that day above the sound of the vehicles, above the twin siren of the ambulances, above the screams of the people running, above even the emergency Tannoy bellowing over the tops of the tents. Only the hiss of steam marked the epicentre. Water vapour rose like a misplaced cloud above the green hedge, the stalled headlights breaking through in uplit shafts. There was an injured stillness here, like the eye of a storm unfolding across the entire green space that day.

Please allow the ambulances through. Please move to a place of safety, Anna called out over the sound system, even though unable to picture what was going on. She even doubted anyone could hear her above the screeching and the sirens. She muted the system with the touch of a button, logged out and grabbed her lanyard. Bursting through the tent flaps, the smell and sounds were overwhelming. The ground was torn up and people were running in all directions. Fragments of time like miniature incidents, surrounded her on every side and for the second it took Anna to gain her wits, she was the only still point in a scene of mounting panic. The horse had bolted past only seconds before she left the tent. She was just in time to see the leap, a perfect arc of escape, as the horse took the hedge.

The favourite part of her reccy in the days before the event, had been the horses. Entering the then deserted field, she had walked through the space enjoying the natural orchestra of birds and insects lighting up the summer's day. She had spotted the horse and foal, already alert to her presence. The foal was not newborn but was small enough to be nuzzling still. The guardian mother locked its senses onto her as she approached, cautioning her movements to be slow and steady. Soothing her as she neared, Anna spoke continuously in a low voice.

She had worked with horses over one summer after she left school, volunteering with an organic farming scheme in Portugal. WWOOFing, they called it. Three blissful months on the coast, grooming horses and mucking out. She'd learnt a lot from Andreas the owner – that horses feel you first, know when you're edgy or angry, that grooming the horse is as much for the human as it is for the horse, and that if you want to do yoga *and* ride, you'd better be an early riser. It was the one summer in her twenties when she had felt grounded. The horses gave her that. They were rooted if they could eat and stand and feel the warmth of other beings. She liked that, it was about as much purpose in life as she could handle then.

The spin off was a smattering of German (Andreas) and a natural affinity with horses (becoming chief stable hand) both of which had served her well in a host of unexpected situations. How to tell a gropey drunken tourist in Brandenburg airport to fuck off in German (necessary), as well as how to calm down someone exhibiting nervous anxiety (herself).

The mare allowed her to move up close. After a few minutes of soothing talk, she was able to stroke her until the foal approached with curiosity, nibbling the fingers of her other hand. By the time she left, she had become as protective of their territory as the mother herself. She fired off a quick yet detailed email to the staff who were organising the Hospital Fete, recommending they get in touch with the horse owner and the farmer whose field it was to ensure proper preparations were in place to safeguard the animals over the coming two weeks.

The moment the horse took the hedge, Anna ran for all she was worth towards the home field to find the foal. People were streaming through the open gate in both directions, so she could not see where the young horse was. Sprinting up the slope, she shouted as she ran. Have you seen a young foal? Anyone? Has anyone seen a young foal? A man sitting on the grass pointed towards the trees. She spotted it immediately, ears back, feet agitated, sheltering under a low hanging branch bordering the woods. The trees were huge, deciduous oaks and ash, behind them tightly packed larch.

As she moved slowly forwards, she took her fleece off, the horse now blocked by the fencing behind. She was alongside it now, her right hand making smoothing movements until the foal had calmed and she was she able to put her fleece around it. Her best option to keep it safe was to tether it to the fence, but if it kicked up a fuss, it might hurt itself. Anna needed help.

Dylan was in no position to answer the phone ringing in his pocket. Tara gently removed it. Hi Anna, I'm with Dylan now, but he's hurt I'm afraid and he's going into the ambulance to hospital. I'll call you back when I can, she hung up.

Anna was horrified, but with one brief call she had the RSPCA on their way. She didn't know why it was Dylan, a man she scarcely knew, who she had called first. Perhaps because he was Mr. Get Things Done, the fundraiser, the man at the top for this event. She had completely bypassed Scott. That Dylan was hurt left her unexpectedly flustered, as surprising to her as the next call that came through on her phone.

25

News

Hello, is that Anna Ainscott? I'm ringing from the tracing agency with some news for you. Is now a good time?

Erm, no, I mean yes, of course. Could you give me a minute? They were going to say she was dead, that it was all too late. She could hardly bear to listen, her chest thumping as if she might cry. Terrified of losing the foal or dropping the phone, she wedged it on to her shoulder frantically saying: I'll ring you back if the call drops, please give me a minute. She tied the two sleeves together around the neck of the foal, then hooked the loop over the nearby fencepost. Yes of course, said the woman on the end of the line, take as long as you need.

The foal seemed to accept its new tether, slowly lowering its head to nibble the grass. Anna did not entirely let go of her shirt, but swapped the phone into her free hand.

Hello, yes, sorry, I mean there's a lot going on here at the moment, but please tell me the news.

Well, we've had a response to our enquiry with your birth mother. We're pleased to say we have a letter for you. Would you like us to forward it for next day delivery?

By the time the call ended, in less than a minute, she was in a daze. Standing in a field holding a foal, unable to move without help, she was filled with hope. All the pain and loss of it, she thought, it was all so *present*, harbouring beneath the surface. Yet she felt happy? For the first time, she knew. She was not bad, or mad, or hateful, or uncaring after all. If she had been, her mother wouldn't want to see her.

Anna felt alive, more than at any other time in her life. The trees shimmered in the sunlight, soughing as the wind passed through them. The horse gently nudged her, its animal warmth alongside so close she could feel its breath on her arm. She gazed out across the scene that a few moments ago had been all consuming. Now, although it was still immediate, there was a distance. Into the long afternoon of that day, it was as if she could cast herself differently.

A second phone call to Scott had two men from the RSPCA heading swiftly up the hill with the right equipment to protect and keep safe the young foal. Hi, are you Anna? I'm Andy, his accent was Scottish. Yes, thanks so much for coming. Ye're doin' a good job there Anna. We can tek it from here.

What about the mother?

Yes, we're sorry, our colleagues are dealing with her.

Has she been caught? Is she okay?

No, she's bin hit badly, she's on the road. I'm afraid we dinnae hold out much hope, sadly.

The news hit her. And suddenly she didn't want to surrender the foal into someone else's keeping. It made no sense, but these kindly officers seemed to present a new and darker meaning. She held the foal's neck close to her body, fearful of the future.

Are you alright there, Anna? Andy was looking at her with a strange look on his face.

Yes, yes, I'm sorry, it's so upsetting to hear that. I don't know what will happen to her.

We'll be in touch with the owner, dinnae worry. Would you like us to let you know when she's safe?

Anna nodded, releasing the shirt from her grip, putting her other hand gently to the nose of the foal. You'll be alright, sweetheart. You'll be alright, she whispers close to its ear, as Andy carefully replaced the shirt with a foal's halter

Walking off down the field, she is her mother walking away. She is the horse's friend. She is the horse bolting. She is everybody on the field that day, the boom and the cry, the scream, the relief of those who found safety. She is the horse on the road, the foal in the field. She is Anna, making her life whole again.

26

At The Hospital

Normally, passing through the double front doors of the hospital was all in a day's work for Anna. But today she was the visitor hoping to see the patient. There was no doubt about it for her - that one message her mother had written had given her momentum: as if there was nothing she couldn't do now if she put her mind to it.

Anna spotted Tara on her way to the exit and quickly made her way over.

Tara. Is Dylan okay? I had to come and check. For a few seconds Tara seemed not to recognise Anna. Her face was grey with fatigue. Oh, Anna? I... um, yes. I didn't expect to see you here. Are you.... I mean... why did you come? she sounded bewildered. There was worry there too, etched into her face. Anna sensed something else too, something deeper that she could not quite place.

I hope you don't mind. I was so shocked to hear about Dylan.

It was only moments earlier we'd all be talking in my tent. I'm sorry, she paused beginning to sense she might be intruding, Tara, I just want to know if he's okay. Anna took a step back, sensing Tara was in need of some space.

Tara took a deep breath. Yes, thanks Anna. He's asleep now but should be discharged later today. He was close to the blast and fell. He's dislocated a shoulder, she paused, her voice shaky. I think he will be okay, apart from smoke inhalation. I'm praying that will mend. But I, well you know, I'm his mother. I feel so guilty this happened to him. This whole hospital thing, it was my idea you see. If I hadn't told him about the League of Friends and our fundraising, he might never have got Goldspiers involved and wouldn't even have been here. Look, I have to go Anna. She walked towards the double doors and was gone.

27

The Letter

It was dusk outside. The number of visitors coming and going through the double doors was dwindling when Anna went to reception to ask after the patients brought in from the incident. Not a relative? We can't, they tell her, give out information. Not even to check if they need anything? I mean I only want to help if I can. No, I'm sorry. Anna couldn't hide her disappointment. Walking away, she wondered if something was wrong with *her* this time. What was going on? Why was she so invested in all this?

On the bus home, her mind returned to the letter. And to Dylan. What was she thinking about him for? This was ridiculous, a man she only met for two minutes. She didn't believe in fairy tales. Surjan's mother used to say *in the west we marry the one we love and in the east they love the one they marry*. It sounded like a good piece of advice, although she couldn't get her head round what it might be telling her to do.

What the hell was this about, this obsession with a two-minute encounter?

Home for Anna, since her life had turned a corner, was a studio on the outskirts of town. She was safe there, and when Surjan and his mother helped her move, his mother had called it *little nest,* which added another layer of security in her mind. She loved her little nest.

Turning the key in the lock, she wondered about bringing her mother here. It wasn't very grand, she thought, looking around the small but homely room, taking in the welcoming plants, the sunlight from the setting sun that cut a shaft across the rug. If they were going to be anything to each other, it had to be real. Dropping her bag by the front door, she spotted the letters lying together on the mat; one bill, one junk mail, and one anonymous envelope. Snatching them up and taking herself over to the small grey sofa by the window, she mused all the while as she settled herself down between a wedge of soft old velvet cushions. They could have tea, or maybe she should make dinner or lunch? What did she like to eat? Would they have similar taste? She turned the brown envelope over in her hands. There would be so much to find out. What she liked, what she didn't, what music she listened to. Anna would show off her books, tell her all about the radio. It would be amazing if she could be a guest on the show even.

An insignificant, typed brown A5 envelope. Anna wasted no time in tearing it open.

My dear, forgive me if I call you that, but to me you have always been that. To say that not a day has gone by without my thinking of you....

For the very first time, she felt she was inhaling the essence of what it is to be mothered, to be loved; to know once and for all who she was, where she came from. The light of the setting sun dipped beneath the trees outside her window, charging the air with the quiet of twilight as dusk gathered while she read on.

…. in any event after so many years I can say I wish him well still.

As for me, the story is a mixed one I suppose. I found some success in my life as a therapist; a career I trained for late in life and for many years I made much of my life around my work. I never found another partner or, perhaps it is better to say, partner for life. That has been one of the great sorrows of my life and I believe that the loss of my beloved child, you, took away something that was never able to fully heal. This, I think, was the reason I couldn't quite build the necessary trust to forge a lifelong relationship.

I gave up work some years ago and moved to a houseboat. Unusual though it may be….

Following each word along the page, she could hear the voice that wrote them speaking inside her head. The journey of her mother's life thrilled her with its sameness to hers, a knowing of likeness. Yes, that's me and this too, a boat, how I have fantasized about living on a barge. She could visit, maybe even travel together, down the waterways of England. She sat back in her chair, her head reeling with the beginnings of a new life stirring inside her, one that would include her mother.

… and partly as a consequence of this there is something else I must now tell you…

Anna was agog. Surely not, she laughed, she's only going to

say she's nearby or will sail here or something. I can't believe it, we are the same. This is my dream. Her eyes followed the words along the page.

... I have been suffering from cancer for some time now and have been in hospital with it. I am, sadly, very ill and do not have a good prognosis....

There was a pain in her heart now. Her breath wouldn't come. No, no, no, no, this couldn't be. Tears began to form, blurring the page. In her mind she was screaming, but she would look after her mother, go to her, her heart's longing, her mother.

...I am rejoicing that before my time which comes soon, I have been able to send these words to you. If I had been in good health, we could have met, but it is with great sadness I do not think that should happen now. I hope you will forgive me, but I could not bear to say goodbye a second time.

It came at her like a blow to the body, stopping her mind, the blood in her veins; her breath stifled in her throat, and for a time nothing moved. Anna dropped the letter to the floor, walked to her bed, pulled back the covers and climbed in fully clothed. All the light had fully gone outside the window; darkness had fallen, heavy as night.

28

Carol

Four weeks earlier

Carol had been in her new job as a post adoption support social worker for over two years now, in which time she'd experienced more emotional reunions than she would ever have expected. At first, most of them seemed likely to fail abysmally, but as time went by, she came to see that something different was happening. It was undeniable. Someone being reconnected to their blood line had meaning. It was something ancient, restorative. Of course, it didn't always go well, yet there was a sense it could put to bed fears on both sides, even if the relationship never developed into the yearned for bond. She had told the panel of trustees for the adoption agency in her first interview that her work in frontline children's social work had primarily been in assessment and support.

Before the interview, the question that had plagued her the most had been: what if they ask me if I have ever recommended post adoption contact?

Paralysed by self-doubt, she was more uncertain about this than any other job. Maybe it wasn't for her after all, but she needed to think it through before, or if, she bailed. She had always thought post adoption contact was iffy at best, so it was kind of mad going for this job. It seemed to her it was doomed to end in sadness and disappointment, and she'd seen nothing to say she was wrong. Except Dylan of course. Back in the day, no contact had always been the go-to recommendation, to ensure there would be a large pool of potential adopters. So many potential adopters had told her they just wouldn't wash it, having to meet birth parents. Oh sure, there was research out there extolling the virtues, providing all the adults could handle it, but they couldn't, could they. Deep down she still believed that what children needed was a substitute family with all that entailed. It had to be crossing the Rubicon with no going back, otherwise how could it work? That had pretty much been her approach before. Until Dylan, there had been no reason to think again.

On the day she walked out of her job at the hospital, all she had known about the change in Tara's life was what she saw; that Tara clearly had some role with the League of Friends and seemed completely comfortable in the hospital environment. That image of Tara with the paper and pins had been imprinted on her mind ever since. She'd looked like the salt of the place, someone who would retire with cake and well-wishers crowding to say their goodbyes, like the sort of woman you would describe as *exactly like a mum*. It made Carol uncomfortable to picture her there, kindly carrying posters and pins.

The hospital's link with Goldspiers Inc as a major funder had become well known by everyone once the new machines had been installed. It had even been in the local paper, a picture of Dylan Downley proudly smiling and handing over a big cheque with giant gold stars. Even though he was now a grown man, she recognised him immediately as the child she had removed from his mother.

The hospital was a landmark in the town, the jobs it brought, the sense of community. It had been transformative for a small industrial town which over time had begun to lack the very industry that had been its beating heart. Then came the day when Carol had been in the supermarket. Seeing Dylan in the flesh, a grown man, doing something as mundane as shopping for groceries with his mother Tara beside him. It had shaken her to the core. He was holding a box of tea and smiled at her, unaware that she knew who he was. Before Tara noticed, Carol had rushed towards the nearest exit, abandoning her trolley on the way.

The references were too old now to be much use, so she'd put down only the recent - the hospital and a private nursery where she'd been a governor for a while. No one would look back further than the last ten years.

What she'd hoped for was a job that could bring families together. A sort of butterfly effect to atone for past misdemeanours. With luck, and a positive vibe, Carol believed she could help birth mothers come to terms with what had happened, for better or worse, or help them if they wanted to try and trace. The adult adoptees might even see her as a force for good if she was rebranded as a post-adoption counsellor. That's the reinvention she was looking for. I want, she said aloud, to be a peacemaker.

With that as a kind of work bucket list, she set out to provide as sympathetic an ear as she could. Never one for wasting time in professional interviewing, she looked online for workshops and courses that could improve her skills at listening and compassionate interviewing.

That's it, she wanted to be able to listen, to properly understand. Take the heat out and help them make changes, if it's what they wanted.

For the first few weeks she did nothing but help prospective adopters. She had a desk in a large sunlit office by the water machine. *Hi Carol*, all day was soon overtaken by *How's it going, Carol? You settling in okay?* This from Janice in Accounts whose hair which reached her waist was pulled back by a velvet alice band; soon followed by *Carol! What's happening? Give me some lowdown*, from Jake whose role she didn't fully understand, but seemed to be lie somewhere between caretaker (he was always clearing up) and chief therapist.

Jake, can I get some help on this? came from her colleagues on the adoption support desk so often in her first month that she soon realised her mistake. Jake was one of the managers. Carol, you look like you need tea! a voice called from across the other side of the room behind a row of computers, allow me, as chief clearer upper and cheerer upper to get you one? Carol swivelled her chair to find herself looking into a pair of smiling eyes. How do you take it, sugar, milk? Right you are, lass.

It was from Jake, with his big heart, she learnt that reunions were not to be resisted. If they want to know, then they want to know, he said. Let them, Carol! he said the first time she came to him for advice after adult children and the birth relatives had expressed a desire to meet, but had fantastical expectations. They'll be better off finding out by themselves, he said, than being told by the likes of us.

And he proved to be right so often that she began to form a new approach. Hungry to read the research, the scales began to fall from her eyes. ... *the overwhelming majority of adult adoptees and birth relatives described reunion as a positive experience and still had a continuing relationship even ten years or more after meeting.* And then came Jo.

I would dearly love to find my daughter Anna Ainscott. She was given up for adoption and will now be an adult....

The letter from Jo was not out of the ordinary, until Carol read the last few lines:

I have been diagnosed with Stage IV cancer and after a hospital stay and some treatment have now been discharged home. Unfortunately they are unable to treat me further and I now have carers who come in to help me remain comfortable. I do not know how long I have got, but I know it is not long.

Carol wasted no time, pulling up Anna's birth records, adoption records and everything she could lay her hands on. With online access, it didn't take long. There were a lot of gaps in the records, periods when Anna seems to have disappeared off the radar, which Carol could not understand, but it did not take her long to find her on the electoral roll.

Two more steps and she had an address.

Carol booked in a supervision session well before she arranged to see Jo, but knew she might be on shaky ground. Jake would be the person to help her sort this one out in her head.

218

Jake, I need help on this one, I can't help thinking that I'm going to blow it before I even get to meet this lady.

They were sitting in his office, piled from one end to the other with books. Jake was a collector of memoir and seemed to have read everything from George Orwell to Henry Thoreau.

Jake, it turned out, had already read what papers there were on file about Jo and her search for her daughter.

Carol, you won't blow it. You think you might give her the wrong advice, but that's not the place to start. You're a good social worker and with all the experience under your belt, you know you can help people make real changes. I've read the file, so tell me, what is your approach to this one?

That's what I'm worried about, Jake. My approach. I'm not sure what it should be.

Let her guide you Carol, go in with a completely open mind. After all the people we deal with in this office are no longer people involved in cases open to social services, you must remember that; these are grown adults with the right to choose whatever they want. So, your role is not a decision making one here, it's a supportive one. Give advice, if that is what is asked for, but otherwise you can let her guide you.

Inside her head was a voice saying: what if she doesn't though? What if she changes her mind right near the end? But instead, she said, yes of course, you are right.

If you are using a person-centred approach, you will be prioritising her dignity and choice. You are there to help, not steer.

Much as Carol warmed to Jake, who seemed more like the father of the team than its leader, the stale motivational platitudes pushed her farther away. She truly was an outsider, with all this person-centred bullshit. What did it even mean? She got that she was supporting her dignity, but didn't that also mean challenging her if she made a crap decision? Carol was going to say this to Jake, but thought better of it.

Yeah, you know, Jake, you're right. I had a wrongheaded approach to this. Jake put down his cup and got up from his chair.

You're not the one making the decisions here, Carol. She has the right to respect for her decisions, even if you think they are wrong. He smiled at her and reached for the doorhandle.

Thanks Jake, really, really useful, she said and got up to leave. As she passed him, Jake placed a hand on her arm. And remember the mantra, Carol. You're a social worker not a magician, he said, smiling.

I am here to support and respect her decision, she recited in her head as she parked up along the canal. Carol's head was pounding and there was a tightness in her chest as if she had come to the wrong place at the wrong time. In the pit of her stomach, she registered something different, but could not name it. She knew this feeling, from a time before. What was she doing here? the voice inside her head kept saying. This was the opposite of what she wanted to do.

Carol did not know it at first, but Jo was not alone when she climbed onto the foredeck to knock on the door, gingerly opening the latch. She knew that Jo would be too poorly to get up to answer the door, but as she put her head inside, she was surprised to see a man in a checked shirt seated on a chair narrowly wedged in next to Jo's bed. Once fully inside she found Jo in a full-size bed that filled all of the available living space, leaving only a narrow margin. The paraphernalia of a medically assisted death lay around the cabin: pills, a walker, and what appeared to be a medical kit bag.

Hello, I'm Roy, he said, getting up, would you like a coffee?

Thanks, but no, I'm Carol and... she faltered, looking towards Jo who was lying on the bed apparently asleep, I am the social worker from the agency. Is it okay to come in?

Yes, yes of course. We were expecting you. Oh don't worry, Roy said lowering his voice and realising Carol's hesitation, she sleeps most of the time now, but I am here to help. I can help her explain how she would like things to go.

Carol was compromised. She hadn't expected this and had not a clue who Roy was. Partner? Lover? Brother? Neither was she prepared to speak to him about it. Is she likely to wake soon? she asked, only I, well, it's an important visit but I am not sure I can stay that long. Are you her....? she trailed off.

Friend, said Roy firmly, only a friend here to help, he smiled. And don't worry about me though, if you'd rather, I can step outside?

Hello? a voice from the bed. Jo's eyes were open and her hand was raised a little but quickly fell to the bed.

Carol nodded to Roy who took himself off. She lowered herself into the chair beside the bed.

Hi Jo, I'm Carol, here to speak with you about Anna. I'm a social worker from the agency.

Jo smiled and nodded to Carol.

Are you happy to continue? asked Carol.

She nodded again and began to speak. Thank you for coming, as you can see, I'm not in great shape. I need to know....and explain stuff.

Although frail, her voice weakened by illness, Jo managed

to explain what she wanted and why. Her immense love for Anna came through, but although she didn't talk about contact, Carol did not feel it was necessary to push it. Clearly, Jo had the means with her friend's help to organise it if she wished.

She spent less than an hour at Jo's bedside, long enough to explain that she had already located Anna. Jo cried then and Carol read out to her some of the letters that had been exchanged with Anna. They were brief, business like, and explained what would happen next. Jo was tiring, so Carol began to draw the meeting to a close.

You have done well, Jo, I realise this has been a big emotional journey for you and probably you need rest now and time to process, she said, standing up. I can come back to talk about next steps if you would like?

All I've ever wanted, Carol, is to see her again, but I can't now. It would not be fair on her.

Winded, Carol immediately sat back down. She had feared this was coming. It was what she dreaded most, the reason she went to see Jake, but with Jo being so positive, she thought she might have been mistaken. Now that it had been said out in the open, the starkness of it horrified her.

Jake's last comment *you're a social worker not a magician* repeated in her head and she pictured his smile. To herself she was repeating the mantra *you're here to support*, but the more she did, the more she felt something was shifting in her. I'm not here to be a passive nodding dog, she thought. I can be so much more than that. *This* moment has to be seized. A chance to do something worthwhile would never come again.

You know, I think I'd have to disagree with you there, Jo.

Now that Jo had said the words, it was as if Carol could think clearly for the first time. Nothing could stop her. What

Jake didn't realise was that sometimes there were things which had to be said. All this support stuff, it wasn't support at all if it was hot air. Like, she *knew* about this stuff. She was not going to offer a lot of mushy tosh to this woman.

On the bed, Jo had closed her eyes and seemed to be listening, but Carol could not gauge how she had reacted.

Trying to reinforce the point, she went on, getting into her stride: maybe have a think about what that is going to do to Anna, Jo. She will know she was this close. She lives near to you as well, you could see her regularly I expect. I would hate for you to make the wrong decision. I think you should see her, I honestly do.

She sat back in her chair, wondering if she had said too much.

For a second Jo made no movement, even her eyes, now open, were fixed on the spot above the foot of the bed. There was a waxy sheen on her forehead and Carol started to wonder if she might need Roy. Jo had still not spoken and although Carol could see the rise and fall of her chest, she was not moving. The air in the boat had become compressed and claustrophobic. There was a smell of decay and Carol could not tell if it was a vapour coming off the river water outside or something inside the structure of the boat.

She was not sure what to do now. Roy was outside, clonking away as he moved around the exterior of the boat. Carol was beginning to feel faintly panicky, the air in the cabin so close. Jo appeared to be asleep again, just the movement of her chest. The skin on her hands was thin, the veins raised. Although her eyes were closed, her face looked strained, giving nothing away. Carol had begun to wonder whether she was slipping away. She was about to get up and call Roy when Jo opened her eyes and looked across at Carol, her face softening with the ghost of a smile.

I have made up my mind Carol, thank you, she paused. I am happy with my decision. She let out a long, constricted breath. I have written it all into a letter for Anna and I'd be glad if you would be willing to pass it on. I know you are here to support my decision and if you don't mind, that's what I need you to do right now.

No, no of course, you're right, so right. Carol was mollified by her answer, aware for a moment she had overstepped the mark. Even this woman knew what Carol was supposed to be saying here. What the hell, she could only be herself in this job.

After she had left Jo, with a promise to pass on the letter, Roy was coming down the path towards her when she stepped off the boat.

How was it? he asked.

She is resting now thanks. Carol was unsure how much to say because she still didn't understand what relationship Roy had with Jo. I've got her letter to pass on and she gave me very clear instructions. Thanks for your help.

Told you she doesn't want to see her daughter didn't she?

Yes, she did. What she wants to do though is up to her of course, Roy. I am only here to support, not judge.

I know, I know, but... Carol isn't it? Roy was looking this way and that. She nodded. There've been so many months, if not years when she has maintained exactly the opposite position, he said. I don't think this, he gestured dismissively at the letter in Carol's hand, is what she wants deep down. I genuinely don't.

It's not my job to change her mind though, Roy. She didn't

tell him what had happened, nor what she had said to Jo.

But I know she wants to see her. I know she does. I'm not saying we should go against her wishes, Carol, but if Anna turned up here I know they would both be happier for it. She could die a contented woman.

What are you saying Roy? I cannot go against Jo's wishes, that would be completely unethical. In her head a chasm opened up, between what she was saying and how she had acted. Look, I need to go. But thanks for your concern, I can see how much you care about her and, well, you know, that matters a lot.

As Carol turned to head back to her car, Roy put his hand out.

Sorry, sorry Carol, look I want to make one suggestion, one that doesn't compromise you. I mean, I get it, you have to support her wishes. But if the file was to be, say, open on your desk, and you went out of the room, well then... Anna could find the address her own way and you wouldn't have done anything wrong, right?

What? her shock was genuine. C'mon that's not how we operate. She was annoyed with this now, it was pushing her into the kind of internal conflict she had put behind her. This is sensitive stuff you're dealing with here, Roy, she said, we have to act in the best interests of .... She trailed off. Oh look here, I'm sorry but I can't do that. I'm going to go now and hey, thanks for your care towards them. She headed up the slope away from Roy who was left standing on the path, looking crestfallen.

I'm only trying to help, you know, he called out to her. Carol waved and started the ignition.

29

The Adoption Support Agency

On the morning Anna had arranged to see Carol about the letter, it was pouring with rain. The streets were heavy with traffic so she didn't even try to dodge the splashes from tyres. She experienced a kind of exhilaration being wet, ruined even, as if anything could be thrown at her. Despite it all, her mother will still be alive on this earth somewhere, living her life and she can think of her even if they never meet. But hopelessness was no stranger to Anna. It carried all the bitter memories of life on the streets, a sense of being abandoned to herself and by everyone she had ever known. I am only as good as my last catch. But what did that even mean now? The fete, the foal, praise she received afterwards from Tara and her friend Gill, her abortive visit to Dylan, it all meant nothing. She had wanted to visit Dylan, but now after the letter from Jo that had become pointless. She could not believe he would want to see her once he got to know her anyway. She was only a girl making a bit of music, no great achievements to her name. She arrived at the office dripping. It was to be her first face to face meeting with the social worker.

Come in, come in, oh my you are soaked. Can I get you a coffee?

Anna dumped herself down into the chair offered.

Thanks, yeah that's great. White, two sugars.

So Anna, how can I support you? This must be emotionally challenging for you, receiving Jo's letter?

Yeah, it's fine honestly, I only wanted, well, to finish it off and find out anything you can tell me about my father. I mean, I get it, she is ill, so yeah…that's it isn't it.

Is there anything I can do to help you process that information?

Like what? Anna was tired of the bullshit psycho talk. I get it, it's all very hard for everyone else and I am supposed to go along with that. They don't like to see me being upset, because everything, *everything* in the adoption process relies on the 'child' not feeling anything, right? Well, I do feel something so they can suck it up.

Like what, Carol? she repeated.

Well, do you want to talk it through with me?

To tell you the truth, no. I don't mean to be rude, but you know, we have only just met. You don't know me, and I don't know you. I don't know my mother. I am guessing you have had the privilege though?

Carol's face fell and Anna knew that she had hit her target.

Yeah, I thought so. Was that when she said she didn't want to see me? Did anyone tell her how I might feel about that or does that not count?

Anyone could see that the tension in the room was stifling:

one woman overwhelmed by feelings of rejection fighting to survive, the other fearing her own fatal flaw that just might screw up every good intention she ever had.

The thing is, Anna, you can come to terms with this somehow, but if not then there's not a damn thing in the world I can do to stop you. If you decide to find out where she is and go there, then it's your decision. I'm just here to support. She got up. Let me get that coffee.

The file on the table was closed. The file she had wanted to see all her life, the one she believed to be hers by right. With Carol out of the room, she got up and moved towards the table. Should she open it? It was about her, so no reason why she shouldn't.

Her hand caressed the edge of the table. Within its private cloak of manila lay the world in which she would have been discussed, her whole life examined. Her mother would be saying something about her, but in there, in secret, the truth she cannot tell her.

On top of the closed file lay a handwritten note which Anna picked up – it was from someone called Roy. My father? she wondered. ...*and the thing is, Carol* the spidery writing appeared to be from someone older *I have known Jo this past year or so, our boats are side by side at Compton Wharf. When I first moved into mine, I was alone so Jo and I got to know each other quite quickly as we were next door. We have been best friends ever since. I spend much of the day helping on Safe Haven, (that's the name of her boat) and I have listened to her talk about Anna for years. The only thing she ever wanted was to see her again. I honestly believe her decision to write that letter was driven by a wish to spare Anna any suffering, but I also know that in her heart of hearts to see Anna is all she wants.*

Carol waited by the kettle in the small kitchen they shared with the accountant from the first floor. He was making himself a drink and chatting to her about the people on the second floor who ran a nanny agency and why they made so much noise. She was not listening but was watching the kettle boil. The accountant had a teaspoon of instant coffee poised in his hand and was looking at her for some response. He seemed content when she smiled and nodded at him and as he stirred his cup drizzling milk into it. He continued, saying he was glad she agreed with him about that because it was not as if he was being critical or anything. He didn't wipe up, the teaspoon slowly leaked coffee onto the counter where he had left it. Meanwhile, he gave her a cheery thumbs up, balancing his coffee and some paperwork in the other hand whilst exiting through the door.

It wasn't as if she had done the wrong thing. She'd done the right thing, only maybe in the wrong way. Or not even that. It took her all of ten minutes, perhaps more to make the coffee, to gently stir it. To urge it towards the right consistency. In no hurry she made her way back to the office, cups in hand. The door stood ajar, the seats empty. On her desk, an untouched file, the letter lay on top of the manila folder, exactly where she had left it.

She picked up the letter from Roy, whispering *thank you Roy* and slipped it in between the mute cover of the manila folder.

30

Dylan

The fallout from the fete seemed never ending. Dylan had met the hospital board of trustees and Scott Marston to examine in detail what caused a day of festivities to end in near fatal tragedy.

His first aim, when he came out of hospital, was to find out who else was injured in the burger van explosion. He visited the homes of over twenty families who had been at the hospital, whose relatives and friends had been brought in by ambulance. There were no major injuries, but the horror and trauma of the events had left an ugly imprint. Most of them remembered the huge blast and many were still experiencing nightmares from it. Others relived being trapped if they smelt smoke. Dylan's first visit, before he was discharged, had been to the burger van owner himself. He was in a room on his own, further down the same corridor in the burns unit, his head and shoulders bandaged.

Hi you must be Matt? he said, head around the door. Would it be okay to steal a few minutes of your time? Slowly, the man drew his eyes away from the television, clearly uncomfortable moving his head.

Err… yeah…sorry, do I know you?

I'm Dylan, I was at the same event…I, um, was the speaker at the event that day. I hope you don't mind my dropping by, but I wanted to know if you were okay? It was your van, right?

He nodded his head, slowly, the pain obvious.

Oh, yeah, I think you were the guy brought in at the same time, right? His smile came gradually, but Dylan was relieved to see it.

How's it going?

Not bad, not bad, the man said, his voice quiet, from the back of his throat.

I wanted to say hi, see you were okay. Matt, right?

Yeah, seems everyone has heard of me now. News travels fast round here. Hi Dylan, I was told you'd been injured trying to help me, thanks man. It's good to finally meet you. He smiled again, this time looking more comfortable. I'd shake your hand, but, well, you know…. He made a tiny wave with his bandaged hand.

Is it too much, I mean would it be okay, to stay awhile? Dylan asked. I'd like to know what happened, well also about your business and how you're going to stay afloat? I may be able to help. I want to be able to help, that's why I'm here.

Yeah, sit down, man, I'm okay. It all hurts rather a lot you know, but the doctors tell me I am going to make a full recovery. There'll be some scarring but, you know, that's not going to kill the love life. What about you?

Yeah, I'm good, thanks Matt. I'm obviously only being

treated for some minor stuff – mostly smoke inhalation, but I'm feeling okay already. Thanks for asking. So we know the horse rampaged after the van went up, but what caused the explosion? Has the fire service spoken to you?

They have, thanks, in fact they were the first in. Followed by the police, the newspapers, the local radio people. The fire prevention team have investigated already and told me it was a gas leak. I had the van and the propane tank and pipes and everything checked for safety only a month ago, so I'll be glad of some advice from the fire service when they do their report. The insurance guys are going to be a pain in the arse I know it, so I'm looking at either total ruin or a new van. He laughed wryly. But it'll take me some time to be confident enough to work out of a van….

Matt trailed off, his eyes straying to the window.

What will you do for money, Matt?

Matt turned, a look of surprise on his face.

I'm sorry, that's a very personal question. Forget I said that. But you know, I suppose what I'm trying to say is: we'd like to help, if we can. I know you've got a lot of local support for all the fetes and events that you do, so no one is pointing the finger. There's room there for some support, for you Matt, whilst you get back on your feet.

Matt had turned his face back towards the window, his face a blank. Dylan couldn't tell if he'd touched a nerve.

Yeah, thanks man, he said with a small nod of the head, but you know it's not my only job. More of a hobby to be honest. I enjoy the company.

What do you do the rest of the time?

I'm a chef, I do catering. The burger van isn't the only way I do it, in fact, the decision has been made for me hasn't it? He managed a laugh, but it looked as if it might double him up.

The nurse said I wasn't to laugh, he carried on, but that's hard. You know you're the second visitor who has come to see how they can help me and nearly killed me with kindness.

I'm sorry, Matt, hey I should go and let you rest.

No, no, you're alright. That young woman who was doing the DJ'ing from the tent was in here yesterday. She told me about all the overdone burgers she's had in her life that she used to call 'burger disasters', but she said this one tops the lot, he grinned.

Oh you mean Anna Ainscott? That's nice she came to see you.

Yeah, she's setting up a support group for everyone affected and wanted my details. Nice idea, it'll bring us together. Maybe you should talk to her?

Yes, good idea, Matt. I'll see what we can get going. Look I know this is a bit previous, but if we fix up some regular meetings for everyone, maybe we could get you involved? I think everyone would want to know you're okay.

Hah, yeah, I could do the catering. No, seriously, I'd like to be involved. It's a good plan.

It was as if there wasn't much to say, and yet it existed: a sense of closeness between the two men, an unspoken bond, a disaster shared. Dylan had seen it before, talked to psychotherapists about victims of natural disasters who had experienced shared traumatic experiences and become friends, a community even, as a result. Goldspiers Inc had a charitable arm that reached out into communities around the world to provide emergency infrastructure after devastating natural disasters. His work as CEO had brought him into contact with volunteers and medics working in the field. But this was the first time he had been at the other end of the process, as a survivor and a key player at the same time.

The tone began to shift towards less weighty topics. They chatted amiably, each comforted by the other, sharing the detritus after the event and their altered perceptions of who was who.

Anna's name came up more than once, as the DJ, the announcer, the calm voice of the hospital radio that Matt said he'd been listening to. By the time Dylan left the hospital, he had set his mind upon seeing her again.

31

Surjan's Big Idea

Anna threw herself into every activity she could think of to help the community. She had stalled after her visit to the social worker, unsure what to do with the information.

As the days ticked by, the conflict between her mother's letter and her desire to see her gnawed away at her. To find your mother and hear her words – *her actual words* – that she doesn't want to see you. That sucked. Whenever it came into her mind, which was most of the day, she was sad to the core, confounded. How could she? was all she kept saying. How fucking *could* she? As if Anna had no rights in this, no say at all.

There was a text on her phone. Hi, can we meet? Dylan.

Since the fete, the one person she wanted to meet more than anyone else was Dylan. When they had met before, albeit so briefly, she knew he would be someone she could talk to about anything. But the scar of that terrible day was still healing. It had been a watershed; there was 'before the fete' and 'after the fete'. No amount of effort to create a support group had made her feel any better either, although she kept going with it. Tara had called in on her one day as well, quite out of the blue.

You're doing a brilliant job, Anna. I have been so impressed. It's made the hospital a bigger and better place you know. Tara hesitated. If there is anything I can do, let me know?

Oh, no it's all under control, I have got the membership list up and running now and Scott has given me the heads up for some publicity money.

No, said Tara softly, I meant for you. Is there anything I can do for you?

Oh. Anna was stumped. Tara put a hand on her arm. Apart from Surjan and his mum, no one had her back. No one had ever had her back. Oh, th-thanks, Tara, you're a star, but yeah, I'm fine. I'll be fine, honestly.

And then, as if his mum wasn't already a total gem, there was Dylan. But as much as she wanted to meet Dylan, she couldn't do it. Yet. Maybe there would come a time when the air had lifted and the shadows pulled back, when life can begin again properly, but for now it didn't feel like somewhere she could go.

The hospital radio broadcast day by day. She was now heavily involved in all aspects of the wellbeing support system too. Scott Marston had become more friend than mentor, turning to her for advice frequently. He wanted to give her a raise and a new title, all of which was welcome, but something had come adrift in her. What it was like to spiral downwards she knew only too well, and in a bid to stay afloat, she tried to keep reasonable working hours, stay busy, but it didn't help.

She was losing the battle against old shadows.

There had been nothing but endless rain since the fete, a flood risk on the flatlands bordering the town. Everything had become waterlogged – the weather, the work, her mind. Communications with colleagues made her feel as if she was underwater, desperate to get out and breathe.

When the day came that Surjan and his mother invited her for dinner, she was grateful. They were family.

I don't know what to do about her, Surjan? Since the fete, Anna had visited the foal every day after work, willingly taking on the responsibility. It was liveried on a farm and was well taken care of for now, but the bills were mounting and despite the farmer's cooperation, she sensed he was going to pull the plug on the money and sell her on.

Surjan was finishing his dinner in the cramped kitchen of their three-bed semi, whilst his mother was leaning against the sink watching them talk. Her hair was silver in the front and lay in a beautiful long plait down one shoulder. Outside the kitchen window the rain continued to fall as it had done all week. The summer flowers full of bloom before the fete now looked battered, circled by petals knocked to their feet.

But I don't understand, Annie, said Surjan's mum (she always called her Annie), why doesn't the farmer keep her on his farm. Animals are always taken away from their mother's, nahin? I feel sorry for this animal. She is only a baby.

She is, Anna nodded, looking at her hands holding a glass of water on the kitchen table, but she is growing and costing more by the day and the farmer sees her as livestock, a bit like he does with all his animals. I think for him she's costing more than she can ever bring in return.

Surjan, finishing up his food, nodded vigorously, wiped his

237

mouth on a napkin and said: Yes, but Anna, think about this. What can you do with a horse? You cannot have it in your flat. You cannot pay for the horse to live at the stables. You cannot trust the farmer, although you can because it is his horse, but you *feel* as if you can't. So what can you do? What is this horse to you now?

Surjan had a point. She hesitated. It sounds stupid I know, but I've come to see her as a survivor of the terrible things that happened that day, because she lost her mother, but is still with us and surviving. I've named her Hope. I mean she has a name, she's called Regent, but you know, it seemed more right somehow.

I know, I have it, cried Surjan, jumping up from his seat. I have an idea. Animated, he started to pace up and down the kitchen staring at the floor, wiping his mouth with a napkin and wagging his finger all at the same time.

Anna laughed and so did his mum. Your ideas are always crazy, Surjan, but always right too. She looked across at Surjan and his mum and her heart began to feel full for the first time since she had left the hospital. It was so good to be at home with them. It had come to mean so much, that this family had taken her into their heart from that day when Surjan found her homeless. His mother even used to drop off Punjabi sweet treats for her at the hospital when she was visiting with a tiffin of food for a patient. There seemed to be no end of loving care this family could provide. Despite her closeness to them, she dared not ask what to do after she got Jo's letter. It was too raw. Jo's address, scrawled on a piece of paper which she had stuffed into her pocket, lay abandoned on her desk at home, untouched. Paralysed, she did not know whether to go to Compton Wharf, to Safe Haven, or destroy the address. There seemed to be no middle ground, nothing in between. Maybe Surjan's mum would have a view, but Jo stopped herself from changing the subject, waiting for Surjan to deliver his Big Idea.

He stopped pacing. Why don't you, he pulled himself up tall, ask the hospital to adopt the horse? Slapping both hands to his thighs he declared: it could be their mascot!

But... where would she live, I mean, how does a hospital keep a horse, Surjan? Anna watched Surjan as he cleared plates from the table and then grabbed paper and pen from the sideboard.

His mother smiled and made towards the door. Another of my son's madcap schemes, she said with a broad smile.

He could live where he is now. Anna interjected, she's a she, Surjan. Yes, she I mean, he said, and wrote at the top of his piece of paper Hospital Horse.

Look, the hospital can pay for her liver or whatever you call it...

Livery. Anna was fully laughing now.

Yes livery, and the horse can be trained by you to be a friendly horse who comes to events or is kept in the hospital grounds.

But Surjan, I've never in my life heard of a hospital having a horse. I mean, it is a bit left field, excuse the pun.

I know it is, but think of it... in the states now they are training therapy horses. Okay they are very short and this one may be too tall. Abruptly he looked up at Anna. Is she short?

No, she's not and what's more she's going to be tall like her mother, she chuckled.

He went on at a pace. But she could be a presence in the hospital grounds they can go and look at. Or be at events, to give children rides?

Well, I suppose I see what you mean. Anna was broadly smiling and sitting back in her chair. I'll give it some serious thought.

The next two days were busy. Anna had pushed Surjan's idea to the back of her mind until a text popped up on her phone.

Horses for Courses – watch equine therapy in action at your local hospital. Love Surjan xx

He couldn't mean this was happening in real life. It must have been a prompt. Impossible to do, but impossible to ignore. It lifted her spirits and when she next went to see the foal, she talked to her about it.

What say you, Hope? She was stroking the young horse's long black neck in broad strokes, whilst Hope munched away on some hay. Could you live here and come to hospital events? I mean, it's a bit mad, but maybe you'd like it? Would Scott think I'd lost the plot if I suggest it?

Hope tossed her head. I know, that's what you think, but you know what, I think I like the idea, said Anna.

Scott looked across at her from his large glass desk. Beyond the window was a view of the hospital grounds, neat slopes of grass bordered by large trees and in the distance the old bell tower. The sun was slanting across the glass, making it hard for her to look at Scott without squinting. Directly outside his office window stood an old ash, one of the oldest remaining trees of the grand estate land that had been bequeathed to the town in the 19th century for the express purpose of building a hospital. Scott's office occupied part of the first floor in the original building where the broad canopy of leaves filtered the light, dappling it across the polished floor. The September sun was deep gold and Anna had walked to the hospital earlier in the day filled with autumn light and warmth. She was nervous about pitching a project, it was new territory for her. Bolstered by the work she had done to put together a watertight proposal to present to Scott, she sat across from him now, ready.

Although she was new to this kind of work, her development as a radio host had honed her skill as a storyteller. She had put together some simple storyboards to help present the idea to Scott. As far as she knew, and she didn't in truth, this was exactly the kind of initiative taking he had been suggesting to her. We need to widen the reach of our concept of wellbeing, he had said to her at the outset. You're an ideas person Anna. I believe if given free rein, you could transform this hospital's atmosphere and make it a leader in the softer skills of welcoming patients and relatives.

He listened to her presentation without interrupting, a good sign, nodding as she went from board to board, explaining her concept and the hospital's potential take on healing the dreadful events of that day.

But this is Never Never Land, Anna.

He put his pencil down, his other hand rotating a paper clip round and around his fingers. The idea you've put forward - to buy the foal and keep it stabled, then bring it out for events is way off, he said. The proposal that in between it could be a sponsored riding horse for the disabled, there isn't a close enough connection to the hospital.

Anna had worked up the idea since Surjan's text. She had even been to see the livery owner, a local farmer. Riding for the disabled was a weekly event at the stables, and on her visits to the foal she had seen them having the best time in the paddock with a lively team of volunteers. On a mission to put something together, she asked one of the volunteers about the riding costs (it's free for the riders) and who was in charge. The Riding for the Disabled Association gave her all the information she needed about becoming a sponsor and how the horses were trained. They were no strangers to corporate sponsorship, and she had noticed that some of the horses already wore neat little badges with the logo of some local companies whose names she recognised.

The thing is Scott, even if the foal is only a riding for the disabled horse that wears the hospital logo, we would have done her a service and in a way, made something good come out of that tragic day. A lot of people might become invested in the idea, you know.

I know, I know. I'm not against it, Anna, honestly. Look, how are we going to get around the optics that it was our fete that killed her mother though? I mean, when I say it's never never land, I'm not poo pooing the idea, but trying to be realistic.

Anna was uncomfortable. It wasn't her style to push ideas when they weren't well received. Hospital radio and all of the wellbeing stuff was a different bag – it was about making people feel better, feel like they wanted to do something.

The corporate world, even if it was a hospital with the known ethos of making people better, was alien to her when it came to budgets and the kind of 'market thinking' Scott was hinting at.

You know a well-known ad for food that offered free tights to women was a disaster, Scott said. It was back in the seventies, and the ad led to consumers associating the food product with feet, so the sales went down as a result. We have to be sure that the association the community might have with a project like this won't invoke the very fear we are trying to heal.

Oh, I guess I'd not thought of that, I'm sorry. Anna was beginning to feel so far out of her comfort zone it seemed better to pull out, rather than try to manoeuvre the project across the line.

Look Anna, I know you're new to this side of the hospital's work, but we have to make sure we proof the project and get a lot of eyes on it before I can give you a decision. But hey, don't be disheartened, I'm not turning it down.

No, no, you're fine, I didn't want you to think I'd come up with an un-thought through idea. Anna was grateful for the honesty that had been a feature of their working relationship since the start. I suppose for me, it was an extension of the hospital as a care giver, and something that has a bigger perspective than tending to the sick, which is of course huge in its own way. I want people to know that the hospital is there for the community, for what happens, for the shit that happens too sometimes. And that we're there for when it needs a helping hand to clear up as well.

I like your thinking, Anna, that's why I wanted you on board for the wellbeing side of the hospital. I know that's where your heart lies and I'm aware that's your focus and not corporate bullshit, Scott laughed.

That's a relief, she smiled up at him, the conversation had shifted to safer ground. I guess health for me is so much more than the body, or even the mind. It's the community, the willingness to recognise that stuff happens to people, to animals and sometimes that's when they most need the support, even when things can look as if they are taken care of on the surface.

I mean, to be honest, I love the idea, Scott said, I don't want to get it spectacularly wrong. Do you still visit the foal regularly?

Yes, every week, sometimes more. She's a dear thing, I've called her Hope. The owner had already named her, obviously, but I prefer my name, she responds to it now. You know, when people think of the fete, the awful explosion, the people running, the horse getting killed, I wonder if they think about the foal and what happened to her. It's that extra bit, where I want them to know something came out of it that is restorative.

Scott sat back in his chair, his face wore a distant look as if something she had said had stirred a memory. It wasn't the first time, when she'd been with him that he seemed to be slightly elsewhere. Then he'd boost her up and say nice things, hold her arm a little too long.

Can I come and see her with you sometime? I know Dylan would want to know about this project too and get involved. Maybe we could call it a proper site visit?

Yes, of course. I am sure we can do that.

You know Anna, you are doing a great job. It is thinking outside the box that I want. Let's get Dylan on board and we can debrief at the pub afterwards, what do you say?

Thanks Scott, that means a lot you know. I didn't want to strike a wrong note either. Let's have another look at it when you've spoken to Dylan. Meantime, I'll see what the livery costs are and get back to you. The owner is quite keen to sell, but I think he'll wait given the press is still all over the story about the fete and the horse. They want a story out of it that will please their local readers.

Well, this could be it I suppose, if we play it right?

Exactly. Anna got up to leave and Scott walked towards the door with her. He put his hand on her arm when she was about to exit and said: Well done, Anna, that was a hard one to sell in some ways, but you brought me into the zone where I could see it the right way. Thank you for that. Oh and by the way, I heard you got to know Dylan's mother at the fete. Sorry, but I forgot to talk to you about it, we've been dealing with so much since then. She's a real trooper in the League of Friends here.

Yeah, I did. She's a nice woman and her friend Gill, they're lovely and went all out to give me that playlist.

Didn't they just, and Dylan and Tara have grown to have such a remarkable relationship considering.

Anna stopped, her hand on the door handle ready to leave. Considering what? she asked.

Well, he was adopted you know, and they found each a while ago – not that long - but now they are close, you can see that. It was Tara that brought Dylan on board with Goldspiers and their sponsorship here.

Not a bombshell to Anna, more a sign there were others out there that would get what she was going through at exactly this point in her life.

Oh, I didn't know, thanks for telling me that, Scott. It means more than you could possibly know, she said and laughed. I know, I'm being enigmatic, ignore me this time. Anyway, look forward to meeting up with you and Dylan. Text me with a date and we can go see the foal.

As she walked down the corridor towards the stairs, a smile

spread across Anna's face. Well, she said to herself. Well, well, well. Blow me if there isn't a bit of a story there. And it has to be me that finds out, but this isn't the time.

32

Project Hope

An arc of blue sky weighted with black thunder clouds was spreading from the east as Dylan swung his car into a visitor's parking bay at the hospital. Summer was fading fast towards autumn, with intense colours appearing in the trees as the season breathed out.

He had made the decision that the best way to get some help out there for Matt and others affected by the explosion was to collaborate with those who were already doing it. Anna's name was coming up left right and centre, first from Matt and then he had a voicemail from Scott talking about visiting some farm with Anna. It wasn't clear why. He figured it was something to do with the aftermath, but held off ringing back until he had spoken to her himself. And besides, there was that drink outstanding.

Good morning, Anna had her headphones on, let's start the morning for all of you with something truly calming, Max

Richter, On the Nature of Daylight. I hope you can all enjoy this as much as I did. It's looking mixed weather out there today folks, but perhaps we're in for an Indian summer before the days get colder, so let's relax back and enjoy the music.

Not wanting to break her flow on air, Dylan ducked his head down and peered in through the tinted side window that let onto the studio where Anna was broadcasting. He recognised her profile though the window, her long hair caught up in a loose pony tail. Even with restricted vision, he could see that posters covered every inch of available wall space.

He was happy to wait till she had a break, if time stretched out, he planned to hang out at the League of Friends. He checked his phone for messages unaware that Anna had seen him, switched off the On Air sign and was moving towards the window. There was a tap on the glass and he swung round to see her beckoning him inside.

Pushing open the door he paused halfway across the threshold, Hi Anna, I hope it's okay I've dropped by? Still beckoning, she said, yeah, of course it is c'mon in! It's great to see you, and especially that you've come to my lair, she grinned.

Ah yes, well I wasn't sure... he looked around the room at the poster heaven she had created, spotting old vinyl covers of some of the greatest – and his all-time favourite – records. She'd made a music lover's den. Posters of every kind that represented, he guessed, her favourite musicians (Durutti Column, Dylan) were nestled in amongst a million thank you cards covering every available piece of wall. Creativity shone from every corner of the small room, even the fact that the headphones she had wired up were her own choice: magenta pink. Against Anna's dark hair they were a bright pop of colour that sizzled with energy. He gazed around

248

the room taking in the bands he knew, those he didn't. There was the magnificent cover of Freewheelin' Bob Dylan and It's a Beautiful Day, The Miseducation of Lauren Hill, Leonard Cohen's Ten New Songs. It was a feast for the music junkie going all the way back to the Abbey Road zebra crossing. There were some surprises in there too, the mark of a serious musical aficionado: Fatamouta Diawara, Caoimhín Ó Raghallaigh, and others he had never heard of.

You're a legend, Anna, if you have these in your collection! Wow, I'm gobsmacked.

Why? Is it that you expected something less of me? Laughing, Anna pulled out the other chair and gestured for him to sit. I'm on again in thirty but thought I'd take a quick break. You want something to drink?

Her hair was longer than when he'd seen her last, it was loosely knotted in a pony tail that draped her left shoulder. In plain black, she looked as if she was more 'at work' than he'd expected, a gesture to being business like, apart from her Doc Martens which he liked. Not for the first time he was struck by her beauty, the casual sinuous movements of her body.

Dylan pointed at the Freewheelin' album. I was named after that picture, he said, a perfect shot of Bob Dylan captured in all his glorious youth and freedom. It reminded him of himself when he had been younger, except that what it felt like to love and be loved like that he could only guess at. He loved Tara, and in some part of himself, and with a twinge of sadness, he wondered where his adoptive parents now fitted into his world. They were complicated people and the less he saw of them, the easier it became, but with that came guilt. It followed him like a ragged dog searching for food, so he would regularly make a quick call to them or send a card. His dad was always the last to phone and his mum would complain when he rang that he *didn't phone as often as he should*. Whenever something he'd turned to or showed interest in was not to their liking, they'd always said: *you should be grateful, we sacrificed so much to take you in*. It made him into a charity case, and his visits had become a duty rather than a pleasure.

Anna's headphones were around her neck. Tea or coffee, we have both? she was filling the kettle in the corner of the room where there was a small sink and an assortment of mugs.

There was something strangely awkward in the air. I wanted to drop by and well, you know, check in on what we can do to support and help those guys – well all of us – since the fete. I mean, there's a lot of damage out there from those terrible events and I think I can help. He paused. And check on how you are doing too of course, I mean, he hesitated, you were right in the centre of it all.

Thanks Dylan. It was awful, I'm not gonna lie. I've felt a bit wobbly since. But, you know, I didn't get injured, so I reckon I can do something still for those who were, she said. Have you been okay since? I know your mum was frantic at the time, although she didn't show it. She's such a trooper.

Ha, yes isn't she. The mention of his mum made him feel even happier to see Anna. I'm fully better thanks. I had a lucky escape too. I wasn't in hospital for more than a few hours. I've been back there to visit and your name come up a lot – I went to see Matt, the burger van guy.

She had her back to him. He noticed how her dark hair shone a deep copper under the studio lights.

She set two steaming cups of tea down between them, answering him as she went along, arranging cables on her desk, putting stuff away. He was surprised at how articulate she seemed to be about the likely effect on everyone. He said he knew there were plans afoot and he'd got a meeting scheduled in for the following week. This was the way the conversation meandered, easy, low key. He was comfortable in her company, watching her hands move things across the desk. Her hands were long and slender and she wore no rings. As she talked, she made a movement where she cupped her two hands towards each other, when she was explaining something and then moved them apart, as if they were reacting to a force field. Her words were carefully chosen, but her hands even more eloquent. And then there was her voice. A voice made for making people feel as if they want to live. No wonder Scott Marston had taken her on.

You have to have a lot of creative ideas in this job, I think, am I right? She smiled and something in his chest skipped a beat. He didn't quite know how to be.

I try my best, but it's easy to care about them, you know? I think the League of Friends share that too. A flicker of sadness passed across her face, he didn't know why.

Tara is a force, and my mum, but you know those things already, he laughed, it's not as if she doesn't tell everyone she ever meets.

You're very lucky, you know, she looked straight at him, but as soon as he went to answer she looked away and began to stand up.

Hey, look at the time, that's gone quickly, I am so so sorry, but it's time to start up again in five. Can we meet up, I mean I know we are with Scott anyway, but perhaps we can talk again about... I can....

Yeah, yeah of course, I am sorry we've hardly started on what to do. Let's hook up again soon? Meanwhile, she said, we've got Project Hope to think about and I can't wait for you and Scott to meet her.

He wanted to see her again, not in a way that was urgent or desperate, but so he could be easy in her presence. Drink tea, let the time slip by. He wanted to see her hair in daylight, the burnt auburn of it, to see if it shone like chestnuts in autumn.

33

Compton Wharf

Anna didn't feel guilty. It had taken her barely a minute after Carol left the room to clock the letter lying on the folder, read through it, scrawl down the address and walk. She'd been tempted to take the whole lot and run, but thought better of it once Roy's letter revealed Jo's address. That was all she needed.

For weeks after Jo's letter and the meeting with Carol she had been paralysed, trying to pretend that it had all been in vain; that it was pointless lying to herself that there might some connection. A real connection. Maybe they were right to say 'birth' mother, not real mother.

She wanted to bin the note with the address on it, but gnawing away at her was a feeling that this had been written by a sick woman, a woman who says she is dying. Dealing with patients was her speciality, trying to understand what they are going through, to get underneath the sickness and rediscover some real joy, especially near the end. She had made it a mission to do just that at the hospital. She wondered if Jo had ever been an in-patient there without her knowing. There were so many questions, but neither Carol nor the adoption agency had been able to answer them. It still made her mad: what right did they have to decide what she can be told? Withholding parts of her life, *her* life, not anyone else's life, not their life. The feeling of having been discussed by this woman, Carol a stranger to her, and her own mother, was like being a child again, as if you had only second-class rights.

One week after driving out to visit Hope with Scott and Dylan, Anna was on her day off. The visit to Hope had been short, but both men seemed delighted by Hope's friendliness, her glossy beauty. The conversation on the way back into town had soon fired up, before long they were looking at ways the hospital could prioritize promoting healing and wellbeing through Hope's connection with it. Project Hope they would call it.

Anna had been out to the stables every weekend since the fete, mucking out, moving Hope outside with a halter and a surcingle, so she could acclimatize to different starter weights, rugging her to practice getting ready for winter. It had been a lifeline for Anna. Project Hope had done what it said on the tin: given her a sense of hope, something to completely focus her mind beyond despair. This weekend was the first time she felt confident enough to stay at home, knowing that without a visit, Hope would still be thriving.

She didn't set out that morning to stake out Compton Wharf, it was just a leisurely stroll that might take her in the general direction. She briefly considered the disaster scenarios it could lead to: being recognised, outright rejection, even shouting. A ring on the doorbell came to mind, but she was inclined against it. She just wanted to go there, see Safe Haven for herself, maybe catch a glimpse of her mother putting the bins out or something. It would take more courage than she could muster to knock on a door that she had been told was firmly closed.

She grabbed her bag and coat and set off. The weather was warmed by autumnal sun, bringing people out of their houses. Compton Wharf was all the way across town. Her heart was beating fast, but she told herself this was just an afternoon's walk, nothing else.

Once you head out of the centre towards the canal, warehouses made way for old mill cottages and back lanes. Anna had been this way before and knew that there was a pathway running down to the narrowboat marina, which was popular with dog walkers. Just before the canal there was a natural boundary in the shape of an old stone wall with a narrow gap that gave onto the wharf. From the wall you would have a clear view of the boats gently rising and falling on the swell. Anna wasn't sure if she should stop there, or take a walk along the towpath.

A family with children and dogs were making their way down the path behind her, the dogs running on ahead, sniffing at the ground. It seemed a good idea to hang back, let them get ahead of her so she turned onto the grassy sward bordering the wall and leant there, readying herself for the next steps.

She heard them call the dogs, and watched as the woman put them on the lead. We don't want to disturb the residents, the woman said, to no one in particular. Anna sat down on the ground bordering the nearside of the wall, the shaded grass damp beneath her. What's it like, being in a boat with a

255

thousand people passing, peering in?

More walkers were coming down the path and Anna was beginning to feel paralysed by indecision. What if she really is ill? What if she isn't, and she sees her hanging about? Her mind was telling her either go for it and knock or just get out.

People nodded at her, as if she might be a local. She felt obtrusive, sitting on the wrong side of the wall facing back up the path. Thoughts about her mother's illness dominated her mind, stymieing even an innocent walk. It was all beginning to seem unfair. She didn't want to become unwelcome intrusion, even if it meant she could see her just once.

Anna got up, paused for a split second then grabbed her bag decisively and walked off up the path, retracing her steps. By the time the canal was out of sight she was crying, overwhelmed by the confusion of mixed messages. It was all too much. This. Just too much.

By the time she emerged from the top of the path near the warehouses the rain was falling thick and heavy and she headed for home.

34

Safe Haven

You heard her, Jo. You *heard* her, her actual voice on the hospital radio. Who could have foreseen that? I mean, it has to be a sign.

Roy was sitting beside Jo's bed, holding her hand between both of his. For two days she had slept through most of the hours of the day, including when he had been there visiting. The 'hospice at home' carers' visits had to be increased to manage the levels of medication she needed to ease her increasing pain.

Roy had brought with him the local newspaper for Jo to see. It carried a photograph of Anna on the front page with the headline: Hospital Radio Host Helps Fete Tragedy Victims. The Gazette had offered Anna the chance to place a fundraiser within the pages of their weekly paper and offered to match donations. Her work so far had brought the hospital into the public eye with such phrases as *much loved radio host leads the way to help victims* and *she's the voice we love to hear, now she's a voice who speaks for all of us,* with glowing tributes to the hospital for its community outreach.

Jo was awake, but her eyes were unfocused, her movements barely a flutter within the tips of her fingers. Roy stared down at the floor, supporting Jo's hand in both of his, whilst he fought to bring his emotions under control. The air in the tiny cabin was hushed, broken only by the sound of Jo's breathing.

He leaned in nearer and stroked her hair tenderly. I've brought a picture of Anna for you, darling, would you like to see it?

Time seemed to slip beneath the surface. He gazed across the bedcover to the view beyond the porthole window, where the shifting shapes of trees rose ink black against a blue dusk. The waterway had been choppy overnight, rocking the barges in their moorings, raising a clatter of ropes. It was warm in the cabin from the stove which Roy had set and lit that morning early, before the carers arrived.

Memories of summer passed through his mind. The birdsong and the last time he had shared drinks with Jo on his foredeck, before unmanageable pain had confined her to bed. Her head thrown back, she had laughed at his attempt to guess at her hair colour as a young woman. Wait, I know, he said, blonde! You were a blonde! It was hilarious. His last best guess was that she'd been a redhead, but she denied even that amidst fits of giggles protesting that auburn wasn't the same *at all*. Whatever it was, he laughed, you'd have knocked 'em dead whoever they were. At seventy years old, Roy was delighted to have found a friend to share the evenings with. He wanted nothing more. His long years on the barges had made him a quiet man for the most part, content with his own company, but Jo's arrival had brought new light into his life. He was devastated when she told him she was dying. He'd spoken the only words that made sense at the time: I'll do whatever it takes to help you through, whatever I can do I'll do, so that you can manage. Now, as autumn fought it out in the skies above, his direction was all inwards. In his mind, he had nothing but respect for Jo and a belief that the most he could do for her now was keep her warm and hold the best of her in his mind's eye, hold the best of her for the life she was, the life she is.

Yet. Roy had seen such unfulfilled longing in her constant references to Anna. It was as if he'd witnessed first-hand her unfinished life. His attempts to persuade Carol to bring Anna had fallen on deaf ears. *We must respect her wishes,* the social worker had said, adamant that no meant no. *One hundred percent we will do what she has instructed us,* he was told. Even if, according to him, they were not her real wishes.

Roy? Jo's voice was thin as if she had woken from a deep sleep a long way off. What's that you're saying? She smiled at him and her hand tightened a little around his.

I've brought something to show you, and tell you about, love. He had only begun to call her affectionate names in the past few days, but she seemed to rally a little whenever he did.

The thing is, he said, I've been doing a bit of digging since you received Anna's letter. I know she said she was a DJ in her letter, but what we didn't know is she works at the hospital, our hospital, where you were, Jo. That means...he paused sensing she wanted to say something.

Jo's voice came then, stronger. It means I heard her doesn't it, Roy? It means I have heard her actual voice speaking to me. She was staring into the space ahead. Roy waited, giving her time to take it all in. A single tear appeared at the corner of her eye and rolled slowly down her cheek.

That means, she said, her voice reduced to a whisper, that blessed voice I waited for each day, was my daughter speaking directly to me. *To* me. Oh, it can't be real, Roy, she turned towards him, tears coursing down her face. I'd know that voice, from a million others, that's why I waited for her to speak, every day that I was there I waited for that voice. It filled my world, made me want to live. He held her tight, her shoulders shaking.

And I have something else for you Jo, my love. A picture. He held the newspaper in front of her, the picture of Anna, taken with her headphones around her neck, smiling directly to camera.

Is that her? Jo's other hand went to hold the paper but was too weak. She is like my mother, she said, and her head gently fell back onto the pillow, exhausted with the effort. She put her hand over the picture, stroking it, then drew Roy's hand which was still holding it towards herself and with a supreme effort moved her head towards the picture brushing her lips against it.

As evening drew on, he made her some soup and she asked for tea, both signs of improvement. A half bowl of soup she managed, before fatigue got the better of her. The carers came and went and he settled her for the night. Before she fell into another deep sleep, she said, you know Roy, I love her. I have always loved her. She is, her breathing was so shallow he had to bring his ear close to her lips, the best thing that ever happened to me.

He settled her to rest and said, I'll see you in the morning, my love. You sleep now, and think of Anna's wonderful voice. He was reluctant to leave this time, even though it had become their regular routine and the news he had brought had so obviously lifted Jo's spirits. There had been a change in energy, he'd noticed, when he'd read to her. It was the first time she'd eaten for a few days too, and she had managed to drink a whole cup of tea. He had been convinced the news of Anna would give her more strength. Now he had watched this very thing come to pass in front of his own eyes.

He would make a plan, see if, with a little encouragement, she might agree to a short visit.

Roy brought in some more wood from under the tarp on the roof and banked up the stove, turning it down to a slow burn. The wind which had relentlessly stripped the trees all day, rattling every spare rope in the rigging of nearby sailing boats, was a distant whine. The logs in the stove flared up when the door was opened, stoked by the rush of air. The flames licked and curled around the new wood, drawing energy into translucent blue-yellow flames. He decided to stay after all and pulled up a chair beside the bed.

The hours passed, the flames softened. At some point during the small hours, ghost flames danced behind the glass like northern lights, evanescing from blue through to green until they disappeared, leaving an afterglow among the embers.

A life reaches its natural ending. Roy would no more be able to fathom how it was that Jo took her last breath whilst he dozed beside her that night, than make sense of all the other mysteries he had encountered in his life. He knew only that as he woke to the familiar chill of a spent fire, there was something else. She had gone. This was a different kind of atmosphere, it was powerfully quiet. There was a sharpening of the silence, not because of an absence, but in her missing presence. He touched her still hands, placing the photo beneath them, sorrow coursing through him like a wild river.

The resolve to be the one to tell Anna first hand, was born in Roy that morning in the fragile hours before dawn.

35

Dylan and Anna

A week after the visit from Dylan at her studio, Anna's phone lit up with a message asking if he could visit Hope again with her sometime. Anna had thought about Dylan constantly since she last saw him, his voice, his laugh.

They agreed to go out to the farm on her day off when he would be in the area. Anna felt embarrassed about meeting Dylan at her 'nest' and made an excuse she had some errand to run for the hospital in the morning fixing that as the appointed place. When the day came she was full of anticipation getting ready, unsure how to appear. Casual? Worklike? She dressed up, dressed down, changed into something more comfortable, added hoop earrings for effect, let her hair down, put it back up again. Racing to the hospital, she felt as if she was on a date, but kept telling herself it was just a visit to check out the horse.

Dylan's car was so understated, just a regular Skoda, she

almost laughed, but then wondered what she had expected. He was in jeans and workboots, which she approved of. On the way out to the farm conversation came easily, just like it had at the studio and Anna soon began to feel relaxed. She admired his hands on the steering wheel, tapered fingers, the backs of his hands brown as if he'd been in the sun.

So come on Anna, I'm on the music in here, he laughed, what is it to be?

Half an hour of R.E.M. later they were singing Losing My Religion at the top of their voices and the glory of it all was between them.

Morning turned to afternoon, the sky deepened to a forgotten summer blue, tapestried by clouds, reshaping as they scudded across the autumn sky. They had walked Hope around her field, Dylan taking the lead rein, then both mucked out her stable together. Afterwards, they sat on the haybales in the yard watching a scatter of rooks investigate the ploughed fields. As the sun faded towards twilight the lightness of a day in the sun brought easy laughter and warmth between them. Anna was savouring this companiable feeling between them, as if they'd bring friends a long time. When a light breeze carried over the fields, cooling the air, they took shelter in the barn. With Hope securely homed, they stood a while, side by side, watching her toss her head up and down over the stable door. Dylan turned to Anna and said, I have really loved this afternoon, Anna, being here with you.

Me too, she said, and moved closer towards him. She rested her head on his shoulder and he held her close, breathing in the softness of her chestnut hair.

A trip to the pub for something to eat seemed a perfect end to the day. Over dinner their conversation turned inwards, away from the many projects, ideas and musical greats they shared an interest in. Anna couldn't help noticing that Dylan avoided talking about himself, whenever she asked a question about his life, or the lead up to his career. Despite his obvious talents, he became self-effacing when she expressed her admiration for his success, especially what he was doing with the company to help the hospital. She had hoped he would confide in her, they had so much in common.

What about you, he asked, your connection to people is such a skill, did you train in radio or does it run in the family?

Anna hesitated, the 'how I came to be here' question seemed random in her case, she didn't want to disappoint by recounting her chaotic journey. Yet there was magic happening here with Dylan, as if a moment without truth would be a moment lost.

I was adopted, she paused, wondering if this was the moment he would share his own story, but he said nothing. She went on and before long the whole journey of her life, towards her mother, towards herself, towards a place of belonging had come out. She told him about her letter, the agony of waiting to hear back. Although her world collapsed when she received Jo's letter, Anna touched on it only briefly, describing it as a 'please go away' letter. She didn't tell him about her visit to Compton Wharf. Dylan listened without interruption until that point. That must have been heartbreaking, he said, I mean, that would floor me totally. He stopped there and they both fell silent. It was as if the room held only the two of them then, wrapped in each other's feelings, enriched with a known unknown.

Moments passed, but when he lifted his eyes to look at her, they were filled with tears. He told her she was beautiful. He said he could only imagine how much her mother must feel her absence every day. Reaching for her hand he took it in his and she felt the warmth of his body. They sat like that for a time, hand in hand across the table. She felt Dylan close to her in his silence, in his breath.

They were both quiet on the drive home. Anna began to wonder about him. She realised she knew almost nothing about Dylan, beyond his role at the hospital. He appeared reticent to open up about his life, but why? It had all seemed so natural to her, the visit, the afternoon together, but now doubts began to enter her mind. Maybe she appeared too needy, spilling everything about her mother. Whatever it was, she felt certain he was holding something back.

A week later Anna took herself off to visit Surjan and his mother. She felt as if her world was imploding. Since that day with Dylan, she had not returned his calls. He had said nothing about meeting Tara, his feelings about the essential stuff they had in common. When she began to pick through every minute of the day: what she'd said, how he reacted, she began to think she had misread him. She was nonplussed, confounded by his reticence. He must be married, or perhaps none of it meant as much to him as it had done to her. Why, why did he not say? She couldn't very well bring it up since Scott had been her source. Wasn't something missing if in all that time they had spent together, including telling him her backstory, he responded only with silence about his. It would have been better to have said nothing at all about her mother.

266

Perhaps this wasn't what she'd hoped it was after all.

Surjan was astonished she had not returned his calls after she gave him a trimmed down version of the day. What? he said, you women are crazy. The more you like a guy the less you talk to them. It's insane.

His mum was making food, chipping in with the occasional remark. When Anna said she hadn't returned Dylan's calls, she came over to the table, put her hand on Anna's shoulder and asked, is this man someone you really have feelings for? Hard as it was to make any sense of the jumble of emotions crowding her, Anna's answer was immediate: yes, she said, I think I do.

Then you should return his calls or texts or whatever, Surjan's mum said. That way at least you'll find out if it is going anywhere.

36

Roy's Mission

Roy thought for hours about how to tell Anna. He didn't want to make things worse for her, but couldn't shake off the belief she should know. If she wrote another letter to the agency in the future and found out from them that Jo had died and no one had told her it would be a cruel blow. Of course, the Adoption Support Agency had to be informed and he wondered if in the normal course of things they would even contact birth children. Probably not. He didn't want it to be that way. He owed it to Jo and, for that matter, Anna to let her know she had gone peacefully and that just before she died, her thoughts had turned only to Anna. It filled him with sadness to think of them so near, yet never meeting each other. A contusion of memories passed through his mind, Jo's hands upon the picture of Anna. He decided he must make sure she is told.

A letter would be best, but keep it short saying he had some sad news, if she would be willing to meet him.

When a note was hand delivered to Anna in her studio, her first thought was that it must be from Dylan. But seeing Compton Wharf at the top of the letter and Roy's name at the bottom, she knew immediately. Since the day she had walked away from the wharf, she had tried to tell herself it had been out of respect for a dying woman's wishes, an act of kindness, of forgiveness even, yet the sadness of not having taken that last step lingered in her, forsaken. Had she done the right thing? It was only two weeks ago, she still didn't know if she had done the right thing. And her heart ached.

Autumn brought cold mornings and mist, a harbinger of winter. They had arranged to meet inside at the hospital coffee shop – his suggestion – for which she was grateful, not knowing what the meeting might bring. When Roy walked in, she knew it was him immediately: older, bearded, and a kind face; an open book which told her everything.

Hi I'm Roy, he said as she rose to greet him. Words left her as she searched his face waiting to hear the words. I'm so sorry, he said, your mum has passed away. I wanted you to be the first to know.

She tried to answer, but tears came instead and suddenly here she was, silently weeping. Roy placed a tender hand upon her shoulder.

He said he wanted to make sure she heard it from him, had written as soon as he could. Anna was overcome, thanking him from the bottom of her heart: for recognising her, for acknowledging her as a daughter. It means a lot, she said.

She liked Roy straight away, his compassion, and told him

about the Compton Wharf visit two weeks earlier, how she had lost her nerve at the last minute. Roy nodded, emotions working his face. Anna grasped his hand and said she wished she had asked for his help long ago.

You're a good lass, Anna, what with your amazing work here, Jo knew about that before she died. She was so proud of you, I know she was.

Thank you, Roy. I am so glad you came, she said laughing a little through the tears, I haven't even bought you a coffee yet, I am so sorry. Come on, please let me get you something.

The hours passed swiftly, Roy's words as he described Jo's sense of fun, her kindness, her outrageous humour, were shaping her mother inside her mind's eye. He told her that but for the illness, he believed it would have been different. It was out of love, he said.

Anna did not know why, but the first person she wanted to tell was Dylan. He sounded relieved to hear her voice when he answered.

Hey stranger, he answered, I'm so relieved you've called back. Listen, I think I must have upset you? When you didn't return my calls, I began to wonder if it was something I said? Did I misread things? He sounded cautious, uncertain.

No, no, Anna said, and you know, me too. I thought I must've misread things too. Look, can we meet? I'd really like to see you, there's stuff going on and, well, it would be good to talk.

Anna invited Dylan to her place, saying it's only a studio, so please don't be disappointed. If I am seeing you, I'll be happy wherever we are, he said.

He arrived at her door holding a jar. It's jam, he said, I made it from plums from my garden for you. She hugged him and brought him in from the rain, shy because there no space to put his coat, his boots.

I'm so glad to see you, he said, I have missed you.

She didn't know where to start, give him a chair? She sat down beside him at her small table where she had placed some autumn leaves in a fluted stone bottle. She told him about her mother, straight off, unable to hold back the tears. Dylan was visibly shaken, at a loss for words. He asked if he could hug her and when he held her close, there was a feeling like home, the pain lifting. Then, unprompted, he told Anna he was adopted. I know, she breathed, but why didn't you tell me before? Because, he said, I couldn't bear to hurt you, Anna, you were just dealing with your mother's letter and it had all seemed so unfair. I didn't want to be gloating about how lucky I have been. Adoption hurts, he said, but it's a bitter pill to lose your mother twice in a lifetime. He held her away a little so that he could look at her: You know, it's you that is the best thing that has happened in my life. Everything else comes second.

37

Dylan, Anna and Tara

So, what, are we like horse parents now? Dylan was puffing his way with a large shaped grooming brush across Hope's flanks, whilst Anna did the twiddly bits with her mane.

Something like that, Anna laughed.

If we can show her at her shiny best, it will do the hospital proud. Me as well. Something to help those families recognise their incredible courage in coming back onto the hospital grounds after what happened. Hope is the one to do that job, I think.

The hospital board had driven the project in the end, especially when one of the patrons turned out to be a well-known competitive rider. Livery was sponsored by the hospital and Anna became the regular trainer for Hope at the Riding for the Disabled days. She was still too young to be ridden, but was developing into a stately horse with a gentle nature, as comfortable around children as the Board could have wished for. Goldspiers had set up a regular donation from their charitable arm and all that remained was to get Hope and the support group together. It wasn't the first event they were preparing her for, but it was the most important, the only event to take place on the hospital grounds since the fete a year before. Matt was going to be on hand, this time with a buffet instead of burgers, which he had decided was an altogether safer way to make a living. Lunch would be in the hospital canteen and there were to be strictly no marquees outside. The League of Friends was billing it as the event to bring the community together and heal the past.

Dylan stood back and admired her glossy black sheen. Anna, still on the other side, was working her way towards Hope's forelock. Where would I be without this as a project, Anna?

Having a nice quiet life, I suspect, she laughed. Right! That's it, she's good to go. Anna took a few paces back until she was standing beside Dylan.

Later that afternoon as she walked Hope up and down the hospital grounds, stopping to greet children and patients alike, her mind turned to Dylan and the time they had been spending together.

Once the year began to turn Anna started to gain her colours as a Wellbeing Ambassador for the hospital. It became her sole focus, that and Hope. Telling Dylan about Jo had been a turning point too. As soon as she understood why he had held back, it made way for something else that had been waiting to emerge.

He told her it had been Tara that gave him the confidence to keep going when Anna didn't pick up or return his calls. She needs you to come and get her, corny as it may sound Dylan, you've got to reach out to this girl or you'll lose her altogether

273

and she'll lose herself.

Unbeknown to her, he had pitched up at her work more times than was sensible, risking everything including his Important Guest status at Scott Marston's table. But he had known then, and deep down so did she. It was never work, the fete, or even the adoption that brought them together, it was the love of someone to be peaceful with, someone to weather the storms with, to hold steady with, to feel whole. He looked at her now and saw a woman whose peace of mind meant more to him than anyone. And what is love after all, if not something by which you can know the world as a kinder place.

The thing is, he said slinging an arm around her, no matter how much I love this horse, Anna, it's not a match for what I feel for you.

When snow falls in October, it is uncommon, rich with metaphor and silence. We are shrouded, held fast in mythological stories. A deep winter sleep, being lost in the woods, the safety of a warm cottage, tales of hardship and survival, being hidden and then found.

So it was when Anna first spoke her mother's name to Tara. The snow had been a foot deep on the ground for two days and she had stayed over with Dylan at Tara's home, enjoying the enforced quiet comfort of hot drinks and a seat by the fireside. No cars were on the road and for the first time in a long while, it was as if she belonged, it was a home that had come to mean something to her as October turned towards winter. When her visits with Dylan increased, so did the warmth of Tara's welcome. Tara already knew Anna had been adopted, but had not spoken to her about it, waiting for the time to be right.

The afternoon drew in towards early twilight, Tara closed the curtains and made tea for them all. A walk out in the road early in the day where the snow lay light as feathers, untrammeled, had made them all sleepy and ready for the glow of the fire.

Over hot buttered crumpets, Anna had asked Tara about her early life, her experience of losing Dylan. It was, she told Anna, the worst day of her life. Dylan did not hear this. Busying himself in the kitchen, he heard only the joyful story of reunion, the first time she saw him, her pride in him.

Can I ask you something, said Anna.

Go ahead, Tara said. Ask away. I mean it might help with understanding your mother a bit too.

Did you ever, you know, get help, therapy, or counselling, whatever? Anna's question was freighted with contradictions. The desire to get help had been growing in her the more her relationship with Dylan developed, but the last thing she wanted was to end up sabotaging her chance at happiness. There was so much fear of loss in her. It was confusing.

Tara was thoughtful, considered, not wanting to rush to judgment about Anna, who she admired and liked, yet she was mindful of Dylan's privacy. The more she learnt about Anna's life, the more she wanted to wrap her arms around her and draw her in close.

Yes, I did have help, but at the time I was terrified of social services and young and pretty much at the mercy of the world, looking back on it. My therapist, Jo, was her name....

Anna sat bolt upright. No way, she said. She looked as if she might cry. What was her surname, Tara? She was sitting forward now on the edge of her seat, I do not believe this. My mother was a therapist called Jo.

Tara was unnerved, unsure whether to trust the moment.

I can't believe this, she said her voice freighted with emotion. That would be just too amazing, Anna, I can't even make sense of it. A pang of remembrance of her young self surfaced at the mention of Jo, and with it a came a wave of sadness. But it was so many years ago. Jo had been the only person who was truly kind to her back then.

Juniper. Jo Juniper, that was her name. She was a wonderful woman to me. Her voice dropped to a whisper, but honestly, tell me we are talking of the same woman and I'll believe there really is a god.

Sometimes the light falls across the glass and refracts, so bright it is as if it cannot pass through into the room, it breaks, curves and finds a home in the leaf and the eye. Autumn leaves, still clinging to the trees outside Tara's window, a year beyond a time of realisation were as new to the eye, yet rich with colours of maturity, that it seemed as if it was the first autumn she had ever witnessed. Experience shapes the way we receive, yet receiving it, we are changed. In that moment at Tara's house, on an ordinary day in late autumn, a cascade of experience came together in one place. Some would say it is just coincidence, yet meaning and purpose are evanescent and made new each time. One thread crosses another and something sparks, brightens. At such times relationships shift, the path curves and winds in towards the light.

Tara became a little more of a mother that day, the realisa-tion she had something to offer that could help Anna came to her as clearly as the image of the girl's mother crystalized in her mind. It wasn't only memory she could offer, of her mother certainly, but what Anna was looking for was a way to make sense of it all and Tara, above all, knew that it didn't. Sense was not what it made. Rather the richly painful, unjust, bloody, shape shifting, glorious fuck up of it all, was what it made, and Tara knew a lot about that. And what she also knew was that even if you crossed the rubicon, if you believed hard enough, loved true enough, heard the universe in those moments of despair, then you could retrace your steps.

Anna, for her part, was like a stem that would bend towards the light; of security, of knowledge, of warmth, of stability. She would always find love where love itself found her.

Acknowledgements

I could not have written this book without having had the privilege of meeting the many mothers whom I represented over my career as a barrister. Their love for their children and their courage was never, in my experience, dimmed by any life experiences they may have had. I have always believed that it could have been any one of us, had we suffered the kind of lives they have had to endure. I thank them all.

Thank you to my editor and old friend Dexter Petley whose encouragement and astute editing has put this book on the road. Thank you to my talented illustrator, Eva Polakovicova, whose superb designs spoke to me.

Brenda Reid, Gill Hyton and Sara Cooke I am indebted to for their willingness to read the book and their encouragement and belief in the project. Thank you to my adopted friends who have so generously shared their own stories of adoption with me, and friends whose lives have been an inspiration.

My family, all of them, have been and continue to be the best teachers about love, relationship, ancestors and the ties that bind us. The idea that we are all, in the end, only seven degrees separate has been evident to me in so many ways throughout my family and beyond.

I thank Matthew for his endless support with my writing and his reading of the book. He is such a great supporter of creativity in all its forms.

And last, but not least, I thank my children, who are my greatest champions, whose lives are an inspiration to me. Always.

About the Author

Judith spent her early years moving house more times than she likes to remember, as a young adult she spent some years living in Scandinavia and Holland. When still a young woman she searched for and met her birth mother, an experience which has shaped her life and continues to this day to underpin her values. On returning to the UK she studied law and became a barrister, practising in the family courts representing mothers, fathers, aunties, grannies and children. Having completed 23 years practising in the field of child protection Judith moved into journalism and hovering around the world of books.

Judith has written op-eds for the Irish Times and Irish Independent on access to records, mother and baby homes, as well as articles in Counsel Magazine and others.

Judith has been a been winner of Counsel Magazine's poetry prize, shortlisted for The Plough Prize (short category), and has published poetry, articles etc in notable journals such as The North, The Interpreter's House.

Judith is married with two children and the family share a lively interest in drama, music and the arts. When not writing she can often be found wandering the lanes of Shropshire or hanging out in the Poetry Pharmacy, Bishops Castle.

You can connect with me on:

🌐 https://judithtrustmanauthor.com
🅕 https://www.facebook.com//judith.trustman.author.s.page

Printed in Dunstable, United Kingdom